LOVING JOSIE

A TOREY HOPE NOVEL

A.D. ELLIS

LOVING JOSIE

A TOREY HOPE NOVEL

A.D. ELLIS

WWW.FACEBOOK.COM/ADELLISAUTHOR

NOTE FROM AUTHOR

I had no intention of writing this story, it had never even crossed my mind. But when loyal readers wanted more Torey Hope after For Nicky and Because of Beckett, I started thinking about how the story could continue and I absolutely fell in love with Kyle and Josie. I have to say that there's a little paranormal twist in this story that I NEVER saw coming since I'm not much of a paranormal fan. But the twist came to me while I was writing and it worked so well that I couldn't help but include it.

I hope you love the newest residents of Torey Hope! I'm madly in love with this town, these families, and these characters. These stories prove that life isn't always easy, but the love and support of family and friends makes it a little easier.

Thank you for reading!

QUOTES OF INSPIRATION

"'Tis better to have loved and lost
than never to have loved at all."

Alfred Lord Tennyson

***

"Don't cry because it's over,
smile because it happened."

Dr. Seuss

PROLOGUE

"Hey man, you coming over tonight? I feel like beatin' your ass in some basketball." Jeremiah Jordan laughed and clapped his best friend, Kyle Martin, on the back as they headed out the doors of their high school.

"Hiya, Izzy. You ever gonna leave this loser and come see what it's like to love a real man?" Jeremiah laughed as Kyle put him in a headlock and Izzy elbowed him in the gut. "I'm kidding, I'm kidding!" Jeremiah broke free of his friend's hold and grinned at the two of them, thinking of how perfectly matched they were; like bookends, they complemented each other so well.

"I know, I know, you two are perfect for each other. I'd never try to break that up. Plus, if you were with me, Izzy, you'd have to pine away for me when I leave for the military in a couple months. This way you can comfort Kyle when he cries over me abandoning him." He jumped out of the way as Kyle grabbed for him again and Izzy giggled over their antics. "Now, now boys. Jordan, you know I'm too much woman for you to handle." She grinned at Jeremiah as she teased him and tucked herself under Kyle's arm.

The two young men had been friends for quite a while. You couldn't get much different than Jeremiah Jordan and Kyle Martin. The only thing they had in common was that they were both good guys at heart.

"Seriously, both of you, I want to spend as much time together as possible. We should just enjoy our time being stupid teenagers and having fun before everything changes." Jeremiah spoke in a more somber tone to his friends.

Kyle and Izzy, recognizing their friend's apprehension over leaving soon, hugged him close between them as they walked down the sidewalk away from school and toward the freedom of their weekend. The three of them knew that changes were coming; life was all about changes. But, like most, they just didn't realize how life-altering some of those changes would be.

CHAPTER 1

Josie Decker

"Whatever course you decide upon, there is always someone to tell you that you are wrong. There are always difficulties arising which tempt you to believe that your critics are right. To map out a course of action and follow it to an end requires courage."
~Ralph Waldo Emerson

I've never felt loved, not one single moment in my life, until I arrived in Torey Hope. Every memory I have, from the beginning of my existence, is one of being a bother, an afterthought, and a hassle, disposable. I was only good for the positive gain in social status for others, and when I disappointed again and again, I was pushed aside time after time. Then I knocked on my Uncle Robert's door and I knew love and acceptance for the first time in my life.

My name is Josie Decker. I'm the unwanted child of Richard Joseph and Corinne Ruth Decker. My father, a business mogul, married my mother for two reasons. First, she was already a highly successful business woman in her own right. *Her* connections would be good for *him*; *his* connections would propel *her* much higher in the business world. The second reason was that, in addition to the business world, they were both very high up on the social ladder. The wedding of Richard and Corinne Decker was the event of the year in New York; everyone who was anyone clambered to be invited or at least involved in some way. My parents weren't just high society in New York; they rubbed elbows with billionaires and movie stars out in Los Angeles as well. Even in Tokyo and London the name Decker was associated with wealth and success.

Getting pregnant with me was a tragedy in the eyes of both of my parents. Richard and Corinne did not love each other; they didn't dislike each other, but they were in the marriage only for mutual status climbing and gratification. I'm not sure how they got pregnant with me; in my entire life I never saw a loving touch between the two of them.

The story that was told to me several times over the years

was that Corinne had an IUD so she never suspected her early pregnancy symptoms could have been what they were. She was six months along when she finally had to admit that the IUD had failed and she was expecting. Richard was furious with her; how could she let this happen? They couldn't be saddled with a child if they were going to continue their climb up the business and social ladders. Corinne lashed back that he was just as much at fault; she was devastated at what this would do to her body, her career, and her social standing.

They attended a secret appointment with a doctor they knew from their social circles. Their hopeful idea to terminate the pregnancy was dashed when it was confirmed how far along Corinne was in the pregnancy. My mother told me numerous times over the years that she should have just admitted her symptoms to herself earlier so she could have terminated me. *Yeah, love you too, Mother. Seriously, what type of person says that to their child?*

So, she hid the pregnancy as best she could for the next few months; she didn't want her business associates thinking of her as a weak female who didn't know how to not get knocked-up. I was born 3 weeks early; not because I was ready to be born, they paid the doctor a hefty fee to induce delivery because there was a trip to Tokyo they both needed to be on. I was born on a Wednesday. Having not cared enough to find out the sex of their baby before delivery, disappointment reigned when it was announced that I was a girl; at least a boy would have been a more rightful heir to their business fortune. As a punishment for not being the boy they would have been more satisfied with, they named me Josephine combining my father's middle name and my mother's first name.

My parents left for Tokyo on Saturday; I was left with the first of many nursemaids and nannies. Richard and Corinne were gone on their business trip for thirty days. Upon their return, they walked to the nursery to look at me and inquire of the nursemaid about me. They did not pick me up or kiss me; they did not speak to me or make over me the way most new parents would have. They left the next morning for a 3 month trip to London; never once did I come before their business ventures. These stories were told to me by various nannies over the years, passed down from one to the other before one was let go for various infractions; most were for showing me any physical affection. My mother told me that the idea of hugging or kissing me made her shudder; Corrine Decker did not show affection.

My parents hired only strict and unloving nannies and help. They did not want me babied or coddled. If I had to come along and put such a kink in their plans, I may as well serve a purpose. They decided they would groom me to be a business guru right along-side of them. I was to be schooled and trained so that I could one day step right into their world.

Josephine Decker would become a business force to reckon with.

The joke was on them though. I was a girly-girl. I was creative; constantly singing and dancing and drawing and painting. This was frowned upon by my parents and discouraged and ridiculed at every turn. Josephine Marie Decker would not have an artistic flair; business women were not successful for creativeness or uniqueness. A strong business woman should be disciplined, brilliant, and proper. I learned to celebrate my parents' months-long trips; I could let loose and be me when they were gone. Well, as much as someone can be free with staunch rules and nannies around every corner.

I had one nanny who nicknamed me Josie; she was later fired for hugging me when I fell and scraped my knee. But, the name of Josie stuck for me; I called myself Josie to anyone who would listen. This infuriated my parents; they insisted that I be called Josephine and severely reprimanded me if they heard me use the nickname.

Imagine their disdain and embarrassment when the school I was attending suggested that I enroll in the Creative Arts program; they had noticed my flair for the arts. A generous donation was given to this school in hopes of keeping my artistic talents a secret and I was enrolled in a boarding school overseas. The school was for future business men and women; I did not fit there.

I attended my classes, sitting quietly, trying to understand the numbers and facts and figures all while my brain painted pictures and created paper designs. My classmates were geniuses, acing every test and competing to be the best in each class. My struggles got me Cs on most assignments. A grade of C was average; Richard and Corinne Decker did not accept average. Every phone call brought ridicule and reminders of what an embarrassment I was to my parents. These phone calls were few and far between which was actually a blessing; saving me from slipping further into the shell I'd put around myself. I cherished my shell; inside of it I was able to be me while I showed nothing to the world. My shell showed a stoic and docile and obedient daughter to my parents; inside of that shell I was my own unique person, creative, a wild spirit, longing for love. Just wanting to be loved.

I survived boarding school; I did my best to pull Cs on topics that I didn't like or understand. I had a private room; only the best for a Decker. My room was what I lived for; it was my refuge. I set up a small area to paint and lost myself in my creations. I experimented with water colors and oils; I played around with mixing colors; I fell in love with painting. This was a form of therapy for me. When I painted, I traveled to a different world; I wasn't unloved or unwanted or a disappointment. In this world I was free; like a wild horse breaking free of restraints thrown onto it. My parents couldn't enter this world; no one could bring me down in this world.

I also enjoyed playing around with paper designs. Cards

and scrapbook pages were my favorite. My parents would have died of embarrassment to see me covered in paint or cutting, snipping, and gluing paper bits. But these two things saved me; they saved me from the nothingness that was my life. I faced uncertainty when I left school, but if I had my art, I would survive. I may not be happy, but I would make it.

CHAPTER 2

Josie

"We must be willing to let go of the life we have planned, so as to accept the life that is waiting for us."
~Joseph Campbell

And I would have made it if my parents had just let me be. However, they found out about my art and forbid me to do it any longer. They felt it was a waste of time; if I wasn't going to play along with their business plans, I wasn't going to be allowed a shred of happiness. I was watched constantly. It was reported to my parents if I so much as got a dreamy look on my face. I was to sit straight, walk tall, work briskly, speak with authority; all of these things were drilled into me and watched for by everyone in my day-to-day world. I failed daily; these things weren't me. I was a soft spoken, dreamy girl who got lost in her thoughts; I was not a shrewd business woman.

My parents finally admitted that I was never going to be a business woman; at this point they had become used to my disappointments in their life. I was ignored, given an allowance that could only be spent on what they deemed appropriate and left on my own. The best thing I did was to swindle this allowance away; spending just enough of it on proper clothing and books so that my parents were satisfied. My small secret stash of cash grew and became a safety net for me; one day I would break free and this money would help me.

They insisted I go to college; I was sent to a private school overseas; I always felt that my parents picked overseas because there was less chance of my being recognized and embarrassing them further.

My college years were a repeat of earlier schooling with the exception of the fact that I actually enjoyed most of my classes. Since they had accepted that I would never enter the business world, my parents allowed me to take classes in the history, theories, and methods of art. I think they had given up on me so completely by this point that they just let me take art classes so they could sadly shake their heads with business and social connections and speak of how simple-minded I was. Seriously, I heard them once tell a business associate, "Our daughter, bless her soul, is not very high-functioning; we've paid for her to dabble in art classes so as to keep her occupied and not bother those around her."

I also secretly squeezed in some classes on web design and small business ownership. What I would do with these classes and my degree I had no clue; my parents would never allow me to operate a small business to sell my scrapbooking or paintings. But, I felt proud when I finished my degree. It was mine and no one could take it from me. Maybe one day I would break free and use what I had learned; use the passion and spirit that flowed inside of me. I should have known they would find a way to squash my feelings of pride.

My parents weren't home when I returned to the house upon graduation from college; they had not attended the ceremony, stating they couldn't be bothered to come if I couldn't be bothered to make them proud. I knew my degree was an embarrassment for them and they wouldn't stoop low enough to attend my graduation from a lowly art school. However, there were strict instructions from the new housekeeper when I arrived home that I was to dress to impress; the driver would take me to the restaurant where my parents were dining with business associates.

I arrived at the dining location and immediately felt my apprehension rise. My parents did nothing with me unless it served their purpose. Why would they want me to dine with them? I was lucky if I ever shared a meal with classmates or a random housekeeper over the last several years; dining with my parents was rare indeed.

Rounding the corner with the maître d, I spotted my parents sitting with Wayne Erickson. Wayne was the son of one of my father's closest business partners; he was about 10 years older than me and had been slowly stepping into his father's business dealings over the past few years. My parents were delighted with Wayne Erickson and his future; they spoke more highly of him than they had ever spoken of me.

I was confused as to why I was being invited to a business dinner with my parents and Wayne. My confusion intensified when I was seated at the table. "I took the liberty of ordering for you, Josephine." My father spoke to me in a way that made it clear it was all for show. Wayne shot me a sickeningly smarmy smile as he winked at me. My stomach was in knots facing this unknown situation.

As the meal progressed, my parents and Wayne spoke of business dealings and I let myself drift to another world in my head. "Josephine! You must stop daydreaming; it's very unbecoming of a woman. Your father is speaking to you about an opportunity you won't be able to pass up." My mother's embarrassment and disdain was evident through her fake smile.

I turned my attention to my father. "Josephine, we

brought you here today because Wayne has offered a deal; a business transaction if you will." My father turned to Wayne.

"Well, Josephine, it's no secret that you're not exactly business material and you'll not be taking over for your parents at any time. You're definitely not going to be a model any time soon..." He said this as if it were a joke, but I could tell he didn't find me attractive and was letting me know as such.

At this, my mother let go a long-suffering sigh and spoke sharply, "She could at least be somewhat attractive if she'd do something with that God-awful hair. Seriously, I don't know where that hideous red came from." My thick, auburn hair had always been a point of contention for my mother; she felt red hair was much less powerful than a head of dark black or platinum blonde.

Wayne looked as if he would have agreed if it hadn't been inappropriate. He just nodded slightly at my mother and continued. "What I'm proposing, Josephine, is a win-win for all involved. I will get something I need, your parents will get bragging rights both in the business and social circles, and you will never want for anything again."

My stomach was fighting with itself to contain the meal I had just consumed. Wayne hadn't spoken the words just yet, but I knew what he was going to say. My breathing was shallow as I waited for the words I knew were coming. The wild horses in my head were circling like mad, attempting to avoid the lasso they sensed was coming.

"Josephine, I'm offering to marry you. I will provide for you and you can do anything you'd like. Your parents have spoken of your little art hobby; I'll set up a studio for you in my home. If you'd like, I'll even allow you to sell your work online, under an alias of course; I can't have my name tainted with selling amateur art online." Wayne puffed up as he presented this "opportunity" to me.

I glanced at my parents and saw that they were completely on board with this business deal. My future was not mine, I would never escape my parents' reign; Wayne's offer was not appealing, I did not want to marry him. However, there was nowhere I could escape to; my parents' far-reaching status would find me. They would never let me leave and embarrass their good name. I had no friends to turn to, no family I knew of.

Wayne was not an ugly man physically, but I did not find him attractive thanks to his abhorrent personality. Taking a moment to contemplate his offer brought me to a conclusion; he offered to let me do my art and possibly sell it. This was more than I was going to get from my parents. My heart was breaking and I felt like I was suffocating, but I turned a forced smile towards Wayne and said, "Thank you, Wayne, that's a very generous offer." The smile he returned and the hand-shake between he and my father sealed my fate. As the discussion around me faded into the background I pictured those wild horses in my mind being lassoed, bridled, and corralled behind fences; I had just been captured and the breaking of what was left of my spirit would soon commence. The only hope of survival I had was this: I would crawl deeper into the shell of my existence and survive by escaping to my other world; my art would be my savior. Inside of that shell I would celebrate my passion and spirit, while on the outside I would portray the wife Wayne needed.

CHAPTER 3

Kyle Martin

"In all the world, there is no heart for me like yours. In all the world, there is no love for you like mine."
*~**Maya Angelou***

I was born to hippy-wanna-be parents so it was no surprise that I was different; my parents accepted and celebrated my uniqueness, they encouraged me to march to the beat of my own drummer. Hell, they often bought me the drums in the form of punk clothes, hair dye, and piercings.

Growing up I was allowed to make my own choices, learn from my mistakes and failures, and to be the person I felt like being. My parents' leniency led to me experimenting in a safe environment; I quickly learned that I didn't give a fuck what anyone thought of me. I wore my hair in a different style and color almost every day. I had several piercings that I put in and took out as the mood struck me. Vibrant colors drew me in but black was a staple in my closet as well. I could often be found wearing black jeans, a black t-shirt, black biker boots, and a splash of color either on a belt, hat, jewelry or hoodie. Once I discovered tattoos, the vibrant colors made their way into my drawings and the ink I put on my skin. When I was old enough to drive I didn't save my money for a car, I bought a motorcycle. I couldn't afford a fancy one at first, but the fixer-upper I bought kept my dad and me busy for months before I got my license. I never drove anything except my bike if I could keep from it.

My parents allowed drug and alcohol experimentation; they didn't offer me hard stuff, just the usual tobacco and marijuana. I think, because they were so lax about it, and because it was sort of 'expected' that I would be into those things by others, I never really got hooked on them. I found I'd rather get my high from the looks I got from people or the ink gun searing my flesh. I didn't need alcohol or drugs to fill my life. It's not that I didn't drink, I just didn't need it. Now, saying and doing things to piss people off or shock the shit out of them? Yeah, that was my drug of choice.

People who knew me, loved me; they knew I was genuine, respectful, and a good-guy at heart. People who didn't take the time to know me usually hated me; they feared me because of my clothes, my "fuck'em all" attitude, my piercings, and my tattoos. I didn't care if people liked me or hated me; I loved my parents and my friends, I did my best in school, and I lived life to the fullest each and every day.

My sweet Izzy didn't have it as easy as me in the parents department. They didn't mistreat her, but they weren't as lenient and 'free' as mine.

I met Isabella the summer before second grade. She was the most beautiful girl I'd ever seen; shiny black hair, large violet eyes, and lips so pink you'd think she had on lipstick all the time. To look at her, you'd expect a shy, reserved, girly-girl, and that's what I thought had moved in next door to me as well. I didn't care what type of girl she was. From the moment I laid eyes on her I was hooked; I'd deal with girly and reserved if she'd just let me spend time with her. Much to my surprise, Isabella was nothing like what her looks made you expect. This was also much to her parents' dismay.

"Hi, I'm Izzy, what's your name?" The tiny girl with huge violet eyes stuck her hand out as she stood in front of me in my driveway. "Come on, don't tell me you're shy. You've got green in your hair and you're wearing punk clothes, you don't seem like the shy type. What's your name, Punk Boy?" She put her hands on her tiny hips and waited for me to speak.

Finally shaking off the shock of her forwardness when I'd been expecting a tiny, quiet voice and shy actions, I swallowed the lump in my throat and stuck out my hand to meet hers. "My name is Kyle Martin. I guess you can call me Kyle or Punk Boy, your choice." I smiled at her; I'd just given this girl permission to call me Punk Boy, I was obviously smitten already.

"So, Izzy is a different name. Is it a nickname?" I began to walk, and she fell in step beside me. I had decided I needed to keep her talking just so I could spend as much time with her as possible

"Well, my parents named me Isabella. I was to be their princess, their little china doll, delicate and fragile. Imagine their shock and awe when their princess turned out to be me! I'm much more an Izzy than an Isabella!" She threw her head back laughing, and I couldn't help but join her. "So, they try to make me comply, and they attempt to dress me up in frilly dresses, but I rebel against them every chance I get. I can't stand ribbons and lace, I'm more of a jeans and t-shirt type girl. I don't want pretty ballet flats or sparkly sandals; I'd much rather wear my old Converse. As soon as I'm old enough to get my hair cut on my own, I'm getting it chopped off into a spikey style and I'm going to add all sorts of colors to it. I'll get tattoos and piercings and it will drive my parents crazy; but it will feel more like me, and I'll love it." She turned those gorgeous eyes towards me, possibly to gauge my reaction.

I shook my head and smiled, "I think I'm in love with you already Izzy; we're going to be the best of friends."

From that day on, Izzy and I were inseparable. I was her

"Punk Boy" and she was my little rebel, my Izzy, my "Izzy-bel."

~

There was never a question about Izzy and me; we were a couple before we even knew what being a couple meant. We were the perfect match; she was the yin to my yang. Our friendship was easy; our more serious relationship later on down the road was easy. We never had to question our feelings, they had been clear from that first day in my driveway. Izzy-bel completed me and I complemented her; we were, by all standards, the perfect couple.

Sex with Izzy was beautiful because our friendship was beautiful. We waited until we were married to have sex; I'm not sure why, it just became an unspoken agreement that we would wait. It wasn't hard, we had spent this much of our life together and we had the rest of our life together, so waiting was not a hardship. We did plenty of other stuff leading up to our wedding night, but always stopped before it went too far; who would have thought that the punks, the rebels, the bad boy/bad girl couple would be saving themselves for marriage? Maybe that's why we did it; neither of us ever liked predictability, we didn't ever do what people expected of us.

Izzy took my breath away the day we got married. Her short black hair was a messy array of black, green, pink, and blue all over her head as she walked towards me in the court-house. The black flouncy skirt she had paired with a ripped up blue shirt and black tank swayed around her mid-thighs and she winked at me as a reminder of what she'd whispered to me the night before, "Tomorrow, when I marry you, I won't be wearing any underwear; just keep that in mind while you're trying to sleep tonight, Punk Boy." I smirked at her and held my hand out to her as she reached my side. I wore a black t-shirt and dark blue button-up shirt with the sleeves rolled past my elbows so that my tattoo sleeves showed. My jeans were gray and my black boots were unlaced as usual. "Happy wedding day, Punk Boy." She leaned in to kiss my cheek.

"I'm glad you get to marry me, Izzy-bel", I smiled at her and winked as I kissed the top of her head.

Her parents had relented to the fact that their Isabella would never be their pretty, perfect, princess; they liked me just fine and were begrudgingly happy with our marriage. My parents adored Izzy; she was like the daughter they never had. I could see four pairs of teary eyes watching us as we exchanged our vows and made our relationship official and forever.

"I'm nervous, Kyle, maybe we should have practiced before our wedding night." Izzy, my little rebel who was never afraid of anything, looked at me warily. "What if we don't do it right?"

I laughed at her. "Izzy, I love you, you love me, we've been together since second grade; us coming together tonight will be as perfect as we are. Now, come here and let me love on you." I grabbed my wife by the hand and proceeded to show her just how much I loved her.

I didn't expect fireworks and stars like the movies glorify sex to be; making love to Izzy was not mind-blowing but it was perfect. Making her mine, finally, was like putting the last piece of a puzzle in place. My life was complete with my wife by my side.

CHAPTER 4

Kyle

"Letting go doesn't mean giving up, but rather accepting that there are things that cannot be."
~Author Unknown

As was normal for Izzy and me, we settled into a perfectly normal, perfectly comfortable routine. Izzy had worked at a record store since high school and she had recently become co-owner of the business that she loved. I had developed my talent for designing and inking tattoos; I opened a shop next to the record store.

We had waited for a while after high school to get married; then we waited five years before we even attempted to have children. We knew we wanted kids, but we also knew we wanted to be Kyle and Izzy Martin and establish our businesses before we added a baby to the mix.

Five years of dinners, movies, setting up house. Five years of traveling, learning how to live together, forming a stronger bond than the strongest bond we already had. After five years, we gave up birth control and decided to have a baby. Imagine our sadness, shock, and disappointment when getting pregnant took years rather than months.

Izzy took it like a trouper and we were determined to keep our strong bond throughout this leg of our journey. It wasn't always easy, but we clung to each other and carried on.

We had been discussing adoption for about a month; it wasn't what we had originally planned, but it would allow us to be parents if the baby we so desperately wanted never came along.

CHAPTER 5

Josie

"The eyes of others our prisons; their thoughts our cages." ~***Virginia Woolf***

I blocked out most of my wedding day. I didn't want to remember a single moment of the day I completely lost my freedom and what little bit of spirit I had left.

While my life was not terrible, it was not what a person would hope for. Although, not much had changed for me except I was now living under Wayne's rule rather than my parents' reign. I wanted for nothing; attending social events, speeches, galas, and ceremonies became second nature.

Dressing as an object and plastering on a fake smile, I would attend those functions with my husband as his "trophy wife." I was expected to smile, giggle, and only add to the conversation if I was spoken to directly. Soon most of Wayne's associates decided I was just a ditzy female with nothing between my ears; this worked to my advantage most of the time because I could smile and let my mind journey to other places while Wayne paraded me around. In my mind I would critique the artwork in the venues we attended; I visualized my own paintings on the walls. I imagined all the stiff suits and their arm-candy in regular, everyday clothes; I pictured the more attractive men with piercings and tattoos while the women spoke their minds, wore clothes they wanted, had careers they dreamed of. My mind was wild and free even if my body had to be confined to the sparkly dress, plastered-on smile, and Wayne's arm around me.

The singularly good part of my new life was that Wayne was true to his word and set up a small studio for me. He had a web designer create a site for me; I could have done this myself but I didn't want to question him and have it taken away, so I settled for the less-than-stellar site that was made for me. Wayne had numerous canvases and paints and brushes brought in; he set up an account at the local art store, and I was allowed a certain amount each month to spend on supplies. Like a father providing for a spoiled child, Wayne purchased practically every paper-cutting machine he saw in the catalog I had been looking at. I truly wanted for nothing. I was told only to avoid using my real name, Josie Erickson, so I set up my site as "Art by J."

The first time I sold a painting online I was ecstatic; I ran around my studio whooping and hollering like a banshee knowing Wayne was gone and wouldn't hear me. Quickly, I tempered my enthusiasm in case the household staff would report my outburst to him. I silently continued to dance around my studio for a few minutes basking in the glow of knowing that someone liked my work. I sold three more paintings that week along with 2 scrapbooks. I had orders coming in for paintings and custom-made scrapbooks. For the first time in my life I felt like I was an actual somebody. I wasn't Richard and Corinne's unloved and unwanted daughter. I wasn't Wayne Erickson's arm candy and simpering little wife. I was Josie, I was "Art by J." I was as close to happy as I was probably ever going to be.

That happiness had to carry me along throughout most of my dealings with my husband. Wayne expected me dressed for dinner at 8 pm every evening unless I was informed of an altered meal-time. My husband told me that I was "attractive in an unconventional way;" he said that my lack of voluptuous beauty was the reason he struggled to perform in the bedroom. From our first night together, sex with my husband was a belittling, disgusting, painful event. Thankfully, Wayne did not have a strong libido so I only had to endure this 2-3 times a month.

A normal intimate moment together involved Wayne

making me watch pornography so he could get "in the mood." I didn't find the images stimulating and often stared unseeingly at the screen so as to make him think I was watching. He once told me that "we'd never fuck if I had to get hard just looking at you." I was usually grateful that Wayne couldn't get it all the way up; it made penetration less painful. I was never wet for him; this was another point that he rubbed in my face.

"How the fuck am I supposed to get turned on when I know all that awaits me is measly little tits and a desert between your legs?" Wayne would sometimes resort to using lube just to get us through the act. He never lasted long and I would just close my eyes and drift off to my own little world. In my own world, the man hovering above me loved me. He kissed and caressed and spoke softly to me. His touch brought me intense pleasure; his words reached my heart, my soul.

I once broached the subject of children with Wayne; we had never used condoms but he'd had me taking birth control since our wedding day. "Fine, if a baby would keep you satisfied, stop taking your birth control. Just know that I'm not taking care of a snot-nosed kid; it will be your responsibility 100%. Your obligations to me will come first, we will have nannies for it when you're needed at events."

This was not an ideal situation, but I had dreamed of being a mother and I knew that I could love a child and care for him in a way I'd never known. I pictured holding him to my breast, hearing his first word, watching him take his first steps. Baby-fever hit me and it hit hard. I even took to initiating sex with Wayne when I knew I was the most fertile. After a year, there was no baby. Wayne took me to the doctor to see what my problem was; stating that he shouldn't have been surprised that there was one more disappointment associated with me.

A week later I received a report stating that I only had a 1% chance of ever conceiving. I was devastated; my dreams of having a child to love and share my world with vanished. I withdrew even more into my shell.

Wayne was getting more and more disgusted with me; the more he despised me, the angrier and meaner he got. He stopped coming to me for sex, though, which was a blessing. He flat-out told me that he just couldn't get hard looking at me and he had found a couple women to pleasure him so he would no longer need me in his bedroom. He moved me to a spare room near my studio; I reveled in the fact that I no longer had to endure sex with my husband. The sounds of loud, raunchy sex coming from our bedroom at all hours didn't bother me. I often listened and smiled to myself before entering my studio to block it all out; if he was in bed with her, or them, it meant he didn't need anything from me and that made my heart soar.

～

My art was selling, my husband was supposedly screwing someone other than me, and I only had to see him about once a day; my life was acceptable. I didn't love my life; I didn't cherish what I had, but I knew many people had it much worse. In my own mind I longed for happiness, I longed to be the strong woman I knew I could be, I longed to break from these chains and run free. Thoughts of surviving like this for the next 50-60 years were depressing and daunting; I adopted an attitude of one-day-at-a-time. I had a secret wish that an opportunity would arise in which I could escape; I didn't know what that opportunity would look like, but I kept my eyes open.

The first open door came when my parents were tragically killed. Their private jet went down in the mountains as they were returning from a business excursion. The pilot, an older employee of my father, had fallen asleep at the controls and crashed; there were no survivors. I felt extremely guilty when the first thought I had upon hearing the news was relief. My parents had been killed and all I felt was a jolt of excitement and freedom. That night I dreamed of those wild horses running free; I wanted to be like them. I wanted to shake off all restraints placed on me and be free to run until I made the decision to stop.

The reading of my parents' wills brought another open door for me. I did not expect a large inheritance and I did not receive one. I was given a good amount of money which was to be used "for keeping up appearances." Wayne, as their son-in-law and business associate, was the biggest inheritor of property and business holdings. Much of their wealth went to charities and foundations so that their names could live on. My ears perked up when the lawyer read the closing statement of my father's will, "My brother, Robert Decker, is to receive nothing of my property or wealth."

How did I not know my father had a brother? I filed this information away in my brain thinking it could be useful one day. Was Robert Decker like my father? Or was he the complete opposite? If my Richard had never mentioned him, I held hope that Robert was nothing like my father.

After my parents' death, Wayne's disposition changed and not for the better. Nothing I did was good enough. It was if, now that he didn't have to put up with me to please my parents, he was angry with me and himself for having agreed to the marriage in the first place.

He was not satisfied with me coming to dinner or attending events; he began having women over for dinner and demanding I stay hidden. He hired women to attend functions with him; telling his friends and associates that I was under the weather or at a spa vacation or in treatment for a mental illness. He gained much sympathy for having to put up with a wife such as me. I gained a new appreciation for being away from my parents and my husband. I kept waiting for the chance to leave.

I secretly had a lawyer draw up divorce papers which I would serve him with after I had fled. I continued swindling money away every chance I had. I had the lawyer in charge of my parents' will deposit the money I was gifted into a newly opened personal account under my maiden name. I looked up Robert Decker and memorized directions to get to his home in Torey Hope, Illinois. Then I waited.

My opportunity to leave didn't arise for another whole year. During that time, I got a little more courageous and daring; I would venture out into town and browse the little stores. Wayne would have forbid this had he known about it; I usually tried to disguise myself, wearing a hat and large sunglasses. My husband was of the impression that anything his wife would need could be ordered and I shouldn't be rubbing elbows with the locals. He also told me more than once that it would be an embarrassment if any of his clients or associates saw me. We lived in a huge, thriving city so I didn't understand what his issue was with me going out. True, I was usually drawn to the more 'indie' or 'bohemian' areas of our large city, but his rule of me not venturing out had just gotten to me and I decided, no matter the backlash, I would take little walks around our city.

On one such day, I happened upon a newly opened tattoo parlor. I was drawn to the artwork displayed in the window. Wiping my sweaty hands on my jeans, I entered the shop. I was instantly in love with the rich, vibrant colors and the strong, solid lines of the designs on the walls, the patrons, and the artists themselves. I spent an hour in the shop, chatting with the artists and some of the patrons. I was amazed at the creativity and devotion the artists showed. A tattoo became something on my bucket list; a list which was ever growing. I knew most of what was on my list would never be deemed appropriate for a Decker/Erickson to do; that didn't stop me from keeping a mental list of the things I dreamed of doing one day.

Upon returning home from my walk, I found Wayne waiting for me. I was taken aback because he shouldn't have been home for at least three more hours. The backhanded smack against my cheekbone and the ringing in my ears were the only warning I got that he was angry.

"You disgusting little waste of space. Did you think you could go slumming it in a tattoo parlor and I wouldn't find out about it? Imagine the embarrassment I felt when my secretary came back from picking up lunch from my favorite little deli only to tell me she swore she saw you walking down the street. I only send her to that part of town for the deli; it's a slum area, there's no way my WIFE would have been there! I sent my driver to look for you and he reported back that you were indeed in the area and he observed you walk into a tattoo shop and spend over an hour in there. So help me God, if you marred your body with that dirty ink, there will be hell to pay. No wife of mine is going to be seen in public with trashy ink all over her body. What were you thinking, Josephine?!" The second smack landed harder than the first, but it also woke something up inside of me. I held my cheek and took a moment to gather myself as he continued ranting and raving.

I took a deep breath and closed my eyes; I imagined those wild horses, corralled inside a gated fence, busting out of their holdings. I watched in my mind as they broke free and ran away from their prison. *Be smart here, Josie. He mustn't know you've left until you've had time to get away. Appease him until you can leave.*

"Wayne, I'm sorry. I noticed the artwork in the window and I was drawn to it as an artist. That's all. I didn't get a tattoo; I'd never embarrass you in that way. Please forgive me." I groveled to him and prayed that he would accept my apology.

"Damn straight you'll never embarrass me that way. I think this art hobby has gotten much too out of hand if it's pulling you into dirty tattoo parlors. Your punishment for your actions today is the loss of your business for the time being. Your studio will be locked and your website will be shut down. In time, IF you can prove you can be the respectable woman I need you to be, I may reconsider letting you back into your little hobby." Wayne sneered at me as he watched the life drain from my face; he knew he'd taken the only thing that could hurt me.

My final door had just opened.

The plan I had hatched in my mind involved my art business; I was counting on it for income. Now it was gone. Luckily, thanks to the sales I'd already had and the money I'd been saving and the money from my parents, I had enough to live on for quite a while; I could attempt to set up my business again once I was settled.

I left the next morning; Wayne was going on a three month business trip to Tokyo. The timing was ideal. My hope was that he wouldn't know I was missing for the entire three months; although, I knew he would check up on me with his staff. I had to hope I would get as much time and distance between us as possible.

My entire plan hinged on getting to Torey Hope and finding my Uncle Robert. I was so very nervous, but I had nowhere else to turn. If my uncle was anything like my father maybe I could at least find a hotel in Torey Hope and stay there long enough to plan my next destination.

I was giddy with the excitement of being out on my own; the fear of Wayne and the uncertainty of what was ahead of me almost overpowered that excitement, but I allowed the giddiness to bubble to the surface. Being on my own, being the real me, making my own decisions; these were things I'd never done before, and I was looking forward to them even though the huge change was scary as hell.

I wore only the clothing I had on and took enough clothing for a week's worth of living. I had an exorbitant amount of clothing, but I feared it would be noticed if I packed too much. Wayne had gifted me with a cell phone early in our marriage; I was allowed to phone my parents or Wayne. I did not use it much, but Wayne expected me to be available on it at all times. The decision facing me was whether to take it with me or not. If I left it in Wayne's home, he would get suspicious when he couldn't reach me. If I took it with me, he could use it to track me down quicker. I decided to text Wayne and hopefully buy myself some time.

ME: Wayne, I need to relax and recover from the consequences of my poor decisions. I'm going to have the driver take me to the spa so that I can spend the week there. I will probably be unavailable by phone since the reception is so bad.

After sending the text, I hid the phone deep in the closet under piles of shoeboxes. I also turned it off and took the battery out; I didn't know much about phones but I hoped this would prevent Wayne from tracking it for a while.

I left nothing for Wayne. I would contact the lawyer when I reached Torey Hope and have the divorce papers served. I was asking for nothing from the marriage other than being done with it. I had taken pictures of my face after Wayne hit me; the local authorities had written up a restraining order for me thanks to the lawyer. My lawyer called ahead to the Torey Hope authorities to get a restraining order on file there as well. With luck, if Wayne found me, he would be stopped and arrested before he could hurt me; I knew, after the anger he exhibited the day of the tattoo shop incident that he would not stop himself if he found me. He had been getting angrier and meaner as our time together went on; I felt he was now a loose cannon and finding out I left would be the light to his fuse.

CHAPTER 6

Josie

"Look at life through the windshield, not the rear-view mirror." ~**Byrd Baggett**

The driver did drop me at the spa; I had to walk all the way up to the door and enter before he would drive away. Quickly, I detoured to the side door in hopes that none of the staff would see me; I was grateful I had worn my hair pulled up under a large, floppy hat with oversized dark sunglasses. Even if someone saw me walk out the side door, I hoped they wouldn't recognize me. The spa would be the first place Wayne checked when he realized I was gone.

I made my way into the nearest town, walking on side

streets and through backyards. Once there I bought a pay-as-you-go phone and asked the store for the number of a taxi company. The cab driver ended up being a kind old man who reminded me of a grandfather; I never knew my own grandparents, but he seemed like what a grandfather should be. He took me about an hour away to the nearest Greyhound bus station. I paid him and told him thank you; I had not spoken of where I was going or why so I was shocked and touched when he replied, "Just so you know, miss, I'm an old forgetful man so if anyone ever asks me about delivering a beautiful girl to the bus station, I'm pretty sure I won't remember it. You have a good life and just love yourself." With a final nod of his head and a small wave, he drove away.

I turned, with tears in my eyes, to face the bus schedule. According to the times and miles listed ahead of me, it would take me two days on the bus to reach Torey Hope. I made a quick stop at the restroom to wash my face and comb out my hair; my head was hot from having all of that hair piled up under the hat I'd been wearing. After my pit-stop, I gathered my hair back up under the hat and donned the ridiculously large sunglasses. I paid cash for a ticket to Torey Hope, Illinois and then sat on a secluded bench to wait for the bus to arrive.

An hour later, as I climbed on the huge vehicle, I couldn't help but breathe a little easier and I felt a weight lift off of my shoulders. I didn't know what lay ahead in Torey Hope, but I didn't think it could be any worse than what I was leaving. I'd keep taking it one day at a time. I already felt better than I had in years because I was free.

~

I arrived in the quaint little town as the sun was setting. I realized quickly that it was the day after Thanksgiving when I saw Black Friday signs and ads all over town; I'd been so distracted with planning my escape that the thought of the holiday had passed me by.

My hands were sweaty as I made my way up the stairs to what I hoped was Robert Decker's home. I was nervous to meet him and doubly nervous because it appeared that he had a house full of company. But, keeping the picture of those wild horses in my mind and grasping to the promise of freedom and a new start, I knocked on the door.

The man who greeted me upon opening the door looked very much like my father, but I could tell this man was nothing like Richard Decker the moment he spoke. "Good evening, ma'am. How can I help you?" He was kind and considerate, and I saw immediately that he was a genuinely kind person.

"Hello, are you Robert Decker?" I willed my voice to stop quivering.

"Well, yes, ma'am, I am." Robert smiled and looked at me with curiosity.

"Um, I think I'm your niece. I mean, I think you're my

uncle. Ugh, sorry. Are you Richard Decker's brother?" Robert's eyes showed recognition as I spoke.

"Yes, Richard is my brother. I never knew he had a daughter. What's your name dear?" Robert took hold of my hands as he spoke.

"My name is Josie. My father and mother were killed in a plane crash over a year ago. He mentioned you in his will. I had to leave a bad situation, and I didn't have anywhere else to go. I won't bother you or stay long, but I was wondering if I could stay with you for a couple days." I prepared for Robert to turn me away as I saw four adults walk to the entryway behind him just as he reached out and hugged me to his chest. My heart soared as I felt acceptance flow from this man. He turned around and practically ran into the two couples standing behind him.

"Dad?" One of the women whispered her question as she and the woman next to her took me in with their wary eyes.

"Well, everyone, I'd like you to meet my niece, Josie Decker." I didn't correct him as he used my maiden name; I hoped to legally be a Decker again very soon.

"Josie, this is my family. We're a very large group; I'll introduce everyone, but don't even try to keep us all straight just yet." My uncle began making introductions as the two women, who looked to be just a few years older than me, exchanged looks of confusion and uncertainty.

"I didn't know you had a cousin, Angel." One of the men spoke in a soft whisper into the ear of the blond woman. I watched as she shook her head and replied, "Neither did I." I felt bad that I was obviously intruding and taking everyone by surprise.

The dark haired woman turned to the other man and mouthed, "I have no clue who she is." He raised an eyebrow towards the other man and they both shrugged.

"This is Jack and Judy Jordan. They are the parents of my son-in-law, Jeremiah, who is married to my youngest daughter, Audrey." Robert rotated me around to meet the Jordans.

"This is John and Cindy Morgan. Their son, Nate, is married to my oldest daughter, Libby." Again, he led me around the room doing introductions.

"This is Nate's brother, Nicky, and his wife Carly." Uncle Robert led me to a chair and had me sit. "The children are all downstairs, you can meet them later." I was glad there were no more names or introductions, my brain was on overload from nerves and meeting so many people.

One of the men, I thought he was named Nicky, bluntly stated, "I didn't know Audrey and Libby had a cousin. How do you not know you have a cousin?" The rest of the group cringed a bit at his question, but it was something I'm sure they were all thinking.

"It seems I have a story to tell. Everyone grab a drink and get comfortable." My uncle indicated he was settling in and the rest of the group followed suite. As he began his story, a deep love for his deceased wife was evident, as was the pain that he still carried with him. I gathered quickly that my Aunt

Lois had been gone many years, but the hurt and the missing her were as fresh in his eyes and his voice as if he lost her yesterday. Uncle Robert began his story and every single person in the room, including me, was drawn into it immediately. His words brought his past of love, loss, hurt, and anger to life.

The long and short of his story included my father and uncle not being close growing up. Then my father fell for my uncle's girl, Lois. She loved Robert but Richard wanted her for himself. He physically assaulted her and tried to bully her into marrying him. She clung to my uncle and they married and had a wonderful life until she passed away suddenly at a fairly young age. Uncle Robert and my father never spoke after the incident between Richard and Lois. Robert didn't even know Richard's whereabouts and certainly didn't realize his brother had married, had me, and been killed.

When Uncle Robert stopped his story and he took a moment to gather himself; I could tell from his face and voice and the sincere interest from the other members of his family that the memories he had shared were ones he had never spoken of with those gathered around him. He took a deep breath and swallowed. Turning to me he spoke earnestly and my heart both broke and soared; this man was welcoming me into his family. "Josie, I don't know what brings you here or what you've been going through, but I want you to know that you've found family here with me."

As he finished his story and spoke to me, I watched as the

adult family members, who had been submersed in the story, all began to move and stretch as if to shake the story from their heads. The two older women, Cindy and Judy, had eyes glistening with tears; it was as if they thought of how easily his story could become theirs; nothing was guaranteed and they could lose their spouses at any moment. I could see how this story of loss really hit home for these two women.

Libby and Audrey, cousins I didn't know existed until an hour ago, sat still on the couch, tears clearly drying on their cheeks. I could tell they missed their mother. I watched, feeling like an intruder as Robert and his girls spoke in hushed tones and hugged each other.

I tried not to listen in but their conversation drifted to my ears. "Girls, right now, I think we need to concentrate on Josie. I can't imagine my brother as a parent and I doubt that being his child would have been very easy. I know it's strange to welcome a perfect stranger into my home, but she looks so much like Richard that I *know* she's his daughter and I just have a gut feeling that she's not been treated well. Will you girls help me to help her?"

Libby and Audrey didn't look at each other, they seemed to know what the other was thinking; I held my breath, would they accept me? "Of course we'll help you and Josie, Daddy." After a group hug, the three of them came to me and welcomed me into their family with no questions and open arms. I barely held back the tears as they wrapped their arms around me. In the two hours I'd been there I had felt more love and acceptance from these virtual strangers than I had ever felt from my own parents or husband.

After all of the sleepy children were loaded up and good-byes were exchanged, the majority of the family members drove off into the night with promises of getting together soon.

"Well, Josie, it looks like we've got a lot of time to make up for. Come on, I've got a spare bedroom and it's got your name written all over it. Let's get you settled in." My uncle spoke with a smile in his voice.

I knew he was taken by surprise when I threw myself at him, wrapping my arms around his middle, "Thank you so much, Uncle Robert. I didn't know where else to go, and I was so scared you'd turn me away. You've treated me more kindly in the two hours I've been here than my parents treated me my entire life." I wasn't ready to bring up Wayne just yet, but I knew I'd have to talk about that part of my life soon.

With his arm around my shoulders, my uncle, who I had recently learned was called Captain by his family and friends, carried my single bag into the house. "I'm sorry about your past, Josie. I'm glad to have you here; you're family."

CHAPTER 7

Kyle

*"You will lose someone you can't live without, and your heart will be badly broken, and the bad news is that you never completely get over the loss of your beloved. But this is also the good news. They live forever in your broken heart that doesn't seal back up. And you come through. It's like having a broken leg that never heals perfectly—that still hurts when the weather gets cold, but you learn to dance with the limp." ~**Anne Lamott***

A year or so earlier...

Izzy and I had our first argument on a Wednesday morning; although it was more of a misunderstanding than an argument. The stress of trying and failing to get pregnant month after month, year after year, had finally brought us to a breaking point. We weren't talking about divorce or giving up on each other, we were just tired. Tired of scheduled sex, tired of hoping and having those hopes dashed, tired of doctor appointments that made us feel like failures.

"Kyle, I'm running late for the doctor appointment. I need to stop by the record shop quickly to open it up for the day then I'll rush to the appointment. You'll be there, right?" Her eyes were red from crying the night before; she was a nervous wreck knowing that we would find out today if we had been successful or failed yet again.

Even with the help the doctors had to offer us, Izzy had been adamant that we would do this the natural way and keep love involved in it. We had tried; of course we still loved each other, but sex because a thermometer says it's the right time or cervical mucus is the right consistency isn't exactly intimate and spontaneous.

She must have noticed my fatigued look. I had every intention in the world of being by her side; it just got so very hard to hold your wife as her hopes and yours were dashed month after month. In her stressed state she snapped over my reaction.

"Oh, I see how it is, Kyle. I can't get pregnant and you're the one who's tired of it?!?! Tired of the appointments? Tired of the scheduled sex? Tired of seeing me cry? Yeah, well, I'm even more tired of it, Punk Boy!" That was all she had time to say before the tears started to fall and she collapsed into me. I held her, like I had done so many times over these many years. I no longer tried to use words to comfort her; I knew nothing I could say would help. I was just there for her; I held her and rocked her gently and kissed her head.

"I'm sorry, Izzy-bel. I didn't mean to look like I was tired of all of it; I'll continue doing this for as long as you want. I want a baby with you so badly, but I also don't want to lose 'us' through all of it. I feel like we've done a really good job up until just recently. Maybe we should take a break from all of the charts and temps and schedules and just love on each other for a month or two and then hit it again when we've recouped ourselves." I looked at her expectantly.

"Kyle, I'm so sorry for blowing up at you. I don't know what happened; I just feel guilty sometimes when I see how this is wearing you out. Thank you for sticking by me through all of this shit. I agree; no matter what the results are today, let's just take a two or three month break and see what happens. I love you, Punk Boy." She leaned in to kiss me and the sparks immediately lit; she was going to be a lot later if I had my way.

"I'll go unlock the shop for you and you can head straight to the doctor. That should give us a good 30 minutes. Come on, my Izzy-bel, let's see what kind of fun we can have in those extra minutes." I kissed her again and carried her to the bedroom. Making love to Izzy just because and not because we wanted a baby was a welcomed and sweet distraction.

Thirty minutes later Izzy rushed out the door to her appointment with me promising to open her shop and meet her there. I was about to leave when I saw some paperwork on the table and wondered if it was something she would need at the doctor's office. Before jumping on my bike, I shot her a text:

ME: Hey, I grabbed the paperwork on the table. Didn't know if you needed it or not, but I've got it just in case. Love you. Be there in a bit.

After getting the shop open and making sure the morning employee was there and ready to man the place, I hopped on my bike and sped toward the doctor. If I didn't hit many lights, I should be walking in about the time they called her back. I prayed this would be the day our appointment took a long time; I envied those anxious couples who got called back and stayed to make follow-up appointments for tracking their baby's progress. We had fought this for five years and for the last year and a half we had partnered with the doctors even though we had been continuing to go with natural conception; every month we went to the doctor for bloodwork and every month they called us back, gave us a quick yet sympathetic negative report, and sent us on our way.

I strolled through the door of the office; none of the ladies behind the desk even blinked an eye at my hair or piercings or tattoos or clothing anymore. Other patients, however, reacted in one of two ways: The first type would ogle me and look like they wanted to lick me from top to bottom. These were usually younger women or very pregnant mothers. I'm guessing the hormones had something to do with both. The second type would crinkle their nose in disgust and quickly try to protect themselves or young children from me. None of this bothered me, it just continued to strengthen my "fuck'em all" attitude.

I glanced around and saw that Izzy wasn't in the waiting room. "Hi, Lisa, I'm a little late. What room did they take Izzy to?" I smiled at the receptionist and silently chuckled to myself as I watch her blush and stutter around on her words a bit.

"Oh, hi Mr. Martin. Um, I haven't seen Mrs. Martin arrive yet. Let me check and see if they've already called her back and I just missed it." Lisa stepped to the back for a moment. When she returned I took in the fact that she was already shaking her head to confirm that Izzy hadn't gotten there yet. My stomach started to churn; how could she not be there? She left in plenty of time, she should have been there by that time.

As I stepped out of the office to get better reception and call Izzy, my phone rang. Seeing her name on the screen, I breathed a sigh of relief. "Hey, Izzy-bel, where are you? I beat you to the office already." I laughed at her, knowing how she hated to be late.

"Mr. Martin? This is Officer Johnson. Your wife has been in an accident; we need you to meet us at Benton Memorial Hospital. Go through the emergency department. Mr. Martin, are you still with me, sir?" The officer sounded hesitant.

"What? Yes, yes, I'm here. How is she? Is it bad?" I was already heading toward my bike to race to the hospital. It was only a mile away.

"Sir, we'd like to speak with you when you arrive rather than over the phone. I will meet you in the emergency department as soon as you get there. The ambulance has already taken your wife there; we were searching for a number to call and found your name in her phone." His voice trailed off and I reached my bike.

"I'm heading that way." I clipped out. My mind was swirling with what-ifs. What if she was injured severely? What if she was already dead? What if she hurt someone else? As I drove toward my destination, I noticed the other side of the road was littered with debris; my heart sank as I realized this was the location of Izzy's accident. I saw her little black car; no one could have survived that. I went into auto-pilot mode; I arrived at the hospital but I don't remember getting there. The officer met me at the door and I could tell from the look on his and his partner's face that my prediction after having seen the accident site was correct. I don't remember dropping to my knees and sobbing in the entry way of the emergency room, but at some point both officers assisted me to my feet and walked me to the room where my Izzy-bel was.

She was black and blue, from head to toe. I hadn't spoken to a doctor yet but I would have guessed there were very few bones in her body that weren't broken. She was hooked up to multiple machines; I saw the ventilator breathing for her. The officers stood outside the door, not leaving me but giving me privacy.

"Oh, my God, my sweet Izzy-bel. What happened, baby?" I gently took her hand and my heart broke even more when I felt how cold it was. This was my wife, the woman I had been making love to just an hour before; she had been warm and sexy and alive. Now she was cold and hurt and still. So very still.

"Hello, I'm Dr. Dannick. You're Mr. Martin, the husband?" An older gentleman with white hair and a white coat walked to stand opposite me beside Izzy's bed.

"Yes," my voice croaked, "I'm Kyle Martin, her husband."

"Mr. Martin, I will let you talk to the officers in more detail about your wife's accident, but it appears she may have been distracted; she veered left, over corrected and hit a tree." The doctor paused to let me take in his words. Izzy was distracted? By what? My stomach revolted against me as I recalled the text I had sent her; did that simple message cause this hell we were living? I had to sit down; pulling a chair alongside the bed, I sat while still holding Izzy's hand.

"Can she hear us? Does she have a chance at recovery?" I spoke to the doctor with a raspy voice; I felt it in my soul that she was already gone, taken from me much too soon.

The doctor's eyes were kind, but his words and expression were grave, "Son, she has no brain activity. Her body has stopped functioning, the only thing keeping her with us is the ventilator. She's not really breathing, she's not alive."

The man's words confirmed what I had known from the moment I took her hand in mine. My sweet Izzy-bel was gone. I would never see those huge violet eyes again; I'd never kiss those bright pink lips. My best friend, the love of my life, gone.

"Mr. Martin, I have some other news that I need to share with you. Were you aware that your wife was pregnant?" And just like that, my world was wrecked even more. What a cruel twist of fate; we had tried so hard and failed for so long. Now we succeeded and Izzy was taken away from me?

"We had been trying for five years. No, I didn't know; we were supposed to go to an appointment today to find out." My voice croaked as I said the words; the gravity of this fucked up situation sinking in a bit more.

"The trauma of the accident caused a spontaneous miscarriage upon arrival. I'm sorry for the loss of your child, Mr. Martin. As delicate as this situation is, I must ask you to make a decision about life support. If you have questions, please don't hesitate to ask; I'll leave you to yourself. Take all the time you need, but I need to know if you want to continue life support or let her go. You can let a nurse know when you've made your decision. The nurse will also speak to you about organ donation if you know of your wife's wishes on that topic." The doctor patted my shoulder in a grandfatherly way and left the room.

CHAPTER 8

Kyle

"Unable are the loved to die. For love is immortality."
~Emily Dickinson

My wife, my best friend, the love of my life was pregnant.

Was pregnant.

Was.

Not anymore.

Why? Because I made her late, because she was distracted by something, wrecked her car, suffered severe trauma, miscarried our baby, and lost her life. Sitting in the hospital room, holding her hand, I had to make a decision. It wasn't a hard decision; I knew what I would do because I knew what Izzy would have wanted. She would never have wanted to be kept 'alive' in this manner; she was a huge proponent of organ donation as well so I knew she'd want her organs to help as many people as possible. I knew what I had to do. But, I didn't want to make the decision; not so soon, not right then.

I sat for over an hour, crying at her side. I told her about the baby and made her hand give me a fist bump to celebrate our final success.

"I'm so sorry this happened, Izzy-bel. I'm sorry I made you run a little late, but I'm also grateful for the last moments we had together. If my text to you was the cause of your accident, I swear I'll live the rest of my life hating myself. I'm going to have to let you go soon, Iz. You've got a baby to meet in Heaven. I'm jealous that you get to know if it was a boy or a girl. I hope it's a girl with your beautiful eyes. I don't want to say goodbye, baby, but I think you've got places to be; if you get a chance, come to me sometimes, even if it's just in my dreams. I love you so very much, baby. I will miss you every second of every day. I don't understand why you were taken from me, but I will love you for the rest of my life." I had let the nurse know of my decision and I held tightly to Izzy's hand as the nurse took away all of the life support. Leaning in to nuzzle her cheek, I whispered, "It's ok, Izzy-bel. Go ahead and let go. I'll hold you in my heart always, baby." My tears fell on her cheeks as the monitors became silent. My Izzy-bel was gone.

~

Hours later, after speaking to the hospital and making the necessary arrangements and meeting with the officers who arrived upon the scene of the accident first, I was done at the hospital.

I was done.

I could leave.

But I didn't want to leave; my sweet Izzy was still there, I didn't want to leave her alone. Rationally I told myself that it was just her body, her heart and soul had left her just moments after the accident; but my grieving, irrational side felt like leaving the hospital was giving up on her. I hesitated in front of the doors which would lead me to my bike; if I didn't leave here, I wouldn't have to start the next part of my journey without my best friend by my side. I turned around quickly and began roaming the hospital. I knew I'd have to leave soon; I needed to make calls and arrangements. But leaving here and going to our empty home was not something I was ready for just yet.

I found myself on the labor and delivery floor; I stood, mesmerized, in front of the glass partition which allowed me to see the new babies. My heart, already shattered beyond recognition, wept inside my chest. I played out how this day should have gone; we should have been laughing and cele-brating our pregnancy. Izzy had plans for a nursery; we should have been looking at paint samples. I knew we would have ordered in and spent our evening in awe that we had finally succeeded.

Instead, I was lost; wandering by myself, crying, staring at babies. I had imagined Izzy and me as parents many times; I wanted so badly to be a daddy to our child, in my mind it was always a baby girl. I pictured Izzy holding our baby to her breast, hearing her first word, watching her take her first steps. The tears in my eyes blurred the babies in front of me; like the image of our own baby, they faded away. I turned and walked to the main floor.

As my heart and mind struggled with the emotions I felt upon leaving this place, I powered through the door and into the evening air. I took a shuddering breath, "Izzy, I don't want to go on; I want to be with you and our baby. But I know you'd tell me to buck up and live my life. I will keep trying to breathe; I will survive for you, but I'm not sure I can actually 'live'." Letting out the breath I had been holding, I climbed on my bike and headed to my empty home.

Izzy's funeral was beautiful.

Fuck that. It wasn't beautiful, it was a fucking funeral.

People kept telling me what a beautiful service it was and that she looked so peaceful.

Fuck that shit! What was beautiful about burying my wife? And peaceful? I've never seen a dead body look peaceful. Izzy looked...well, she looked dead. She wasn't my Izzy. The mortician, while he had done a great job covering her bruises, just couldn't capture her hair and makeup; she didn't look like she was supposed to.

I opted to have the casket closed after close family and friends had paid their respects. Alone with her for one last time, I brushed a lock of hair out of her face, kissed my fingers and placed them on her lips. "No kissing a dead body, baby. I know you'd be in agreement with me on that one." I chuckled as I slid my wedding ring off and placed it carefully on her finger. I pulled a pair of pink baby booties out of my pocket. "Give these to our baby girl, Izzy; tell her that her daddy loves her more than she'll ever know." Again, rationally, I knew that she couldn't hear me, she wasn't taking these things with her, she was already where she was meant to be, but it gave me some closure to go through these actions.

Hours later, as the line of people began to dwindle, I looked up to see the face of my best friend from high school. Jeremiah Jordan had been best buddies with both Izzy and me. The tears in his eyes and the emotions I felt over seeing him after all of these years finally did me in, and I let the tears flow. I was grateful that he had waited until all of the others had gone through the line before he approached.

"Jordan, man, thanks so much for coming. I didn't expect you to make such a long trip." I clapped him on the back, but he grabbed me into a full-blown hug.

"Man, there's nowhere else I'd be right now. It fuckin'

sucks that this is how we meet up after such a long time, but I knew I needed to be here with you; Izzy would kick my ass if she knew I left you to deal with this on your own." I smiled at his words, knowing he was right. He had loved Izzy like a sister and they had teased and bickered just like siblings all those years ago.

"I think I'm done here until tomorrow morning. Do you have some time? We can grab some coffee or something." I understood if he needed to head out right away; he had driven a long distance. But I was hoping he'd have an hour or so to catch up.

"Man, I'm yours for the next few days if you'll have me. I thought maybe I could sleep on your couch, see your shop, help out with anything that needs done to get through this part." The tears started again, my teeth were going to be ground to little nubs if I kept this up. Even with the tears, my heart felt slightly lighter than it had since the accident; having my friend there to help out and distract me was just what I needed. I had my own parents and Izzy's parents, but it wasn't the same as having a buddy there.

After all of the funeral necessities were completed the next day, Jeremiah and I spent the next three days reliving grade school and high school memories, drinking a little more than we should have, playing basketball, and just catching up. For three days my heart wasn't as broken as it had been. For three days the pain wasn't as severe as it had been. But, life had to go on and Jeremiah had to get back to his family. We promised to keep in touch. I watched him drive off in his old Bronco and felt the dark clouds roll in. I could feel the heavy blanket of sadness and hopelessness settle over me. I kept trying to breathe through the heaviness; I would survive, but I couldn't live.

CHAPTER 9

Kyle

"There are things that we never want to let go of, people we never want to leave behind. But keep in mind that letting go isn't the end of the world, it's the beginning of a new life." ~*Author Unknown*

A year or so later...

I couldn't stay there any longer. I had already moved out of the house Izzy and I shared, and I was living in the back room at my shop. But it had started to feel like the town was closing in on me more and more. I kept trying to breathe, but it was getting harder and harder each and every day.

Everyone in town had moved on. People had expectations

of me; some thought I was too sad, some thought I was too happy, everyone had an opinion on how I should be acting now that my wife had been gone a year.

My parents were travelling the world. Izzy's parents had retired to a warm beach. I had a few people I considered friends in town, but no one and nothing was truly holding me here any longer. It had been a year since I lost my wife. Part of me felt like it had happened yesterday; part of me, the piece that was so very tired of trying to keep breathing and surviving, felt like it had been a million years. Every day was the same; I fought all day, swimming against the tide of blackness that threatened to overtake me. I visited with a therapist for a trial run; she suggested that I make a fresh start, get out of town, away from the memories. She promised that the memories I wanted to keep of Izzy and me would remain, but letting go of the extra would free me up to keep moving along. For some reason I liked her phrase "moving along" better than "moving on." Moving on felt like I was turning my back on what Izzy and I had. Moving along seemed more like I was just living life and taking on what came at me next. I liked that.

Packing up my shop and listing it for sale didn't hurt as much as I thought it would; I was actually feeling somewhat relieved to be getting away. Jeremiah had invited me to stay with his family for as long as needed. I'd be moving in with them within the week. I didn't plan on staying indefinitely, just until I could get a new job set up and my own place to stay. Knowing I was going to be closer to a good friend was a strong attraction for moving to Torey Hope, Illinois.

~

Moving in with Jeremiah and Audrey Jordan and their children went as smoothly as can be expected. Their kids were great and Audrey was perfect for him. The entire extended family welcomed me as one of their own; feeling welcomed softened the blackness to more of a dark grey.

I had feared feeling like a third wheel in this large family. Jeremiah had Audrey and their three children. Audrey's sister, Libby, was married to Nate Morgan and they also had three kids. Nate's brother, Nicky, had a wife and child as well. Then there were the older couples; John and Cindy Morgan, Jack and Judy Jordan, and Captain Robert Decker. The Captain was Libby and Audrey's dad and a widower, but even he seemed to be moving on and beginning to date again.

However, instead of being the third wheel, I met Josie Decker. She was the niece of Robert Decker. I hadn't heard her entire story, I'm not sure the rest of her family had either, but I knew she had just recently arrived in Torey Hope and was staying with the Captain until she could get her feet under her.

If I hadn't been so focused on just breathing, I would have found my breath taken away by Josie Decker. She was about 5'6" which made her quite a bit shorter than my six-feet. Her skin was like porcelain; had I wanted to hold her hand it would have contrasted starkly with the olive tone in my own skin. Her hair was a deep auburn color that hung past her shoulders and made her bright blue eyes pop from her wary and gentle face.

I felt a connection to Josie the second I met her; she was going through something like I was. I didn't know if she had lost someone or what her situation was, but I could tell she was still reeling from something big. We both had a past we weren't completely ready to share; we both had memories and demons we were battling.

I loved that she was easy to talk to, we struck up a friendship right away. I think with us being the two "extras" in the family, it was likely for us to be paired up a lot of times. I didn't mind; Josie was kind and gentle and fun to be around. I got the feeling she was like a wild animal that had been caged; her will had been taken from her, but I didn't think she had been broken. I saw a flicker of something in her eyes now and then which led me to believe that Josie wanted to break free from the prison that was holding her back. But she needed to love herself and believe in herself first; she was too restrained, too uncertain, too wilted. I hoped that our friendship would bring that life back to her and also help me breathe easier.

I knew the whole family hoped that Josie and I would become something more. I didn't want to go into details, but I wasn't ready now, or ever, to love again. Friendship though was something I needed, something I could offer, something I wanted.

I had just taken Josie on her first motorcycle ride and she was still riding the high from the thrill of that. I felt guilty popping her with a question like the one I had planned when she was so full of adrenaline, but it was something I needed to ask and I wanted to get a move on my plan. We had already had a conversation earlier about both of us being ready to move out on our own, so maybe this plan wouldn't take her as much by surprise as I worried it would.

I battled the internal struggle within me and finally just overpowered and delivered my question. "Okay, here's the deal; I've been thinking about what we talked about. I can't or won't talk about the bad shit that brought me here, at least not right now. I'm still fighting pain and demons, but I feel better here than I've felt in a long time. I want to stay; I can't keep living with Audrey and Jeremiah. I want a place of my own, and I want to set up a tattoo shop in town. I know you want your own place as well. Maybe I'm prying but I get the feeling that you've got some stuff going on in your past as well; no need to talk about it until a time when you feel up to it. But, I was wondering, since we're friends looking for the same thing, if you'd like to look for a place with me? We could be roommates. Whatdya think?" From my seat on the bike, I turned my eyes up at her with my question.

"Kyle, I think that's a wonderful idea! I trust you completely since you're friends with Jeremiah; I know Audrey would have said something already if she didn't trust you as well. But, can we look at houses first? I'd really like to get something where we both have a bedroom and then maybe we could use a third bedroom as a studio." At my questioning look she shrugged, "I like to paint. Or, I used to like to paint, and I'd like to try it again. I also do scrapbooking so a studio/office space would be perfect. If we can't find a house in our price-range, we can switch to apartments. I have quite a bit of money saved even though I've not been working. We should sit down right after the holidays and work out a budget. Oh my gosh, I can't believe how exciting this is!" She blushed now, realizing just how worked-up the bike ride and my suggestion had her.

I had to laugh at her enthusiasm, and I brushed aside the stirring I felt in my core as I watched her face flush pink. "Well, Josie-girl, I think you're still a little jazzed from your first motorcycle ride; but I'm glad that my suggestion is so exciting. I consider you a friend and it's good to see you letting loose a little bit. Day after tomorrow, let's sit down and run some numbers and start our search." I leaned in to hug her and Josie hugged me back; I refused to acknowledge the tingly feeling that hugging her left on my body.

CHAPTER 10

Josie

"When you recover or discover something that nourishes your soul and brings joy, care enough about yourself to make room for it in your life." ~*Jean Shinoda Bolen*

Kyle Martin had recently moved in with Audrey and Jeremiah. I know I said I had no plans of ever pairing up with a man again, but Kyle is different. Aside from the fact that I didn't plan on dating, Kyle had made it very clear that he had no intentions of dating. He didn't actually *say* those words but I could sense a wall around him guarding his heart. I didn't know what happened to hurt him so badly, but I could tell dating was not even on his radar.

If I WAS looking to date, I wasn't even sure if Kyle would be my type. He's a very attractive man; about six-feet, tattoos all over his body, piercings, hair that he colors and styles a different way almost daily. His chocolate brown eyes were filled with pain, but I would sometimes see a tiny spark; it was like a damp match that starts to light but just can't burn. His eyes were like that; he would laugh or joke with me and start to look moderately happy. But then, just as quickly as the spark began, a look of guilt would cross his face, and he would shut down.

Kyle is the exact opposite of me. No, that's not accurate. Kyle is the me that I want to be, he's the opposite of the me my parents and Wayne created. I watched Kyle dress the way he wanted, speak the way he wanted, and be whatever he wanted; I desired that. I wanted to let loose and really live, really be me. I had started with baby-steps; riding a motorcycle for the first time was definitely for the new me and was such a rush. I couldn't wait to do it again; one thing off of my bucket list and the rest just waiting for me to get to them. On my own time, because *I* wanted to do them; not because someone was telling me to do them.

I was contemplating a tattoo; actually, I was thinking about two. The first would be like a practice or trial run; the second would be a much larger piece. Once Kyle and I got settled in our new place, I planned to talk to him about the tattoos I wanted.

I didn't even think twice about being roommates with Kyle. Other than Libby, Audrey, and Carly, Kyle was the only friend I'd really ever had. My parents and Wayne really put a kink in friendships for me. I loved my cousins and Carly; we spent a lot of time together and I was really beginning to glow from the girl-talk and their love and support. But, Kyle was almost like my soul-mate; if a person could be your soul-mate without being a romantic love interest, then that's what Kyle was. He and I contrasted and complemented each other perfectly.

We got along great and neither of us was expecting more from 'us' than friends and roommates. I think that's one of the reasons we clicked so well, there were no expectations from either of us; we were truly just friends.

We spent a very long, very disappointing week looking at house after house. We had chosen a realtor and she was very kind, but she just wasn't finding us what we were wanting. We needed at least two bedrooms and we wanted a space for a studio. We also wanted enough room that the rest of the family could come over often; Kyle and I laughed that we had gotten pretty used to the Morgan's, Jordan's, and Decker's family get-togethers and we wanted to have space for them to come to our place sometimes too.

The Monday of our second week of house hunting Kyle picked me up at Uncle Robert's and we went to get coffee before meeting the realtor. I had started making excuses for him to drive so we could ride his motorcycle.

Kyle had taken to shortening my name; I loved it and secretly smiled each time he said my name as something other than Josie. Usually it was Jo or Jose or Jo-Jo. It made me feel comfortable and wanted and safe to have this man, my friend, call me personal little nicknames.

"So, Jose, I'm wondering if we need to give up on the idea of a house. I know you've got your heart set on a house for a studio area, but it's starting to seem like it's just not going to work out. I was thinking that maybe you could set up a studio area in my shop once I get it. It wouldn't be as convenient as having it right in our house, but it would give you a place to work; plus, you could spend your days with me. That's got to be a bonus." He smiled a crooked little smile at me as his warm chocolate brown eyes laughed.

I had to laugh at him; he was such a good guy, so fun and funny and caring. He was so smart but he was also a smartass and sarcasm was a second language for him. I truly hated that he was so hurt inside; I felt like he had so much to give, something was just holding him back. "Wow! Bonus for sure!" I smiled at him and he shrugged his shoulders as if to say, "Yeah, I know."

"You're right though, we should let her know today that she can start looking at apartments for us. I guess I'll just have to let go of my dreams and watch my hopes be dashed and slashed." I sighed dramatically and tried to pull off my saddest face. In all actuality, I really was sad, but it didn't bother me as much as I thought it would. I was just happy I'd still be rooming with my friend. Kyle smiled at me and wrapped his arm around my shoulders as we left the quaint little coffee house. I caught myself inhaling his scent; it was clean, fresh, and male. There was a slight tingling in my belly as I leaned into his solid warmth; he may have been just my friend but I wasn't totally immune to this man.

As we pulled up in front of the realtor's office, the woman who had been showing us houses came running out on her chubby little legs. "Whoa, she looks excited." Kyle whispered in my ear as Sally ran toward us. She was breathing hard when she reached us; either from excitement or exertion or both.

"Oh. My. Goodness! I'm so glad you both are here! You won't believe the deal that just came across my computer screen! I think it's the absolute perfect fit for you! I was ready to give up and convince you to find a nice apartment, but this showed up and it's seriously perfect! Let's go, follow me!" She made an abrupt about-face and headed to her sporty little car. Kyle and I looked at each other, eyebrows raised in excited anticipation.

We followed Sally as she sped along Torey Hope's streets;

I loved the fact that the house wasn't right in town but was just on the outside of it. When we pulled up in front of the house, my eyes filled with tears as I stood in the front yard gazing up at its beauty. Kyle must have sensed my overwhelmed emotions because he walked over to me and wrapped his arms around me from behind. "Like what you see, Jo-Jo? Is this what you were dreaming of?" His voice was quiet and smooth in my ear and it added to the overall impact of the moment.

"This is exactly what I've been dreaming of," I told him as I dried the tears. "Look at it, Kyle, it's the most gorgeous house I've ever seen!" I stood there, barely breathing as I took in the sturdy columns on the front porch, the small portico on the right, the impressive turret on the left. I could already picture my studio in one of the turret rooms and a reading nook in one of the bay windows. I turned worried eyes toward Sally, "I know this type of Victorian usually goes for a pretty penny, are you sure we can afford this?" I had already fallen in love with it, I wasn't sure I could deal with not getting this house.

Sally practically jumped up and down as she exclaimed, "You can totally afford this house! That's why I'm so excited! You wouldn't believe the deal you're going to get! Let's go in and check it out! If you love the outside, you're going to die over the interior!" Sally was seriously about to explode with giddiness. Kyle and I hid our smiles as we followed her into the house.

As we walked up the front sidewalk, Kyle exclaimed, "It's a good thing I'm a sucker for color. You like this color, Jo?" The house was a gorgeous lavender with dark purple trim. I loved it and told Kyle so. "But if you want to change the color, that's ok. Let's just not change it as often as you change your hair color." I teased him but got the feeling that he would let me keep the color if I wanted.

After an hour of touring every nook and cranny of the house, we were both completely sold. I had already envisioned decorations in certain rooms. I had claimed the upstairs "round room" in the turret as my studio and we'd decided to keep the downstairs turret room as the library/office like the last owners had designed it. Kyle laid claim to the upstairs room as his own studio; I knew he was an artist, but I was also learning how much he loved music. He planned to put in a little work space and audio features. Downstairs there were two bedrooms; they shared a bathroom as a lot of older homes did. This wasn't the most convenient setup, but it definitely wasn't enough to deterr us from buying. This house was on the very small end for a Victorian style home, but it had plenty of room for the two of us and met the wishes we were looking for; we'd even have room for the entire family to come over.

Walking out on the porch, I pictured sitting here on nice evenings, sipping tea, reading or talking to Kyle. I wanted this house. This place already felt more like home than either of the homes I'd lived in with my parents or Wayne. I visibly shivered when I thought of Wayne; Kyle noticed, "You ok, Jose? You having second thoughts? We can take a bit and think about it if you want."

I shook my head and smiled at him, "No way. I was just thinking of something unpleasant. I am definitely sure about this house. Can we go ahead and make our offer?"

We followed Sally back to the office and immediately put in our offer. Waiting for the response was torture, but we heard back fairly quickly and within a week we were moving into our new home.

"So, tell me about this 'I used to paint' statement you made. What made you stop painting?" Kyle inquired during a lunch break one day as we were moving in and unpacking our belongings. Kyle had a few more belongings than I did; he'd kept some things in storage when he moved to Torey Hope. Neither of us had a lot so we had been doing a lot of shopping for furniture. Kyle said he'd let the girls and I handle shopping for the decorations. We'd been working all week and had made quite a dent in getting the place ready to live in. We were planning on moving in the following week.

"Well, it's a pretty long and drawn out story; not a very happy one either. So, I'll save you that part and just suffice it to say that I used to paint and was forced to stop. But I very much want to get back to it. I used to have a website where I sold my work, but it was taken away from me. I want to set up another site and this time I want to make it totally mine. Would you help me design a logo?" I was chomping at the bit to get the area set up so I could begin painting and selling my work again.

Kyle watched me for a while, deep in thought, then he nodded his head, "Definitely. We'll work on it as soon as we are moved in completely. What's the name of your website store going to be?"

I didn't want to use "Art by J" again; too many bad memories and I didn't want Wayne to be able to track me down through the website if that were even possible. I had been playing around with a name in my head for a while. I wanted to take my image of wild horses running free and make it into my logo and business name. I had recently found a song called Wild Horses by Natasha Bedingfield and I cried as I listened to it; it was like she wrote the song just for me. Coming out of my ponderings, I smiled at Kyle. "I think I'm going to call it 'Wild Horses—Reckless Abandon Art by J. Marie'."

He smiled and nodded, "That's perfect. Have you heard that song called Wild Horses? I think it sort of fits you." He looked at me to see if I knew the song he was talking about.

Tears filled my eyes, "Yeah, I've heard it. I almost think it was written about me if you want to know the truth. That's where the name came from. And, while we're on the subject, I'm pretty sure wild horses will be the theme of the tattoo I have you do for me one day."

He looked shocked for a moment then grabbed my hand across the table, "I knew you were a tattoo girl at heart the moment I first met you. I'd be honored to work something up for you and ink that beautiful virgin skin of yours. You just let me know when you're ready." I was touched that he got me so completely. I forced myself to ignore the electricity that passed from his hand up my arm with his touch.

"Well, go ahead and plan something small to start with. Maybe for my wrist? I want it to say 'run free' and have a small wild horse with it. I'll start with that and work up to the bigger piece. I want the big one across my back; wild horses and the words 'Reckless Abandon'." I could already see Kyle's artist wheels turning as I spoke; I knew he would design something perfect and beautiful.

A week later we were totally moved into the house and had started staying there. I missed seeing Uncle Robert, but I was so thrilled to have a place of my own. Kyle had gotten along great with Jeremiah, Audrey, and the kids but I knew he was glad to be somewhere with more privacy. We agreed that we'd take the week to set up my studio and then have the rest of the family over to see the house properly; of course, Nate,

Nicky, and Jeremiah had all helped us move our stuff in, but I wanted everyone to come over and help us celebrate our home.

Audrey, Libby, and Carly had expressed some reservations about Kyle and me jointly taking on this house; they worried if one of us started dating it would be somewhat awkward to have the date come over. They questioned what would happen if one of us wanted to marry one day. I pushed their concerns away; neither Kyle nor I were planning on dating. I was completely satisfied with where my life was right then and I had no plans of marrying again. I knew Kyle felt the same; well, I knew he felt the same about dating, so I assumed he didn't plan on marrying either.

I knew Kyle and I needed to get everything set up so we could start bringing in an income, but the time we got to spend together setting up our home, my studio, and his shop were some of the best weeks of my life. I learned to laugh; I made decisions based on what I wanted, not worrying about the reactions of others; I got to be myself. I learned to not concern myself with pleasing others. I knew Kyle liked me, I knew my new family liked me, that was all that was important to me; I was done trying to please others. I was living for me; I was set on learning to love myself.

We started with my studio and took three days. I opted for white walls and black furniture so it was the perfect lighting for my painting. Kyle had shown me a couple drawings of "Wild Horses—Reckless Abandon Art by J. Marie"

He was truly so very talented. We enlisted Jeremiah's computer skills to help us convert Kyle's drawing into my website logo. I had brought a couple small paintings with me along with some blank premade scrapbooks I'd made. I took the pictures of them and listed them for sale on the site. I had started realizing that staging the photos of my paintings and scrapbooks was almost as much fun as creating them in the first place. I planned to have some other items created and for sale within the next couple weeks.

After setting up my studio, we were both exhausted but I felt happier than I ever had. I was away from Wayne, I had family to love me, I had a friend to share a home with, and I had my art and website back; I pushed aside the niggling fear of Wayne tracking me down. I was much stronger now than I had ever been; I wouldn't say that I had yet learned to actually love myself and believe in myself, but I was getting better and better at it every day. I caught tears streaming down my cheeks as I stood in the doorway of my studio; my emotions were all over the place. Kyle finished hanging the paper he'd drawn my logo on and walked over to me. "Hey, Jo-Jo, don't cry. This is a good thing. Whatever that prick did to you, he can't take this away. This is yours, you did this; this is one of those wild horses breaking free from the corral and running free." He gathered me into a hug; I heard his intake of breath as I wrapped my arms around his waist. I didn't know how he knew that my tears stemmed from a man, but I knew Kyle would help take the weight of my past from me if I just asked.

We stood like that for several moments; I felt as if I were drawing strength from him. Each day that we spent together I felt more and more strongly that Kyle and I were brought to Torey Hope for a reason; we needed the place, we needed the people, we needed each other.

CHAPTER 11

Kyle

"Often the thought of pain is actually worse that the pain itself." ~ ***Greg Behrendt***

I wasn't being fair to Josie; I wanted to know about her past, but I wasn't ready to tell her about my past. Other than Jeremiah, I hadn't told anyone what happened to Izzy. Before I came to Torey Hope, the therapist told me I needed to let go of the guilt. The police had determined that Izzy had wrecked before my text even came in; me texting her while she was driving wasn't what killed her. I truly was letting go of that guilt because I had a comprehensive police report to prove I wasn't at fault.

Letting go of the guilt of moving on with my life was harder; no, not hard, impossible. How could I smile when she was gone? How could I laugh with friends when she was gone? How could I set up house with a beautiful girl when my Izzy-bel was gone? I lived with the guilt with every breath I took. I enjoyed Josie's company and I knew that rooming with her was in the best interest of us both. But then I would catch myself laughing and joking with her, smiling at her, breathing in her scent, wanting to touch her, and I'd be bombarded with feelings of guilt as powerful as military weapons. Was Izzy watching? Was she sad that I was moving on? Did she think I was betraying her by moving on too soon? If I forced myself to answer these questions, I knew the answers; Izzy would have wanted me to be happy. In fact, she would have absolutely loved Josie. But, instead of embracing the true knowledge I had of what Izzy would want, I clung to the falsities and guilt; moving on hurt and I wasn't sure I wanted to hurt any more than I already did.

I wanted to tell Josie about Izzy; I just didn't know where to start. "Hey, so I used to be married, but she and my unborn child died in a car accident over a year ago. I came here to escape the haunting memories of my dead wife and child, but I can't escape the guilt I feel over moving on without her." Exactly where do those words fit into a conversation?

So I focused more on Josie. Her confidence was growing; it was slow going, but I was seeing the real her peek out here and there more and more each day. She was making strides, but she still had a long way; if asked point blank if she loved herself or felt good about herself, I didn't think she would have been able to say yes at that point in time.

Something happened to her in the past; I didn't think she was physically abused because she wasn't skittish around anyone. I thought she had probably been emotionally abused. Her confidence was crushed, her will was corralled like those wild horses she was so fond of; her spirit was broken. I wanted to know who hurt her. A husband? If so, she couldn't have been married for long. Her parents? That seemed likely based on what her Uncle Robert had told me about her father, Richard. I was determined to get her to trust me enough to share her past; I felt like she would finally be able to love herself, love the real Josie, once she spoke about her past out loud. *Do you see the irony in this, Martin? You want her to talk about her own past to help let go of it. How about you take your own advice?* I ignored my psyche; talking about my past and letting go of it meant that I was leaving Izzy and forgetting about her. I wasn't ready to do that; I didn't know if I ever would be.

Sally had really come through for us on finding the house and she proved her worth again when she found me a perfect spot for a shop. It wasn't far from the house, so I could walk if needed, but it also had ample parking for my bike and customers. The shop front was perfect for catching customers' attention. I was totally stoked that Torey Hope didn't have a tattoo shop; even better, the closest one was about 30 miles away so I would be able to draw in customers from some of the surrounding towns as well.

Josie helped set up the store front. I showed her some of my work and she painted these huge panels of my four favorite pieces. We put two panels in each window; this gave a little mystery as to what was inside and showed some of my work. Josie had been playing around with my shop's name; she wanted to paint the sign for it. I was going simple with the name; "Kyle Martin Ink Designs" was the name of my shop before, and I thought it still worked well, so I was sticking with that. She designed two completely different signs to hang in each window between the panels; the girl was truly talented.

I had brought a lot of my furniture from the old shop and put it in storage, so I had only a few things to order and set up. Within a week, my shop was functional. Jeremiah and Josie and I worked on setting up a business page online so that I could bring customers in. We decided we'd cross advertise on each other's sites in hopes of bringing business in for both of us.

Josie insisted on being my first customer. I had drawn up

a tiny wild horse with the script "run free" and she fell in love with it the moment she saw it.

"Kyle, it's like you peeked into my brain and saw exactly what I was picturing. This is perfect." The kiss she had planted on my cheek was, I'm sure, meant to be friendly but the burning sensation I felt there left me a bit dazed. It was like I could feel her lips there the rest of the day.

"Ok, Jo, are you sure you're ready for this?" I asked her as I set up my gun and ink. Glancing at her I could see her nervousness, but I also saw excitement and anticipation. "Ahhh, I see you ARE ready for this. That's my girl; I'm predicting this one taste will turn you into a tattoo junkie real quickly." She bit her beautiful lip and her eyes went wide.

"I'm just so excited to be doing something I've always wanted to do without having to worry about repercussions or the image that someone else thinks I should be portraying. I want to portray the real me and this tattoo is part of the real me." I hung on her words as I tried to piece together her past. Her gorgeous eyes were big and bright as she spoke and I felt a jolt in my stomach as I took in her flushed cheeks. Running my thumb across the inside of her wrist, I admired her delicate skin. Without thinking I pulled her wrist to my mouth and feathered a kiss across the skin there; her breath caught and our eyes met. I felt her pulse quicken under my thumb, "Last chance, Jo, are you sure you want to permanently ink your body?" I chose to ignore the heavy breathing and obvious sexual tension between us; I didn't mean to cause that, I just had a gut reaction to seeing her like this and my mouth needed to touch her skin.

On a shuddering breath she nodded her head, "Yes, I'm sure. Let's go." I had to laugh at her demand. I think she was worried she'd back out if she let me wait too long.

Fifteen minutes later her wrist was red from the needle and shiny from the goop I'd rubbed on it. I wrapped it up in gauze and plastic and gave her the care instructions. "Not to worry, though, I think you know a pretty good guy who can keep an eye on it for you and watch to be sure it's healing okay." She smiled at me as I spoke, and I thought to myself that I wanted to make her smile like that every day. And then I felt a shot of guilt straight to my heart; I had made my wife smile, I shouldn't be making other women smile.

Through the guilt, I hugged Josie to my side, "You did great, Jo-Jo. We'll get started on that back piece soon and do it in small spurts, okay?" She nodded her head into my chest. When I heard a sniffle, I pulled her away from me and saw tears. "Jo, what's wrong? Do you regret getting the ink?" Shit, I'd never had someone cry after I had inked them.

"No, no, no. I don't regret it at all. I'm just happy. This little blob of ink represents a lot for me. It's the first time I've done something just for me. It has a message that is important to me. One of my favorite people in the world gave me this tattoo and shared in this moment with me. Sorry, I'm just emotional." She took a deep breath and wiped her tears.

Leaning in, I kissed her head. "I'm honored to have shared this moment with you, Josie. I hope to be here for many more of your firsts."

That night we had the whole clan over. Our backyard was not huge but it was big enough for the kids to run around and explore a new area. Since it was cold, they weren't outside long. After we showed everyone around the house, Josie asked the kids if they wanted to paint. She had bought them all a small canvas and set up little paint palettes for them to use. The older kids, Beckett, Abby, and Megan, took a few moments to think and then began painting. The younger children dove right in; Kendrick, Zach, and the twins, Decker and Sawyer, were covered in as much paint as their canvases were within moments. Luckily, Josie had chosen washable paints for this occasion. Nicky Morgan, Zach's father, joined him in painting; the grown man knelt beside his son and spoke quietly to him as he watched the boy boldly add color to his canvas. Nicky laughed when Zach "accidentally" got some paint on his father's nose. Leaning in to nuzzle his son's cheek, Nick exclaimed, "Oh, you've got paint on your cheek. Sorry, it was an accident." Everyone in the studio room laughed at these antics; my laughter soon turned somber as I recalled the baby I'd never meet, the child I'd never watch grow up, the relationship I'd never have with my own daughter or son. My eyes stung as tears threatened; I turned to leave so that I could gather myself emotionally. I was going to spend a lot of time around these families; I needed to get myself together and not lose it every time I felt regret or jealousy over the parents' relationships with their children.

"Hey, are you okay?" I heard her voice just as her hand slipped into mine. I knew it was meant to be a friendly, caring gesture but the jolt of electricity it sent through my body to feel her skin on mine was just more than I could handle in the state I was in. I removed my hand from hers and moved away; what I longed to do was hug her to me, I wanted her closeness, I wanted her calming. But I shouldn't want that; I couldn't have that.

"Yeah, just got a little caught up in the moment in there. Jose, I promise I'll tell you about all my shit sometime, I'm just not ready yet. I'm sorry." I sighed and hung my head. I hated this person I had become. The real me didn't hide from things, I took everything in stride and faced problems head-on. Then my wife died and I became this broken man who hid his problems and feelings. I knew Josie would be the perfect friend to confide in, but talking about it was painful, and I wanted to numb myself and not feel the pain. The only thing I wanted was to revel in the memories of Izzy, the good memories. But now even the good memories brought guilt and pain; remembering her made my heart soar, until I fell to Earth with the pain of never having her with me again. Remembering Izzy now mixed with thoughts of Josie and the guilt over that mixture made me physically ill. When had these thoughts of Josie started? I couldn't pinpoint a specific moment, but I needed the thoughts to stop. I needed to keep my memories of Izzy alive in my mind, I couldn't let her go. I loved Josie as a dear friend, but I couldn't have more than that. It wouldn't be fair to Izzy's memory, and it wouldn't be fair to Josie; she deserved someone who could give 100% of himself to her, and I could never do that, no matter how much I cared for her.

"Kyle, I think it would do us both some good to talk about our pasts, but please know that I don't want to pressure you in any way. You're one of my best friends, and I want to be here for you, but I don't want to push. We can both talk when we feel up to it." That damn sweet face looked at me expectantly, and all I wanted to do was lean in and kiss her. I couldn't want shit like that. My psyche whispered, *So what, Martin, are you planning to live the rest of your life feeling guilty and lost? Are you really thinking you can live without love? Not to be crass, but what about sex? Never going to have that again either? Be real here, man.*

I pushed the words from my head. I missed sex something fierce, but I'd only ever made love to Izzy, I couldn't see myself with someone else. Ever.

That's not true, I could picture myself with Josie easily, so easily that I felt terrible that I could imagine my body aligning with hers so clearly. So I forced the image of our bodies writhing together from my head and told myself that I couldn't picture sex with anyone but my late wife.

I didn't want to live forever feeling lost and guilty. My heart wanted love. But the problem was that my heart wanted love with Izzy; I wasn't ready to love someone else.

That's not true either. My heart had been telling me for a while that it wanted to love Josie; I wanted to love Josie. I probably could have loved her. But loving Josie meant, in my screwed up mind, that I was leaving Izzy. So I told myself that I wasn't ready to love someone else. It was just easier to believe that. The constant war inside my head and heart was beginning to wear on me.

"I'm going to go get the kids set up to watch a movie while the girls and I chat. I think the guys are out in the garage when you're ready to join them." Josie patted my shoulder, almost as if she recognized I couldn't do the physical closeness right now.

I sighed as she left the room. My head and heart were so fucked up right now. How could I love and miss my dead wife so much while still longing for the touch and closeness of my new best friend? Days like this made me want to crawl in bed and hide under the covers for the rest of my life. Days like this brought the heavy blanket of darkness tighter around me and made it harder to breathe. I had promised Izzy I would keep breathing, but I wouldn't live without her. But now, in fleetingly brief moments, I was feeling like I wanted to live instead of just breathing. And that brought more guilt.

I found all the men in the garage. Our garage wasn't much to look at; at some point we'd probably need to turn it into a fix-up project. But for now it served its purpose. We stood around a portable heater. Jeremiah had brought a case of beer to keep in the garage fridge as a house warming present and we all cracked one open and toasted to Josie's and my new businesses and our new home. After a few quiet moments, Captain Decker spoke up.

"Son, this isn't meant to be an intervention, but all of us here are your friends, hell, I'd say we're more like family. It's not our place to force you to talk about something if you don't want to. But, I wanted you to know that talking about something painful from the past can really help to ease the pain." He paused to see how I would react.

I sighed. "I want to ease the pain, I really do. But my fear is that if I lose the pain, I'll also lose the memories."

"That makes sense, it really does. Something I've found is that talking about the good times helps to keep the good memories alive and also helps to ease the pain of losing her." Captain Decker spoke and I knew he came from a place of experience with this same situation. "Son, it took me way too long to work through loss and move on and I left a path of hurt and regret and heartache in the wake of the years I held onto the pain. Don't take as long as I took; I lost too much during those years and people around me were hurt because of my unwillingness to let it go. It's not easy and I'm not saying that you have to forget. But once you can speak of her and let the pain go, there's more room for just the good." I nodded at the man through a lump in my throat.

"You should practice talking to us. Do it like a band-aid. Just rip it off and tell us something from your past. That way you'll be more ready to talk to Josie when it's time." I glanced up as Nicky Morgan spoke. How did this man struggle in so many aspects of life yet seem so very perceptive in others? My face must have been questioning because Nicky shrugged. "I see you looking at Josie sometimes. It's like you don't want to like her, but you can't help it. Your eyes look at her the same way Nate looks at Libby and Jeremiah looks at Audrey. But your eyes also look like you feel guilty. Our hearts can love more than one person. You can love the person in your past while still loving Josie. Would the person in your past be mad if you loved Josie?" I instantly shook my head in honesty; I knew Izzy would be thrilled if I moved on with Josie. I could just hear her in my mind, *Listen, Punk Boy, it's not like you're cheating on me. I'm dead and gone. We'll see each other in eternity, but until then you've got to live. Josie is about the cutest thing I've ever seen. Give it a chance.*

I smiled as I thought about Izzy speaking those words to me. Taking a deep breath I spoke, "I was married to a woman named Izzy. I fell in love with her in second grade. A little over a year ago she was killed in a car accident on the day we were going to find out we were having a baby after trying for over 5 years." The words left me in a rush and the tightness in my chest loosened marginally.

"Speaking for the group, I can tell you we're all very sorry for your loss. But, I can also tell you that you're a handsome young man with a lot to offer. I can't imagine your wife wanting you to live in the way you've been living. I've known you since you were a small boy, Kyle; you need to get that sparkle back in your eyes. I miss the 'fuck'em all' attitude; I miss the life that used to exude from you." Jack Jordan looked at me with warm eyes as he spoke. I nodded my head to acknowledge what he said because I didn't trust my voice to speak.

We moved on to safer subjects while we finished our beers. The kids' movie was finished and the women were gathering everyone up to head home. Jeremiah found me in the kitchen before he left. He pulled me into a bro-hug. When he released me he spoke quietly, "Talk to Josie, man. I think the two of you could probably help each other just by listening and sharing. Nothing has to move too fast. Just be there for her and let her be there for you. You're not doing anything wrong. I knew Izzy as long as you did; I know she'd want you to be happy and she'd probably want to kick your ass for holding on to this guilt over her. She wouldn't want you to hold yourself back just because of her. Letting go and living doesn't mean forgetting her. You'll never forget her, none of us who knew her will ever forget her. Living without her sucks, but we can live and be happy; she would want that." For what seemed the millionth time that night, I nodded and fought off the tears which threatened to fall. I knew all of the words directed at me tonight were true. However, knowing something is true and acting upon that truth are two very separate things.

CHAPTER 12

Josie

"You yourself, as much as anybody in the entire universe, deserve your love and affection." **~Buddha**

My heart hurt. Hurt for the child I would never have. Watching my new family and friends as parents was touching, but it also brought to the forefront of my mind that I would never have that. My heart also hurt for the man I considered my best friend. I knew he was struggling and I didn't know how to help him; I didn't even know if he wanted help. My heart hurt when I watched the love between the couples who were in our home that night. I had a terrible relationship with my parents and a completely fucked up marriage in my past; I didn't have faith in love and marriage. But, watching those couples, a little spark of faith lit inside of me and gave me hope. That's when the hurt came in. I didn't have anyone to share that love with; the one man who I could possibly consider loving was my best friend, but he had shut himself down to love. So, for various reasons, my heart just hurt that night.

As I climbed the stairs to clean up my studio, I heard music coming from Kyle's studio office. I sat down outside of his door and leaned against the wall. Five songs played while I listened and I learned that Kyle's taste in music was as eclectic as he was. An old Firehouse song, something from the Eagles, a great one from Steve Earle, Something to Believe In by Poison, and Personal Jesus by Johnny Cash all played while I sat immobile in the hallway and thought about the man inside that studio. He was my friend. He couldn't be more. He didn't want to be more. As another song came on, Hurt by Johnny Cash, I realized two things. Kyle was a Cash fan, and he was hurting even more than I had originally thought. The haunting lyrics and music floated on the air as tears ran down my cheeks. I would push aside any personal feelings for this man and simply be his friend; the break in his voice as he sang along with this song broke my heart and sealed my decision. He needed me, and I would be there for him.

I stood from my seated position and rapped on his door.

"Come in, Jose." His voice was raw and tight. I hesitated. Maybe he didn't want me around.

Poking my head into the room I smiled at him. I took in his mussed hair and the sadness in his eyes. "Want to come downstairs and talk?" I knew that I would have to be the first to share if I expected him to ever open up. I would sacrifice and tell this humiliating story if it meant giving him the opening to tell his own story. I watched as he started to deny my request, but then he took a deep breath and nodded. "I'll be down in a bit."

In the kitchen I prepared the margarita mix that Audrey had brought over as a house warming gift along with a tiny bottle of tequila. It was just a two serving packet and the bottle had just enough for the two servings which was good because I had never consumed alcohol before, and I didn't need to get shit-faced before Kyle and I got to talk.

As I heard him coming down the stairs I headed into the living room. "Margarita?" I showed him the two glasses I held, and he smiled ruefully.

"Yeah, that sounds good. I'll probably need one to get through this." He took a drink from the glass I handed him and breathed deeply after a swallow. "That's good. I don't drink much, but you made that perfectly, Jo."

"Well, I'll say thanks even though all I did was follow the directions." I took a drink as well. Kyle laughed at my curled up nose.

"Not a fan of tequila, huh? Take a few more sips if you

want to get used to it. If not, don't force it. You're not a drinker are you?" He cocked his head to the side and studied me as I took a couple more sips. I don't think I'd ever call a margarita my drink of choice, but after about four sips it wasn't as terrible as the first taste.

"No, this is the first alcohol I've ever had." I shook my head almost unbelievably at the statement I just made. "It's not that I never wanted to try it, it was just frowned upon, and I never wanted to push the edge of the proverbial envelope, so I just never tried it." He waited patiently as if he knew I planned on telling him more.

I took a deep breath. "This is going to be hard. I don't want to tell you about my past and then have you think poorly of me for not being strong enough to break free earlier." I watched as he settled onto the chaise lounge part of our new sofa and patted the spot next to him. I sat with my back leaning into his chest and shoulder, my feet stretched out onto the sofa part while he stretched his out onto the chaise section.

"Jo, you don't have to tell me anything, but I'm here to listen if you want to talk." He leaned in and kissed my head. I took strength from that gesture as I also tried to ignore it and the pang of longing it sent through my gut.

"No, I'm ready. The longer I keep it inside, the harder it gets to tell. I should have just told people when I first arrived, but I was embarrassed. After I tell you, I'll share with the rest of the family slowly. Maybe I'll tell the girls and they can pass the information along, so I don't have to retell it over and over. But, I'm tired of hiding behind it." I paused as I gathered my thoughts. I knew in my heart that I would have a sit-down with Uncle Robert and share my story with him before I told anyone else; he had taken me in as if I was his own child and I owed it to him to let him know what had brought me to Torey Hope.

"My parents didn't want me, they never planned on having children. It was too late to abort me when they found out my mother was pregnant, so they were stuck with me. They were high up in society and in the business world, an adoption could have caused scandal because they had so much to offer a child, at least to the thinking of the public, so they kept me but hated me." I cuddled into the soft new sofa and continued my story. I spoke of my upbringing with nannies and boarding school and no friends and parents who voiced their disappointment at every chance they got. During my story, Kyle reached his left hand for my right and held my hand as I went on.

His thumb stroked mine when I spoke of the arranged marriage. His breathing quickened when I told of the horrendous sexual relations with Wayne. He growled low in his throat when I mentioned the other women in Wayne's bed. His breathing almost stopped completely when I spoke of not being able to have children. By the time I got to the time Wayne hit me, Kyle had stood up and was pacing the floor.

"So, I had been planning a way to leave, and I had finally

just had enough, so I put my plan into action. That's how I ended up here in Torey Hope at Uncle Robert's house. Finding out that my father had a brother was my saving grace because it brought me here to family and friends." I startled when Kyle dropped to his knees in front of me and took my hands.

"Josie, thank you for telling me your story. I'm so very sorry you went through that. You deserve so much more. You are a very special person and your parents and Wayne are pieces of shit who were too dumb to notice what a gift they had in you." He climbed back onto the couch and pulled me closer to him. "Now, what about Wayne. Did he sign the divorce papers? Do you think he'll search for you?"

"Well, I just heard from my lawyer that Wayne signed the papers easily and just last week married again. So, I'm free of that hassle. But, I'm not sure about your other question. I don't know what he would gain by searching for me. He has a new wife; I don't know what he'd want with me. But, I wouldn't put it past him to cause problems just because he can." I had been overwhelmed with relief when my lawyer told me about Wayne signing the papers. I was disgusted by Wayne remarrying so quickly, but I knew he felt he had an image to uphold. I laughed out loud when the lawyer told me Wayne had released a statement saying that I had succumbed to a mental illness and had requested he divorce me and move on. Whatever he needed to tell the public was fine by me; the important thing was that I was no longer his wife.

I felt my face warming as the alcohol really hit my system. I was glad there had only been enough for the two servings I fixed because my brain was just hazy enough that I knew I would probably slurp down another glass if one was available. As it was, I was grateful for the looseness the drink had on my words. I had told Kyle my whole story and gotten through it with no problems. He didn't judge me or think badly of me. I should have done it sooner.

I turned on the couch to face him; not wanting to pressure him, I waited for a moment to see if he was going to speak. I took the last drink from my glass as I gave him time.

After draining his own glass, he placed it on the coffee table and took a deep breath. "Josie, what I'm going to tell you serves two purposes. The first will explain why I'm so sad and haunted and why I came here. The second will hopefully help you understand how I can be so drawn to you but unable to act upon it." My heartbeat picked up at that statement. Was he telling me he felt the same for me as I was starting to realize I felt for him? But, if he did feel that way, he was telling me why he couldn't feel that way.

"I met Izzy in second grade. She was my first and only love. We were inseparable from that moment on. We married a few years after high school. A couple years after that we decided we'd try to have a baby. Five years later there was still no baby." He paused long enough for me to reach for his hand; it was meant to be a comforting gesture, but the heat between us felt anything but comforting. He absentmindedly stroked my thumb.

"We were exhausted from the stress of not being able to have a baby. We had just decided to take a little break. I made love to her that day, just because, not in hopes of making a baby; just because I loved her and wanted to hold her close to me. I went to her record store to open it up for her, and she headed to the doctor's office; I was meeting her there. When I arrived, she wasn't there. I got a phone call from her cell, but it wasn't her. It was a police officer; she had been in a wreck on the way to the appointment. At the hospital they showed me to her room; I sat with her for hours, but I knew from the moment I took her hand that she was gone. I had to tell them to turn the machines off. I held her hand and told her to go on without me. In a cruel twist of fate, she had been pregnant. The baby was lost of course. So, my wife and child died in a car accident and my life ended that day." He paused in his story to gather his thoughts and calm his emotions. Tears streamed down my face, and I covered my mouth to hide the sobs which threatened to erupt.

"I promised Izzy on that day that I would go on without her, I'd keep breathing, but I'd never be able to truly live." A sob hiccupped out of me; this man, my best friend was hurting so much, and I ached watching him in pain. My arms longed to wrap around him, but my heart battled with my brain if that was the right move to make at this point.

"Josie, at first I thought that what we had was just friendship. I didn't even suspect anything more. But over the time we've spent together, I realize I'm attracted to you. In my head and in my heart I know Izzy would want me to move along. But I can't let go of the guilt I feel every time I think about trying to love someone else. I know I could love you, you are so perfect for me; but it's not fair of me to ask you to be with me when I can't give you my whole heart. I really shouldn't have drained that margarita because I'm saying a whole lot more than I wanted to say tonight. I'm sitting here thinking about that pencil-dick husband of yours acting like the bad sex was your fault. There's no way you'd be bad at sex; you're too passionate about life. Hell, Jose, you cried when you saw our house. I wish things were different, and I could show you what it would be like to have sex with a man who could actually appreciate your body and give you the pleasure you deserve." I stopped breathing as Kyle spoke these words.

Not knowing what to say to his words, I spoke as if he'd not mentioned sex with me. "Tell me more about Izzy. What did she look like?" I had a strange mix of jealousy and admiration for this woman I'd never meet; I envied the time she got to spend with Kyle in a way that I would never experience. He pulled up his photo album on his phone and handed it to me. Staring back at me from the screen was a beautiful woman with huge violet eyes and almost red lips but she wasn't wearing lipstick. Her dark hair was styled in a short messy look with chunks of pink, purple, and green. Her eyes were laughing and I saw that she was the perfect match for Kyle. "She's beautiful, Kyle. She looks like she was truly your other half."

"She was. She was a little rebel; I called her Izzy-bel. She called me Punk Boy from the first moment she met me and it stuck. We were like yin and yang; we just fit and complemented each other perfectly." His eyes got a faraway look in them, and I knew he was recalling his sweet Izzy.

"Would she and I have gotten along?" I didn't know why I asked that. It's not as if I could compete with his wife, dead or alive, but I was curious.

His laugh shook his chest. "Yes, I think she would have loved you. She would have seen your broken spirit and wouldn't have stopped until she unearthed the real you. She was spunky, my Izzy. It's strange how you remind me of her in some ways yet the two of you are completely opposite in other ways. Yeah, you two would have been friends." He smiled at the thought.

"Kyle, I'm really sleepy. I think that margarita hit me harder than I realized. I think I should head to bed." I needed to remove myself from the situation before I acted on the words he had said earlier. He couldn't love me; he didn't want to love me. The longing I felt to have his body close to mine would have to be tempered because nothing was going to happen. I needed to learn how to put distance between us to fight these new and quickly-growing feelings.

I headed to my room and changed into my pajamas. The short shorts and tank were not warm enough to wear around the house in the winter, but under my big blankets they would be just fine. I heard Kyle leave our shared bathroom, and I went in to brush my teeth. I felt strange about our talk tonight. On one hand, it was so good to have our pasts out there and no longer hiding. On the other hand, it hurt to know what he'd gone through and that he would never be available to me. I understood his concern about never being able to love me completely because his heart would always belong to Izzy. But that didn't make the feelings I had for him go away; well, they'd have to go away. We shared a house, he was my best friend. I'd have to just get over it. My heart hurt at that moment; hurt for him and hurt for me. It was like I watched a dream-come-true float away and crash a fiery death; a dream I didn't even know I held onto, a dream that I had barely had time to embrace, and then it was gone.

I jumped as Kyle entered the bathroom. "Oh, sorry, Jo. I thought you were done." I spit and rinsed, reaching around him to put my toothbrush away.

"I'm done now. Thanks for talking to me tonight, Kyle. I'm really sorry for your loss. Even though we ended up here because of shitty things happening, I'm really glad we ended up here together." Possibly in my best judgment or against my better judgment (my heart and brain were battling on this again), I reached to hug him and closed my eyes as his arms closed around me. I felt his heartbeat against my cheek. In the mirror I saw his chin on top of my head. The tattoos on his arms were beautiful against my pale skin. I'd seen him without his shirt on before but the tattoos on his stomach which disappeared below his waistband were almost more than I could handle. I began to pull away so that I could go be breathless in the privacy of my own room. But I made the mistake of looking up into Kyle's eyes; those endlessly deep, endlessly sad, dark brown eyes. I saw guilt and anger flash before the heat lit up.

"Fuck, Jo, this is a really bad move on my part and I'll regret it in the morning, but I'm being a selfish prick tonight." With his words, he tipped my chin up and feathered a kiss across my lips. As my breath caught, he captured my lips with his and deepened the kiss. Never had I been kissed in that way. I could barely breathe from the way my heart was pounding; my body felt like it was on fire. He drew my bottom lip into his mouth and brushed his tongue along it. As I whimpered into his mouth, he plunged his tongue deep into mine. Then, just as abruptly as he started, he stopped. With ragged breath he closed his eyes and leaned his forehead against mine, "Josie, know that I will never regret kissing you. I only regret that I can't take things further with you; you deserve love and not just sex. Sex is all I'd be able to give you." He hugged me to him again, "I'm sorry, Jo."

I was left in the bathroom, lips tingly and swollen, eyes sparkling, and chest heaving. A thought began to grow in my head. If I decided to act upon it, I'd have to do some convincing, but I had the beginnings of a plan. I also had an art project I needed to get started on.

CHAPTER 13

Kyle

"People have a hard time letting go of their suffering. Out of a fear of the unknown, they prefer suffering that is familiar." ~**Thich Nhat Hanh**

What the hell are you doing you jackass!?!? Do you really think you can just kiss that beautiful, innocent girl and then leave her just standing there? You need to get your head out of your ass, Punk Boy. I'm dead, I'm gone. You're not hurting me to move on with someone else. I mean, if she was a bitch or a slut I may kick your ass, but Josie is absolutely perfect. I honestly think she's more perfect for you than I was. There's such a passion in her. She needs you Kyle. Don't miss a good thing just because you're feeling guilty about me.

I sat bolt-right-up in bed, sweating and breathing hard. "Izzy?!" I frantically looked around the room. I swear she had just been there, talking to me. I padded silently to the kitchen for a drink of water as I shook off the dream I'd just had. It had been so real, I felt as if she was right there with me. I could hear her voice exactly the way I remembered it, it was if I could almost smell her and feel her there. That was the first time I'd dreamed of her in a while; I'd never dreamed of her talking to me.

Turning to head back to bed, I noticed a light on upstairs in Josie's studio. I didn't want to disturb her, but I was drawn to that light; drawn to her, like I had this *need* to see her. I found her in her studio, headphones on, bent over the desk; her back was to the door and she couldn't hear me, so I watched. She was intent on whatever it was she was creating, surrounded by paper and scraps and scissors. I'd seen some of her paintings, but I'd not seen any of her paper crafts. I stood, transfixed as her auburn hair draped silkily down her back; her bare shoulders peeking through the strands. She sat with her legs beneath her, delicate feet barely in view. Delicate. That was a word I would have used to describe Josie. But she was so much more. The old Josie was fragile, but the new one, the one I watched emerge a little more each day, was stronger. She was strengthening everything about her; her spirit, her attitude, her resolve, everything was being repaired from the years she spent with her low-life parents and that fuck-off husband of hers. Yes, she was stronger, but I could still see the fear, the vulnerability, the uncertainty. If I could love her completely, she would thrive. But, if I couldn't give her all of me, I feared I'd break her even more. I couldn't do that to her.

So what are you going to do when someone comes along who CAN love her completely, Punk Boy? Can you just watch her fall in love and know it's someone else loving her and making her smile?

I spun around, almost giving myself whiplash, looking for Izzy. Shit, I was losing my mind. Maybe I had more to drink than I thought. For the second time that night, I was hearing my dead wife speaking to me. With a deep shuddering breath, I took one last glance at Josie, and turned away so that I could go back to bed. I had a feeling I was in for a restless night.

The next day I headed to the shop. I had two pieces to work on for a couple new clients. I was pretty stoked with the amount of customers I had coming into the shop in such a short time since getting everything set up. Being the first tattoo shop in town and being the closest one around for several miles was proving to be a great thing.

I loved being able to lose myself in a design. I took great pride in being able to hear a client's wishes and turn it into a great piece. The guy I was working on first had come to me with the idea of a full back piece to represent his addiction and recovery. He spoke of his earlier years when he'd crashed, head first, into some pretty hard drugs and drinking. It wasn't until a nurse in the ER took pity on him and helped him get clean for the umpteenth time that he finally got the help he needed. He had tried to get clean before, but having her support was what did it. Twenty years later they were still together, and he was still in recovery. He was adamant to include something in the piece that showed he wasn't ever "cured" but every day was a new day and the chance to be a better person.

I loved the piece I had worked up for him. It would take a few sessions at least. First we'd get the outline on and start with a little color. This was not his first tattoo for which I was grateful. I didn't want to have to calm someone down, I needed to zone out and get lost in the buzz of my gun, the scent of the ink, and the blur of color.

Once my client had approved the piece, I got it laid out on his back. As I watched him look in the mirror to okay the placement, I pictured what it was going to look like with color and knew I'd hit it out of the ballpark with this one. I wanted Josie to paint this design so I could display it in the shop. I even thought that it would be the perfect one to use in the next ad I put out. The black and darkness of the demon, the fiery reds and oranges of the phoenix rising from the fire, the greens and blues of the bird's feathers, all of it was going to be breathtaking. I wished that Josie was there to see the drawing and watch as I started the ink on his back.

I stopped shortly, a split second before turning on the gun, and realized that I'd wished for Josie to be there. I didn't wish for Izzy to be there. My wife used to come to the shop and watch me. Sometimes she'd sit and chat with the client. Sometimes she'd watch from outside the little room, but I always loved having her there. She would have loved this design. But, I didn't wish for Izzy, I wished for Josie. Man, I was fucked-up. I didn't want to love her, couldn't love her, but wanted her close to me.

As the buzz of the gun started up, my brain and body went into automatic mode. The black of the ink staining his skin, the constant vibration of the gun, the continual wiping of the blood and ink from his skin, it lulled me. That's when I heard her again. *It's a great design, Kyle. I see how it represents his addiction and recovery. Know what else I see? I see how it represents you. The blackness you fell into when I died. The phoenix shows your chance to start over. It's beautiful. I hope you keep this picture in your mind as you continue to move along.*

My breathing had stilled as I listened to her words over the buzz of the gun. When I stopped to reload the ink, she was gone and my hands were shaking. If I was one of the artists who took smoke breaks, I'd ask for one now. But I didn't smoke, so I told the client he could take break if he needed; I needed to grab a drink. The sleeplessness from the night before had gotten to me if I was hearing her again. I grabbed a cold Mt. Dew from the little fridge I kept in my office and swigged at least half of it down.

Returning to the room, I settled in and got the man's outline completely done before taking another quick break. We decided to start the color on the demon and call it quits for today. I had two hours before the next client showed up. I prepped her design and then decided to take a quick nap in my office before she showed up.

I woke with a start when I heard the door chime. Looking at the clock I realized I'd only been asleep about 20 minutes but I was feeling better. The girl was early, but since I didn't have any other customers waiting it was fine by me to get a start on her design. Walking from my office I stopped short; Josie was walking towards me and my heart couldn't decide if it wanted to beat rapidly or stop completely. Damn, she was so fucking gorgeous. The thought that flittered through my brain shocked me; I couldn't help but think it was true as I watched as those blue eyes sparkled and her hair swayed as she walked. In fact, that wasn't the only thing swaying; I took in her perfect little butt as she walked towards me. Damn it, I shouldn't be thinking about this girl's perfect ass.

Why not, Kyle? It's a cute ass. It's okay to admit that you like her ass. In fact, it's okay to admit you like her period. I'm all for it. I know we were perfect together; you two are perfect for each other too. It's a different type of perfect, but it's still going to be great.

I figuratively pushed at Izzy, willing her to stop talking to me. *What's wrong, Punk Boy? Am I getting to you?* She spoke with a smile in her voice; I wished I could see her, I could picture the little smirk on her face she'd get when she knew she had me on something. I ignored Izzy and walked toward Josie.

"Hey, Jose, what's up? Did you come to watch the master at work?" I decided I'd shoot for casual and relaxed in order to avoid any possible awkwardness after the kiss the night before.

"Oh, yeah, I thought I'd come observe greatness in action. I hope I can handle watching the master as he works his magic." She smiled at me and punched me in the gut as she reached me. Good, she was going to go for casual too. I guessed we were just going to act like the kiss hadn't happened.

"Actually, I *do* want to watch for a little bit, but I also wanted to know if you wanted to go out for dinner tonight?" At the questioning look I gave her, she stammered a bit. "I ask because I've been thinking."

"Uh-oh, Jo-Jo thinking, this could be dangerous." I teased her, but pulled her into my side. "I'm kidding, Jo, go on."

"Well, I don't really plan on dating anytime soon, but I thought I'd sort of like to go on some practice dates just in case anyone ever asks me out. Plus, I've not been to most of the restaurants in Torey Hope so I thought we could do a little tour of them over the next few months. My parents didn't allow me to go to a theater to watch movies; they said it was too low-class. I've always wanted to go to the theater and eat popcorn, drink a big pop, and watch a movie. I've also never been bowling or skating or shopping at a regular, everyday mall. So, I was hoping you could help me on my new venture; it's all part of 'remake Josie'. Whatdya say, KJ? Will you be my man? My arm candy? My date? I can't pay you for your services, plus I think that would possibly border on illegal, but if you train me well enough, I can at least promise a fun date every so often. Please?" Her eyes sparkled as she finished her long speech, and she looked at me expectantly.

Fuck. What was I supposed to do with this request? If I turned her down, she'd be upset, and it would look like I didn't want to spend time with her. If I accepted her invitation, I was going to be spending even more time with her. In a split second I made my decision. I couldn't turn her down. I couldn't let her think I didn't want to spend time with her. It was just some dates. She wasn't asking me to romance her, she just needed someone safe to show her the world of dating and to expose her to so much of what she'd never done. I lived with the girl, I could surely deal with taking her out for dinner or a movie every so often.

I smiled at her as she awaited my answer. "First, before I commit to anything, where did KJ come from?" I knew she was using my initials, and since I shortened her name so frequently I didn't mind it, but I wanted to hear her answer.

Blushing she replied, "Well, you're always nicknaming me, so I thought I'd nickname you. I think I'll use KJ and Ky if that's ok with you. I won't lower myself to Ky-Ky like you do with Jo-Jo though. I do have my pride." She giggled as I laughed.

"Ok, with that explained, I think I can accept your invitation. I will be your practice date until you feel comfortable and have the average dating experiences under your belt. Now, my next client is almost here. Want to see what I've been working on?" I grabbed her hand and pulled her to my office to show her the drawing of the design I'd just done on the guy's back. Instead of concentrating on how right her hand felt in mine or the heat that traveled between our joined hands, I focused on her face as she took in the drawing.

"Oh, my God, Kyle, it's gorgeous. I should paint this!" I could see her artistic wheels turning and knew she was already making the same plans for this picture in her head as I had made in mine.

"Yep, that's what I was hoping you'd say, Jo-Jo. Here, this is the one I'm going to do on the next client. It's sort of cliché, but it's what she wanted and it's pretty apropos to her story. I won't share her story since she told me in private, but maybe if you stay you can hear it from her while you watch." I held up the rising sun I would be inking onto the girl's hipbone. It was rising from blackness and then it became deep golds and oranges and reds of the sun. She had explained her darkness with depression and how she was reaching for the warmth and light of the sun to heal. I hoped she'd like my interpretation of her story.

I like your interpretation, Punk Boy. But I think you've sort of interpreted your own story, don't ya think? The blackness of losing me, the warmth and light of Josie represented in the sun? Hmmm, I'm seeing a connection. Stop fighting it, Kyle.

I took a deep breath and shook my foggy head a little. Hearing my dead wife talk to me was starting to really mess with my mind. I loved her with every fiber of my being, but she was actually starting to piss me off a bit. "Just leave me alone, would ya?" I huffed.

Josie turned her eyes to me, questioning and ready to be hurt. "Sorry, not you Jo. I was just talking to myself." She continued looking at me as if she didn't really believe me but shrugged her shoulders and flipped through more of my pieces.

We headed to the front of the store when the door chimed. Julie, the girl who was getting the sun design today, walked in smiling. "Hi! I'm so nervous! I almost canceled the appointment, but I made myself come. Is the design ready?" She was definitely nervous. I was glad Josie was with me, I knew she could get the girl talking and calm her nerves.

"Yeah, I've got it ready. This is my friend, Josie. Do you mind if she hangs out while I work?" I didn't think Julie would mind, usually the clients were more than happy to have someone to talk to.

"Hi Julie. I saw your design a couple minutes ago. I think you're going to love it, it's truly beautiful." Josie's soft voice instantly put the girl at ease, and I saw the nervousness dissipate, and she was just excited to get started.

"Here it is. Let me know what you think." I handed her the design and heard her breath catch.

"It's absolutely perfect. It's exactly what I pictured. Could we add a little more purple and blue as the black fades and the sun begins?" I loved when a client spoke up and helped me make their design truly theirs. As long as they weren't trying to ruin the picture, I always tried to accommodate their wishes. If what they were wanting was going to go against my artistic design, I'd show them on paper the fault with what they were asking for. Most of the time they agreed with me and then were very happy with the results when they finished. On a couple of occasions I had to have a client sign a waiver saying they were going against the artist's design and they would not hold the artist responsible if the finished product wasn't to their liking. I had a reputation to uphold; I did a damn good job on my designs and ink, I wasn't going to let some jackass who wanted to ruin a great design mess up my reputation.

While I added the blues and purples, Josie and Julie talked quietly. I saw Josie show her the horse on her wrist and explain about the back piece we'd be working on soon. Julie touched the black horse and spoke the words, "run free". "What do those words mean to you, Josie?" Julie's interest was genuine and Josie relaxed into a chair next to where Julie was laying so I could begin my work.

I had Julie pull her pants and underwear down far enough so that I could work and tucked a towel all around so nothing indecent was seen and her clothes were protected from the ink. I glanced at Josie as I did this, and she had her eyebrows raised and a smirk on her lips. I knew a question was brewing, but she would wait until we were alone.

"Well, I grew up in a very unloving home. I was not allowed to really live or experience life. I was roped and harnessed and placed in a corral like a captured wild horse, figuratively speaking. Then I was married off into a loveless marriage and the breaking of my spirit was continued. By the time I broke free and ran, I had almost no spirit left. But I came here to Torey Hope and found family and friends who love me, and I slowly began to love myself again. I'm learning to run free, like a wild horse. The next tattoo I get on my back is going to say 'reckless abandon.' That's part of the name of my art store. 'Wild Horses—Reckless Abandon Art by J. Marie'." Josie was quiet for a second as she watched me rub the design onto Julie's hipbone and then peel back the paper. "That's going to be absolutely perfect," she spoke to Julie, but I could hear her words directed at me as well, and my heart swelled with pride. Having Josie love my art meant a lot to me.

"So, Julie, what's the sun mean for you?" Josie spoke to the girl as I started the gun. I knew she was trying to take the girl's mind off of the pain; the hipbone wasn't the most pain free place to get a tattoo. Although, a needle scratching deep lines into your skin as ink stained your body would lead most to the correct assumption that a 'pain free' tattoo wasn't exactly a reality.

With a deep breath, Julie began, "I don't remember a time when I felt happy. I felt like I was always sad, always in the dark. I didn't want to have friends, I didn't want to go out and have fun. I just wanted to stay in my room, listen to dark, hateful music, and be sad. My parents didn't know what to do with me; they say I was happy as a young child, but I don't recall those times. They let me be homeschooled because going to school was so hard for me. People made fun of me for my dark makeup, dark clothes, dark personality; I was miserable at school, and the blackness settled in more and more with each passing day. At least being homeschooled I didn't have to put up with the teasing; although being at home didn't do anything to alleviate the blackness." She paused for a moment, lost in her thoughts, and I caught Josie's eye. She was holding back tears, I knew this story would affect her. She blinked the sparkling tears away and waited for Julie to go on. I could tell she was intrigued to know how this girl changed from the person she was describing to the seemingly happy girl lying on the chair in front of us.

"As the blackness settled darker and heavier, I contemplated taking my own life. I remember wanting so badly to just sink into that blackness. It would have been so much easier to just stop fighting the blackness and just give into it. It was like this sticky, black, seeping goo; it was everywhere. If a corner of light started to peek through into my life, the goo would seep its way over to it, and the light would eventually succumb to the blackness. That's what I wanted to do as well. I wanted to lie down on my bed, pull the blackness over me, and let the suffocating, sticky, black goo seep over me until there was nothing left." Julie paused again and took a deep breath. I had been working on the outline but was starting the black part of the tattoo. I watched as her skin filled with the black ink as she told of the blackness in her life.

With a slight chuckle, she continued, "It's not like something bad happened to me. I think I was just born predisposed to depression. My parents had doctors look at me to see what was wrong; they prescribed medicine. Sometimes the meds worked, sometimes they didn't. Sometimes I liked taking them, sometimes I'd stop because the blackness was easier to deal with than the blinding light the meds brought to me." Another deep breath and I knew this was the hardest part of her story.

"The night I planned to kill myself, I took a walk. I wanted to breathe the air and see the town once more before I let the darkness win. A vicious lightning storm began while I was walking, and I decided I needed to take shelter. I was going to kill myself, but I was afraid of getting struck by lightning; ironic I know. I saw a large building on my left and started running towards it right as a torrential downpour began. When I hit the front steps, I slipped and hit my head. I blacked out and didn't wake again until about an hour later. I awoke to a steaming hot cup of coffee and an angel sitting watch over me. She was the night cleaner at the building I had sought shelter in; it was a church, and she had found me. For some odd reason, after years of not wanting to speak to doctors or therapists, I wanted to speak to a total stranger. I told her my story. She didn't judge. She just said she wanted to pray for me and invited me to church with her. I wanted to tell her I wouldn't be able to come to church on Sunday because by then I'd be dead. But she had helped me, and I felt I owed her. I'd fought the blackness this long, I could wait until after Sunday. She took me home and prayed for me again. I felt strange as she prayed for me; like I didn't deserve the prayers and, also, like it was such a waste to pray for me; nothing was going to help me by this point if nothing had helped me throughout all of the years I battled the darkness."

Julie stopped speaking again and I knew she was feeling the pain of both her story and the tear of the needle. I watched as Josie sat, mesmerized, waiting for the story to continue.

"I went to church with that lady. Her name was Marty, short for Martha. Turned out she had lost a daughter to suicide, and she was hell-bent to prevent me from taking my life; she hadn't realized the pain her own daughter was in before she took her own life, or she hadn't wanted to admit it. But, meeting me and saving me and hearing my story, she knew she had a second chance to do the right thing. Damn woman was persuasive." Julie laughed. "She kept at me, kept begging me to let her have her second chance. Every Sunday she made me promise that I'd give her just one more Sunday. I was drawn to this woman; I didn't want to let her down. I don't know how she reached me when my own parents and the doctors and therapists couldn't reach me, but for some reason I wanted to keep fighting the darkness for Marty."

"The songs and messages at church each Sunday really spoke to me. I got involved in a group for people struggling with different health problems like cancer, depression, and other chronic diseases, at Marty's insistence of course. I started seeing that I wasn't the only one dealing with this. I started seeing that I was deserving of more from life. I started seeing the light creep into my life and the darkness had a harder time overtaking the light now."

"My recovery wasn't overnight. It was a year of Sundays, with Marty making me promise at least one more Sunday, until I finally started seeing another therapist and really started seeing the light start fighting back with the darkness. That was three years ago. I'm still in therapy about once a month. I still go to church every Sunday, usually with Marty. My parents joined me in attending as well. It's not easy and the darkness still tries to overtake my light sometimes, but I revel in the warmth and glow of the light, so I keep fighting back." Julie stopped and glanced up at the overhead mirror to see that I had added her blues and purples and I was working on the fiery warmth of the oranges and reds on the sun. "The light is just too beautiful to let the darkness overtake it ever again. It's exhausting sometimes, fighting back that seeping darkness, but with the right medicines, therapy, church, family and friends, and a love of that light, I keep fighting every day." Julie closed her eyes, as if the story had drained her. She hadn't told as much of the story when she explained what she wanted on her tattoo, so I had been just as enthralled with her story as Josie had been. I felt her depression to my very core; those feelings of blackness had threatened to claim me so many times after I lost Izzy.

"Julie, that's a beautiful story and I'm so very blessed that you shared it with us. Your tattoo is perfect for that story. I hope you can use your journey to reach others who are fighting that darkness as well." Josie spoke sincerely to the girl.

"Thanks Josie. Yeah, Kyle pretty much captured my story perfectly with this design. Marty and I have been talking to groups at different locations about depression and how to help. Sometimes just letting someone know that you've been there and you understand is helpful. I just hope that I can save someone from the blackness that threatened to overtake me. If I can save one person from it, it's worth telling my story. Marty has assisted so many people suffering through depression; but she still fights the demons of not reaching her own daughter soon enough." Julie stopped to listen to my instructions for care and winced as she pulled up her yoga pants. "Wow, you weren't kidding when you said to wear something with a soft waistband. Ouch." She smiled though and I knew she was very happy with her new ink.

After Julie paid and I cleaned up my work station, Josie and I headed out the back door of the shop. "Did you drive, Jo?"

She smirked and shook her head. "Nope, you know I'd walk all the way here if it means I get to ride on your motorcycle." I smiled at her, knowing it was true. I, too, had taken to liking her riding on my bike. I liked having her behind me, her arms wrapped around my waist, her legs firmly encasing mine.

"Well, then, let's go. We can get cleaned up and decide what we're doing for our 'date' tonight." We climbed on my black, silver, and green Harley and roared toward home.

I decided to play up this practice date scenario. I dressed in gray jeans, a blue long-sleeve button up, and black boots. I put all of my piercings in, rolled up the sleeves so that the tattoos could be seen, and added some leather bracelets to my wrists. I had colored my hair again before my shower; actually, I guess I had removed the color. I was now sporting dark brown hair with a chunk/stripe of white. I styled it into a messy, punky Mohawk and headed out of the back door. I texted Josie to let her know I'd be back by the time of our date.

I drove over to Jeremiah's house to kill a little time. When

I arrived at his front door, Audrey answered and let out a whistle. "Damn, who is this very fine man standing on my front porch? You look a little like Kyle Martin, but you seem more alive than I've seen him look in a while." When I laughed good-naturedly, she got serious for a bit. "Really, Kyle, you look great. Both physically and emotionally. What's the occasion?" She stepped aside while she spoke so I could enter the house. Jeremiah had walked into the living room. He stopped when he saw me and looked me up and down. I saw a wicked gleam in his eyes; he walked over toward me and caressed my arm. "Hey man, I knew you'd come around some day. And I'm touched, really, I am. But, I just can't leave my wife and family for you. Once upon a time, you were all I craved, but now, I've got all I need. I hope you can understand." He almost made it through his words without cracking a smile. Almost.

Putting him in a headlock as I'd done about a million times before, I laughed and told him to "shut the fuck up, Jordan." He and Audrey whooped with laughter, and it felt good to just goof off and laugh with friends.

Walking to the kitchen, Audrey put on some coffee and we all sat down at the table. Beckett came in at one point and looked at my hair. "You sort of look like a skunk, Kyle. But if you are happy with how you look then it's okay." That kid sounded like a miniature public speaker or therapist every time I talked to him. Megan came in later and asked her mom if she could have a white stripe in her hair too. Audrey told her she could do anything she wanted to her hair when she was eighteen. Kendrick came in to check out who was visiting but he didn't stay long. Coffee and grown-up talk didn't interest him.

Once the kids had satisfied their curiosity, Jeremiah turned to me. "So, you look like you're dressed to impress. What's up?"

"Well, Josie has asked me to take her out on practice dates. She missed out on all of that growing up and in her marriage. She's never been to a movie theater or bowling or skating or a regular mall. She wants to get the average dating experience and I guess she feels like I'm safe. I agreed to be her 'date' so she can get used to it all." I spoke as if this was a logical thing. Jeremiah and Audrey, however, looked at me as if I'd grown two heads.

"And you don't see how this practice dating could maybe skew perceptions, mess with hearts and feelings?" Audrey cocked her head and stared at me as she waited for my answer.

Shaking my head, "No, it's just practice. I find Josie extremely attractive, and I wish I could make something more with her. But I can't. It wouldn't be fair to her; I'd never be able to give her all of my heart, it belongs to Izzy and always will. But, as her friend, I can help her with things like this. It's just some casual dates. I mean, heck, I live with the girl; I don't think some dinners or movies are going to be a problem."

Jeremiah, rolled his eyes and shook his head. "So, you're going to get her all ready for some real dates? Then what? Stand by and watch as some other guy comes in and sweeps her off her feet?"

"Fuck off, man. You sound just like Izzy." Two heads snapped to attention and looked at me expectantly. I sighed deeply, not wanting to tell this part, but having no choice now. "Shit, I didn't mean to say that. I've been hearing Izzy a lot lately and she pretty much said the exact same thing you just said." I hung my head, feeling psycho admitting I was hearing the voice of my dead wife.

Audrey excused herself to check on the kids. Jeremiah just shook his head as we finished our coffee. "Well, Izzy and I were always the smartest of our little trio, that's for sure. I think you're setting yourself up for trouble here, man, but I'm not going to tell you how to live your life."

I bristled. "What should I have done? Told her, 'No, I don't want to spend time with you, not even on practice dates?' She already thinks so low of herself because of that ass-wipe, Wayne, I couldn't refuse her."

Jeremiah smirked, "No, I don't think you should have refused her. I think you should admit your feelings to your-self, accept that your wife is gone and would be FINE with you dating Josie, and take that girl on some REAL dates. But, again, I won't tell you how to live your life. Although, when this backfires in your face, you're definitely going to hear a big

'I fucking told you so' from me." He clapped me on the back and laughed as I flipped him off.

Climbing on my bike, I felt irritated. Damn it. I'd come over here to chill out but now I was pissed. I could take my best friend on dates without it being romantic. She knew where I stood about things between us. Didn't she? I probably needed to cut out the kissing if I was going to keep the lines between us strictly friendship. But, a few dates weren't going to hurt anything. I couldn't give her all she deserved, but I could at least give her this.

I found myself outside a little market. Dismounting my bike I walked into the place. Absentmindedly, I purchased a bouquet of flowers, a card, and a small chocolate cake. Putting the items in the small pouch on my bike, I headed back to the house. But, I saw I still had an hour before I needed to "pick up" my date, so I drove to the park. I sat on the bridge and watched a couple ducks brave the cold water and let my mind wander.

CHAPTER 14

Josie

"When one door closes, another opens; but we often look so long and so regretfully upon the closed door that we do not see the one which has opened for us."
~Alexander Graham Bell

I heard the knock on the door as I emerged from the bathtub. I knew it couldn't be Kyle because he said he wouldn't be back until date time. Was I stupid for being excited about this date? Yes, yes I was.

I wanted more with Kyle. I knew he couldn't or wouldn't give me more at this point. So, my plan was two-fold. The first part was to get some real-life dating experience with a safe, attractive, friend. The second part was getting to spend time with him without it being awkward. If he thought he was just playing a part in helping me, maybe he wouldn't over-analyze things between us and would just let us enjoy our time together. This was a great plan in theory. However, my heart knew that it could backfire terribly.

All of this ran through my head as I headed to the door. Why were my three best girlfriends standing on my front porch? I opened the door with a questioning look? "Hey ladies. Can I help you?" Audrey rolled her eyes and pushed past me.

Libby and Carly looked sort of apologetic, but they walked past me as well. I got the distinct feeling they were here to witness an ass chewing. We sat down in the living room, and I waited, not knowing what was going to happen.

"What the hell are you thinking, Josie Decker?" This from Audrey. She continued, "I just left my house after calling in my reinforcements here. Did you know Kyle's over at my house talking to Jeremiah? He's all dressed up, pierced up, tatted up, bleached up, and styled up. Do you know why? He's got a date. Oh, but that's right, you already knew he had a date, didn't you?!"

When I didn't respond, because I wasn't sure if this was a rhetorical question or not, she powered on. "It was bad enough when you bought a house with the man. But now you're going to 'pretend date' him?! This isn't a good thing, Josie. If he weren't so fucked up, I would be cheering you on. And, honestly, I think dating you would be truly good for him. But, he's so damn stubborn, I worry he'll never let go of the notion that he can't love you the way you deserve and, in the end, you're going to end up being hurt."

She stopped and looked at Libby and Carly for their input. Libby spoke first. "Josie, we love you, and we want you happy. I think you and Kyle are meant to be together, but I don't know when or if he'll ever admit that to himself, let alone admit it to you. I just don't want to see you fall harder for him than you already have and then have a broken heart to deal with along with all the other junk you're still dealing with."

"He loves you, I can see it in his eyes." Carly spoke softly, everything about Carly was soft. "But that love makes him feel so guilty. I think one day he may finally let go of the guilt and start to live again, but until then.....well, I just worry that you'll be collateral damage as he fights the guilt." She looked at me sadly.

"Girls, I get what you're saying. I can't and won't try to compete with Izzy. I know he loved her with his whole heart. But, I'm living with a man who is my best friend, and I'm falling in love with him a little bit more each day. I don't know when I started to love him, but I do. I know this practice dating can't go anywhere and there's a very real risk of it backfiring in my face. I'm not trying to trick him; I really do want the real dating experience. I just don't want to actually date any real guys right now. I'm not ready for that. Kyle can give me the real experience and he's off-limits and safe. I love spending time with him. This way I get to spend time with him and hopefully start loving myself a little more. Every day I'm with him I start loving Josie a little bit more because he shows me that I'm worth my own love. Please just let me do this. I'm sure I'll be crying to you at some point and then you can say you told me so, but just let me make my own mistakes here, okay? I've never been allowed to make choices for myself or make mistakes. I need to do this, even if it hurts and even if it turns out bad." I dried my tears and laughed as I realized I was still in my bath towel. "Now, I've got a date to get ready for. Unless you think I should meet him at the door in a towel, you all need to help me pick out clothes or head on home."

"Oh, Lord! No, meeting him at the door in a towel is not a good idea. It's just the first date, after all." Libby smiled at me and Audrey laughed. Carly just blushed.

My girls helped me pick out a pair of skinny jeans, a longer tunic top, and some funky ankle boots. They waited while I dried my hair then helped me apply makeup. I knew I didn't NEED them there to help, but it was really nice having them there to help.

I heard the roar of the Harley coming down the street and

shooed them out the door. They smiled and waved at Kyle as he pulled up, and they piled into Audrey's vehicle.

"Company?" Kyle asked me with a smirk.

"Yeah, I figured if I was going to get the real experience, I would have probably had friends help me get ready, at least for a first date." I hoped that my explanation sounded plausible; I didn't know how to explain they had actually been there to talk me out of this whole crazy practice dating idea.

"Well, if you're ready, head back into the house. A good date should ring the bell." Kyle smiled at me, that perfect, slightly lopsided grin and his brown eyes sparkled. I turned and headed into the house, trying not to smile from ear-to-ear. But I was sure I failed. Badly.

I grabbed my purse and a jacket. I forced down a giddy giggle when Kyle rang the bell. Opening the door, I imagined what this would be like if it was a true first date between us. I knew it couldn't ever be real, but my heart begged me to just play along. My brain agreed but only on the condition that I keep my heart in check.

"Hi, Jo. You look great. Here, I brought these for you. First date impressions and all that." He blushed as he handed me a card, flowers, and a small chocolate cake. "I thought we could have dessert back here after dinner and the movie."

I beamed at him. "Dinner AND a movie? I get both in one night? Wow, you're setting the bar pretty high, KJ." I sashayed into the kitchen to put the flowers in water and the cake on the counter for later. I thought about what it would be like if his eyes followed my swaying behind as I walked away. I knew I wasn't sexually alluring, but it was fun to imagine his eyes on my ass.

In the kitchen, I put the flowers in water and read the card.

Dear Josie,

I'm not sure this is the best idea, but I can't refuse you. I wish like hell this could be real.

But if you can be okay with just friends, I can too. I love you, Josie. I just wish it was enough of the right kind of love.

Love,

Kyle

I wasn't sure whether to smile or cry. I felt so lucky to have this man as my best friend. Was I setting us up to lose that friendship? Was this whole thing going to end in us both hurt and not being able to turn to each other for support? I shook my head sternly at my thoughts. No. This was going to be good for me, for him, for us. As long as we both remembered it couldn't go past just friends, we'd be fine.

Walking back into the living room, I found Kyle sitting on the couch. His gaze took me in as I walked toward him. I watched his eyes close slowly and his chest heave as he took in a deep breath. "God, Jo, I don't know if I can do this."

He walked towards me and took me in his arms. "This would be so much easier if I wanted to just fuck you and walk away. But that's not what I want to do. My body and mind haven't responded to a woman in this way since Izzy. Honestly, I don't recall my body ever responding with this much longing even with her. And now I feel like a total asshole admitting that. In a perfect world, Jo, I'd romance you and love you and make you mine. But, this isn't a perfect world, this is real life and I'm fucked up missing my dead wife. I'm trying so hard to do the right thing here. I could pretend with you but then I'd feel guilty and you'd know that you wouldn't ever have my complete love. Do you hate me for what I'm saying?" He touched the side of my face and I leaned my cheek into his hand.

"No, Kyle, I don't hate you. I understand. I wish so badly that this was that perfect world you're talking about, but I know, maybe better than most, we don't live in a perfect world. I want your love, but I understand why you can't give it to me. I've accepted our friendship. I want more, but I've accepted what we've got because it's better than nothing. I need you in my life, however I can get you." His eyes looked sad as I spoke to him; I knew my words hurt him like they hurt me. We'd just have to be ok with what we had.

He leaned down and pressed his forehead against mine; his breathing increasing and his voice whispered in my ear, "Jo, if for one night, I could just forget it all, I'd take you in my arms and love on you until sunrise. My lips want to taste you. I want to feel your touch. I long to feel you wrapped around me. God, I hurt with wanting you." He stopped speaking, as if he was too overcome to continue.

"Kyle, let's just go enjoy our dinner and movie. We've got to stop putting ourselves in these positions. Friends, right?" I faked a smile and pushed down the tears. My body felt tingly all over; I didn't know mere words could affect me the way his words had. My heart was beating quickly and between my legs felt damp. God, if only we could have that one night.

We pulled up to the little Italian restaurant about 15 minutes later. I'd requested Italian tonight and authentic Mexican on the next date. The movie we were going to watch was starting in two hours so we had plenty of time for dinner.

I was embarrassed to admit to Kyle that I'd never been to a restaurant like this. The establishments my parents and Wayne took me to were upper-echelon. I'd never even been allowed to order for myself. Kyle smiled and winked at me, "Well then, Jo, how about you order for yourself and for me? That way you can sample mine and I can sample yours." The man was perfection. Unattainable perfection.

We enjoyed our entrees. I had picked fettuccine alfredo for myself and chicken parmesan for him. Sharing the entrees was a perfect idea, and we still had plenty to take home. Turning down dessert, Kyle ordered us one glass of wine to share. "Sorry, Jo, but I'm afraid to drink around you. I've got to keep my wits about me so I can stay in gentleman mode." He laughed as he spoke, and I knew he was sort of kidding; I didn't fear him ever being less than gentlemanly with me. But I understood where he was coming from. I knew, if I were to drink too much, I'd lose all inhibitions and throw myself at him; to hell with the consequences.

I'd never laughed as hard as I did during the movie we went to watch. I had really wanted to watch the romantic comedy that was playing, but thought that the straight-up comedy was maybe safer for just friends on a practice first date. Tears streamed down my face as I laughed at a particularly funny scene; I caught Kyle looking at me, his smile very real, but the hurt in his eyes very real too. He pulled my close to him and kissed my head. "You having fun, Jo-Jo?" When I nodded into his side, he released me, "Good."

As we left the theater I asked him, "Why did you look so sad when I was laughing at that movie?" Regret flashed in his eyes as he turned to me.

"I was just reminded of all you've missed out on. I'm glad I get to be here for you as you experience all of these firsts, but I wish I could really and truly *be with you*. I am just feeling sad that Izzy was taken from me and you're sort of being taken from me as well."

When I looked at him questioningly he replied in explanation, "Someday a guy will come along and provide you with all of these experiences for real. And I'll lose you then, even though I never really had you."

I smiled at him sadly and whispered, "You do have me. You just have to be willing to keep me." Disheartened, we left it at that and headed home.

Later, sitting on the couch with our little chocolate cake, Kyle brought up the tattoo I'd watched that day. "So, two things I noticed today. One, Julie's story really got to you. It made you think. In fact, I bet you're still thinking about it, aren't you?"

I nodded. "Yeah, I am. It was a hauntingly beautiful story. So real, so many different ways it could have turned out. The exhaustion from fighting the depression was so evident in her voice. Julie's experience made me think that there are a lot of people who could benefit from just telling their story and hearing others tell their stories. Everyone has a story. But, when you hear the stories of others, sometimes your own doesn't seem so deep or terrible or scary. I've been thinking that I may ask Libby about how to set up a group at The Center so that people who just need to talk can come talk." I hadn't even planned the idea out in my mind, but it spilled out when he asked me about it. I looked at him to gauge his reaction.

"You're right, Jose. Talking about things is pretty darn good therapy. I think you've got a good idea. I bet Libby would be thrilled to let you use a room at The Center once a week or something like that. You might ask Audrey to put you in touch with her therapist, Dr. Xander. I know Audrey, Nate, Jeremiah, and Carly have all benefitted from his practice. Hell, if Jeremiah has his way, I'll be seeing Dr. Xander sooner rather than later. You need to be prepared for those people who come to tell their stories and need more help than just talking can offer." I felt my heart soar, Kyle got it; he got me. He already believed in my idea.

"So, what was your other observation today?" I really wasn't sure where this conversation was heading.

"Well, you looked at me with that pretty little smirk when I had Julie pull her pants down. What was going on in that mind of yours?" Kyle was teasing, but I knew he also wanted to know what I'd been thinking. I bought some time by taking a big bite of chocolate cake. I watched as he hungrily stared at my mouth as I finished the bite and licked the chocolate off my lips. How did I end up in a situation with a man who turned me on like never before, who looked at me like he wanted to eat me alive, but nothing could happen?

Shaking my head to bring myself back to his question, I carefully considered my words. He watched me as I pieced my thoughts together; he looked slightly amused, as if he knew part of what I had been thinking was going to be embarrassing. Settling into the couch, he raised his eyebrows and continued to wait.

"Wellllll, the first thing that went through my mind was, 'I wonder how many private parts he's seen while tattooing.'"

I stopped there and hoped that he'd snag onto that thought and forget the rest.

Throwing his head back, he laughed; a deep, real, actual laugh. "Ahh, Jo, you kill me. Well, yes, I've seen A LOT of 'private parts' in my career. Some just because they are near the tattoo location, but I get them covered as quickly as possible. Some I've seen because the client wanted the tattoo ON the private part." He kept chuckling, "You'll have to set aside some time one day for me to tell you some of my best stories about those private parts."

"Does seeing those things ever turn you on?" I had wondered today, as Julie took her pants down, if he had felt an attraction to her.

He cocked his head to the side for a moment. "The human body can be a beautiful thing and I think it's natural to be attracted to it. I can appreciate the swell of a breast, the curve of a hip, the hint of a scrap of lace covering the most secret of places. Hell, I can even see the beauty in the strong lines on a man's body. But attracted to the point of thinking about acting on it? Never. Not with a client. Not yet anyway." The way his eyes caught fire I knew he was thinking about me having my shirt off so that he could do the piece on my back. To diffuse the sexual tension, I began to gather up our plate and forks but his hand stopped me.

"Nope, hold up. You had something else going on in that mind of yours today. What was it?" Dang it. I had been so close to avoiding this portion of the conversation. I couldn't lie to him. One, I wasn't good at lying and two, he would know I wasn't telling him the truth. He always knew.

"Fine. I was letting my imagination run away. I thought about picking a tattoo for my hip bone so that I'd have to take my pants down for you the same way she did. I wanted you hovering over my body to put ink on me the way you hovered over hers." Stopping to look at him, I bit my lip, knowing that my imagined thoughts were turning him on. "I'm sorry, Kyle, I don't mean to make this harder on you. I've never had someone be attracted to me. I've never flirted. I don't know what I'm doing; I don't want to make it awkward for you. But the things your eyes and your casual touches do to my body are brand-new to me."

He shut his eyes, swallowed deeply, and took a cleansing breath. I could almost see him counting in his head to calm his heartbeat down. I watched his jaw clench. After about 30 seconds he let out a deep breath and opened his eyes. "I'll put a tattoo on any part of your beautiful body at any time, Jo. Just name the time and place. I know I can't give you what you need and deserve, but I'd never turn down the chance to touch you, hover over you, and mark you as mine. Knowing that my design, my ink, is on you, in you, that's one of the sexiest things I think I've ever thought about. Now, before this conversation gets more dangerous than it already is, let's clean this up." He bolted off the couch, and I watched him wince and adjust himself before he picked up the cake plates and forks.

I walked behind him into the kitchen. My arms had a mind of their own as they snaked around his waist. "Ky, I don't ever plan on taking Izzy's place. I know I can't compete with her. She was gorgeous and so perfect for you. But there are times when I really wish you'd just give me that one night you spoke of earlier, just so I could experience it one time. My body feels so alive when I'm around you. When you're near or you touch me or you even speak words like you just spoke, my body feels things it never felt with Wayne. Sex with him was painful and never fulfilling; I know it would never be that way with you and sometimes I wish we could just push pause on real-life and indulge in our fantasy for one night. I want that. I want you." I shuddered against the tears which threatened to fall as I leaned into his back.

In the blink of an eye, he spun me around and lifted me to the counter. "God, Jo, you can't say things like that to me. It makes me want things I can't want, can't have. The problem with that one night scenario is that I wouldn't want to stop at one night. I'd want you in my bed night after night after night. But with every night, you'd wonder who I was thinking of, who was better, who I pictured under me. You're my best friend, I live with you, I love you, I need you. Do I want more? Yes. But I can't risk losing you." His eyes sparkled with tears and I wiped them away with my thumbs. "I can't lose you, Jo."

"You aren't losing me. I'm not going anywhere. I know we can't have our one night. But you CAN kiss me. Even friends can kiss, right?" I watched as he shut his eyes tight, fighting against what he thought was right and what he wanted. I felt guilty, I didn't mean to put him in this situation.

"I'm sorry, Ky. I didn't mean to put you in a bad spot. I shouldn't have said all of that to you. You're worried about not being fair to me, but I'm not being fair to you either. We should call it a night...." Before I could finish my sentence, his hand wrapped around the back of my neck and pulled my mouth towards his. His lips crushed mine, his tongue immediately hot and urgent against my mouth. I moaned as his tongue found mine and slowed to a sensual assault. I slowly moved my hands up his arms and pulled him closer to me. Of their own accord, my legs parted and made room for him to step between them. In an instant I felt my ass being pulled and my center came into contact with him; hot and hard against me, I didn't know what to do with the electric heat coursing through me.

"Jo, baby....." his voice was anguished as he spoke against my mouth. I pressed myself against him in response and we both groaned. "I can't. Jo, we can't. Please know how much this kills me." With one last kiss, he moved slightly away from me and helped me off the counter.

As we both stood and caught our breath, crazy thoughts were floating through my mind. Thoughts I had no business thinking. Thoughts I knew would cause my friends to flip-the-fuck-out. But the thoughts were there. Before I acted on these thoughts which may be the death of me, I changed the subject completely.

"Kyle, I made something for you. I hadn't planned on giving it to you yet. But, in order to get our minds off of whatever that just was, I think now is the perfect time to give it to you. Can you come up to my studio?" I turned and walked away from the man who had just set my body on fire with a kiss. A kiss that shouldn't have happened. A man I couldn't have. Not in that way. Right?

CHAPTER 15

Kyle

"The loss of love is not nearly as painful as our resistance to accepting it is." **~Tigress Luv**

Fuck my life. What the hell was I doing? I loved Izzy. I never would have left her. I never would have stopped loving her. But she was taken away from me. I vowed to never stop loving her. I couldn't love anyone the way I loved Izzy. Right?

I watched Josie walk away from me and I knew I should be struck down with lightning for the thoughts I was having about her. Sex with Izzy had been beautiful but my body had never been on fire for Izzy the way it was for Josie. It was probably just because I'd been without sex for such a long time and my body craved what it hadn't had. At least I tried to convince myself of that.

"Izzy-bel, please forgive me for the thoughts I'm having. I'm attracted to her, and I love her like a friend but that doesn't mean I will ever stop loving you. You're my only true love." My whispered words sounded strangled out of my mouth as I started to follow Josie to her studio.

My heart almost stopped beating when I heard her words. *Punk Boy, you were never this stupid when I knew you. I'm not a fucking priest and this isn't a fucking confessional, stop asking for forgiveness. I know you loved me, and you'll always love me; that doesn't mean you can't love her too. I want you to be happy, Kyle. Just be happy. Stop being so fucking stubborn and just love her.*

I dropped to the nearest stair and just sat there, tears running down my face. "I can't love her. I just can't. I can't let you go. I'm afraid to let you go."

I'm already gone, baby. I can't come back. You can't bring me back. Love her, and let her love you.

"I'm not ready, Iz, I'm just not ready. Give me time." My stomach revolted at what I had just said. Was I telling Izzy that I would eventually let myself love Josie? I pushed the thought to the back of my mind.

Get up there and see what she has for you. It's gorgeous. I love it, and I know you will too.

I stood and walked the rest of the way up the stairs. These conversations with Izzy were getting to be too much. Maybe I should make an appointment with Dr. Xander soon. Whether I was hearing voices, hallucinating, or imagining it all, I needed someone to help me.

Walking first to my own studio, I popped in to turn on some music. I needed the noise to drown out the words Izzy and I had just spoken. I crossed the hall and entered Josie's studio. Right as I walked in, Poison's "Talk Dirty to Me" started blaring from the speakers in my studio. Not thinking, just wanting to escape, I grabbed Josie and began twirling her around and singing to her. I startled her at first, and she screamed. But, realizing what I was doing, she relaxed and joined in my playfulness.

We each picked up our pretend microphones and sang the song to each other. Josie played a mean air guitar on the guitar solo. I about lost it when she grabbed her desk chair and pushed me down into it. She backed away from me as if she was attempting to look sexy, but her grin gave her away and she busted out laughing. I assumed a frown and pretended to be demanding a proper lap dance. This girl had more than likely never seen anything close to a real lap dance, not even in a movie, but what she lacked in experience, she made up for in creativity. Twirling around she bent down so that her perfect little ass was in view and began to wiggle it to the beat of the music. She spun around to face me and dropped to her knees; she crawled toward me, again trying to be serious, but fighting laughter the whole way. Once she reached me, the song was almost over and she whispered, "Talk dirty to me" in my ear. Then she fell over on the floor laughing. I cracked up and joined her on the floor.

"Thanks, Jo-Jo, I totally needed that." We lay on the floor for quite some time. Just replaying our day, our conversations, and the crazy dancing/singing performance we'd just put on. Finally, Jo grabbed my hand and pulled me up.

"Come on, I really want to show you what I made for you. I hope you're not mad. I had Jeremiah get me copies of some things, and I used a couple things from your phone. The rest I sort of had to use my imagination with. This isn't meant to make you sad, it's just my way of showing you how sorry I am for what you lost." My heart started pounding as she spoke, afraid of what she was going to show me. I wanted to keep my guard up, I didn't want her to show me something that was going to make me break down. I started to feel defensive and angry.

Don't you dare make this girl feel bad for what she's made for you. It's beautiful and you need to say thank you.

My heart skipped a beat and I whipped my head around, half expecting to see Izzy in the doorway; that's how close her voice sounded.

Josie pulled an 8x10 canvas out from under a cloth and turned it toward me. My breath caught, my eyes stung, and my heart completely stopped. She had painted my wife, my

Izzy and she had captured her perfectly. I tried to speak, "Jo, it's...I'm..." but I couldn't get the words out. I took a deep breath and gathered myself. "Thank you, Jo, it's perfect and beautiful."

I thought we were done, but she pulled me over to the desk and had me sit down. "This one may be a little harder, but I hope one day it's something you can cherish without feeling too sad." She handed me a little, pink, bound book; a scrapbook. I opened the pages and saw she had made me a scrapbook of Izzy and our baby. Pink. She had made it pink; for the daughter I pictured we would have had. Each page had a picture of Izzy-bel with decorations like booties, rattles, bottles. There were no faces on the pictures of the babies but she had added baby feet, baby butts, baby hands in photographs. Tears streamed down my face as I gazed at each page.

"I'm sorry if this made you even more sad, Ky. I hate that you lost them; I'd give you up in a heartbeat if it meant you could have Izzy and your baby back. But, since it doesn't work that way, I had to do something to show you how sorry I am. I hope both of these can be pieces you hold on to and cherish as the years go on. I only wish I could have put a name on the scrapbook."

Addyson Rose

I sniffed my nose and looked around.

Addyson Rose. That's our daughter's name, Kyle.

Drying my eyes and clearing my throat I strangled out, "Her name is Addyson Rose. Can you add that to the book?"

Tears streamed down Josie's face and she smiled through them. "Yeah, I can add that. It's a beautiful name for your daughter."

I stood up to hug her. I pulled her close to me and stroked her hair and her back. "Thank you, Josie. You've given me a beautiful gift and I will cherish it always."

Taking the scrapbook and the painting, I padded downstairs to my room. I felt drained. Today had been a lot to take in. I needed to sleep and regain my balance. I felt shaken to the core.

CHAPTER 16

Josie

"Don't rush into any kind of relationship. Work on yourself. Feel yourself, experience yourself and love yourself. Do this first and you will soon attract that special loving other." **~Russ Von Hoelsche**

I climbed into bed feeling overwhelmed, sad, happy, and exhausted. The feelings were swirling around me. I pictured those wild horses again, but instead of running in a herd, I watched them break off and run in wild circles, each one going a different direction. I felt like those horses that night. I felt pulled in so many different directions. I wanted to love Kyle. I knew I couldn't love Kyle. I wanted him to love me. I knew he couldn't or wouldn't love me. I wanted to help him remember his wife and baby, but making him remember also brought more sadness and that hurt me. My feelings were an absolute mess. I needed to sleep so I could regain some balance and perspective. I yawned as I fell into my pillows. Within seconds I was out.

Josie? Josie? Can you hear me?

I sat up with a jolt. Someone had spoken my name. I flicked the switch on my bedside table and looked around frantically. My breathing was erratic and I felt as if I should be screaming. It must have just been a bad dream.

Josie, this isn't a dream. I'm Isabella, Kyle's wife. You've probably heard him call me Izzy. I don't want to scare you. You're not going crazy. I just wanted to talk to you a bit. Please be patient with Kyle. He loves you, but he's fighting against it so hard; he's so damn stubborn. Give him time. You're so perfect for him. Even more perfect than I was for him. We were friends forever and our relationship was wonderful, but your spirit challenges his. He needs you as much as you need him. Just love him and support him. I'll work on him from my side; just please give him time, he'll come around.

The voice stopped after that. If she'd kept talking I wouldn't have been able to hear her because my heart and breathing were so loud in my own ears. His dead wife had just spoken to me? His dead wife was cheering us on? Hell, I was more exhausted than I even realized.

The next day I had a lunch date with the girls and Kyle had an appointment with Dr. Xander, the therapist who had helped Audrey through so many of her issues. Many members of the family had seen Dr. Xander at some point or another. Kyle was pretty irritated about going, but Jeremiah kept at him until he finally just gave in and made a few appointments.

The girls and I were meeting for lunch in town then going shopping. Carly wanted to get a few new baby things; they had sold some of the bigger pieces after Zach was a little older so she was wanting to look for a few things they needed. She and Nicky were so darn cute with this new pregnancy. I didn't begrudge them their happiness because I knew it had taken a long time for them to get pregnant. That didn't mean that the hurt and envy in my heart didn't eat at me just a little.

"So, you seem a little off-kilter and preoccupied, Josie. We've got all day, let's hear it." Audrey spoke in her no-nonsense way, and I was overwhelmed with all that was going on. The tears started flowing as we perused our menus.

"Shit, Josie, I didn't mean to make you cry. Let's figure out what we want to eat then you can tell us all about what's going on. If I had to bet, I'd put money on a certain tattooed, pierced, heart-of-gold bad boy being somewhere among those tears." She patted my hand and gave me a moment to regain my composure. "Let's get the sampler platter with four choices. I'm definitely getting that dessert on page 8 too. Do you know how nice it is to look at a menu without having to help little ones decide on their food and drink? Half the time I feel like I just point to the first thing I see when the waitress comes because I've been too caught up in the kids deciding what they want."

We all laughed although mine was a half-hearted one. Libby giggled and sighed, "Yeah, or what about getting the item you really want and then having the kids eat over half of it? Last time we went out to eat, Nate ended up giving over half his fries to Abby and the boys ate most of my salmon. I had a couple bites of their cheese quesadilla, but it didn't take the place of my salmon."

Carly smiled and added in, "Zach is notorious for ordering something then deciding he doesn't like it even though he ate it just fine last time."

The girls obviously loved their children, but I'd learned that moms liked to swap stories about the everyday stress of having children. My heart felt heavy as I thought about the fact that I'd never have those stresses; I'd never get to be a mommy. My tears threatened to fall as I ordered my unsweetened tea. I let Audrey order the sampler platter; I didn't think I'd be able to speak. Once the waitress left, three pairs of eyes turned to me and I lost it.

"Sweetie, you don't have to tell us anything, but it seems you've got a lot on your mind. Why don't you talk to us; sometimes just talking about it helps." Libby's sympathetic eyes met mine and she gave me a slight nod of her head to encourage me.

"I don't want to sound ungrateful; I'm so thrilled with the life I'm building here. I feel like I've been given a second chance, and I don't ever want to take it for granted." I took a shuddering breath and then it all just poured out of me.

"I can't ever have babies, my ex-husband was a complete douche-canoe asshole, he made sex unbearable, I don't know if I'll ever get to have good sex. I live in fear that he's going to find me and mess up what I'm building here; I don't know if I'll ever love myself completely thanks to him and my parents. Kyle and I have been kissing, and I'm pretty sure I love him." I didn't breathe until the last word left my mouth and then I felt like I would possibly pass out. I hung my head, feeling especially sheepish about the last thing I had said. I knew "I told you so" was coming.

But, when I looked up at my cousins and friends, I saw tears shimmering in their eyes and my heart swelled larger than I thought possible. This, this was what having family and friends was all about.

Audrey flagged down our waitress, "Ma'am, we need to add to our order and get it all to go. I'm going to order the chocolate toffee almond brownie." Libby, Carly, and I all added our dessert order as well.

"Okay, this conversation is going to take longer than a lunch, and I don't like people being around to overhear. We are going back to my house, Jeremiah and the kids are over at Nate's I think so we'll have the whole house and as long as we need. Then we can head to shop for Carly."

Once we had our food, we made the short trip to Audrey's house and set up a feast in her living room. Breadsticks, chips and dip, boneless wings, wontons, and desserts filled her coffee table and we settled in among cushions and pillows. I was anxious as I knew the conversation was going to revolve around me. We ate our fill and began on our desserts; I was grateful for the moments I had to gather myself before the conversation I knew was coming.

"Alright, lady, some of what you just told us is old news, some is new. Let's start with Wayne. We all knew you had an asshole ex-husband; we didn't know that sex was so terrible or that you're afraid of him causing trouble. Tell us about that first." Audrey never beat around the bush, but I liked that about her.

"Well, Wayne wasn't into sex with me. It hurt every time. He was my first, and I always thought it would get better, but it never did. He never got very hard, which I guess was a blessing. He said that sex with me was revolting; he blamed me for him not being into it. He convinced me that the bad sex was my fault. He would only come to me for sex about once a month, but then he stopped and started bringing other women into his bedroom. It always sounded like they were having a lot of fun so that reiterated to me that the bad sex was my issue, not his. But, lately, around Kyle, I've felt things

I've never felt before. My body feels alive around him. I think maybe the bad sex was Wayne's fault; but then I remember that Kyle and I are just friends and it can't be any more than that." I stopped for a moment and saw that the girls were all just waiting on me to continue.

"As for being fearful of Wayne. He hit me twice; before that he was just detached, aloof, unloving, and controlling. I left him in secret. There are two restraining orders against him; one in my old town and one here in Torey Hope. I'm not sure what he'd gain from stirring up trouble here, but I'm just afraid he's going to come mess things up for me. I knew he was an asshole but, after he hit me, I worry now that he may do worse to me and think that he can buy his way past the restraining order."

All the women had furrowed brows and sincere looks of concern. "I know what it's like to be fearful of someone coming after you, Josie. Do you have a picture of Wayne so that we all can be on the lookout? The guys and the grandparents need to see his picture too. I know the Sheriff; I'll make sure he gets the picture out to all of his officers so that Wayne won't be able to come to town unnoticed. This is just a precaution." Carly spoke softly and I recalled the nightmare of a story she'd been through in her past. I nodded slightly to let her know that I'd get them a picture.

"Let's take a little break and then we can finish up. I think there's still quite a bit Josie needs to talk about." Libby smiled gently at me as we gathered up our mess. After a restroom break, we piled back onto the couches. Three pairs of kind eyes watched me expectantly.

"When I was married to Wayne I wanted to have a child; I wanted someone to love who would love me back. He agreed I could stop taking birth control, but I never got pregnant. He rubbed it in my face that it was just one more thing I couldn't do right and took me to the doctor to figure out what was wrong with me. They ran some tests and found out I can't get pregnant, unless you count 1% good odds. I was devastated of course. I love being part of this family, I adore your children, it's sometimes just hard to watch something I'll never have." Tears streamed down my cheeks, and the girls joined in crying with me.

"Thank you for sharing this with us, Josie. I know how hard it is; wanting a baby so badly and month after month not getting what you want. Please know that none of us ever want to come across like we're rubbing our children or pregnancies in your face. Now that we know your situation, we can be a little more sensitive to your feelings. And, I'd like to add, someone has to be that 1%. I'll pray that you get your baby someday." Carly wiped her tears as she hugged me.

I was feeling a ton lighter after sharing these things with the girls. I would have happily left the rest of the conversation for another time and headed out to do our shopping. However, I could tell from the looks on their faces they weren't going to let me forget about the rest of the words I had spoken.

"I promise we won't say 'I told you so,' Josie. But you can't tell us about kisses and falling in love and not elaborate. Would you please tell us more about what's going on with you and Kyle?" Audrey's voice softened, and I knew there would be no judgment from these women.

"Well, Kyle and I have found out that we have a little trouble keeping our lips off of each other. His kisses are amazing; they make me weak in the knees and my stomach flutters, and I can barely breathe. I know I affect him too, he sat me on the counter during our last kiss and he stood between my legs; I could feel how hard he was. Wayne never even got a tenth that hard; it thrilled me yet scared me too. I think it scared him too because he stopped abruptly. I know he's fighting being attracted to me. I don't want to make things harder on him. We've talked somewhat about our feelings and how we wish things were different. But, they aren't different. He's still in love with his dead wife and stubbornly refusing to admit he could love me as well. I feel like a complete bitch even thinking about making him choose me or her. And, now you'll all really think I'm insane; Izzy is talking to me. She told me she's on my side and that I just need to give him time." I shook my head as all of it spilled out of me.

Three sets of lungs took in deep breaths as I finished. Then three pretty mouths smiled at me. Smiled? "Why are you all smiling at me?"

Audrey spoke, almost as if she couldn't believe what she was saying, "You love him, he loves you, even if he can't admit it yet, AND you've got Izzy on your side. She's right, just give it time. Before I heard your words, I would have lamented that you were just going to get hurt. But, now that I've heard it all, I feel good about this. He needs to get his shit together and realize he can love you without forgetting her. I don't usually do the whole 'ghost' thing but if Izzy is speaking to you and cheering you on then you know she's speaking to him too. If his dead wife wants you together then you just need to sit back and let it happen. And when it DOES happen, it's going to be beautiful, Josie. You two will be just beautiful together. You already are, but it's going to be even better once he can work his shit out."

It was my turn to take a deep breath. Okay, so my friends were probably the best in the whole world. Talking to them had helped so much. It amazed me how much just talking about something could help. Abruptly, I was reminded of Julie's story and my plan to ask Libby about using The Center.

"Girls, thank you so very much for listening to me today. Talking about things truly helps so much. Libby, I was wondering if I could use The Center one night a week to hold a group? I want to invite people to talk about their problems. It could be open to anyone; we all deal with problems. I want to talk to Dr. Xander about being available if someone's problems are maybe beyond just talking about them. Having others listen just helps to alleviate some of the weight on your shoulders; also, listening to others' problems can sometimes help us realize that our own issues aren't as serious as we thought. It will maybe take a bit to get it set up, but I wanted to know if it was feasible to use The Center before I made other plans to get it set up." I looked at Libby expectantly and she smiled.

"That sounds like a fabulous idea and I know The Center would be a great place for it. We'll get a schedule worked out once you have the details. This is a wonderful idea, Josie. Now, let's going shopping!" We all laughed as we headed out the door to the car.

We headed into the baby store; I felt the girls' apprehension as we entered the door. "I'm okay, girls. It's hard, but it's not new. I'm happy for all of you and want to help Carly today. Just ignore my tears or melancholy." Three shaky and sad smiles flashed my way.

Baby clothes are about the cutest things I've ever seen. So tiny, so perfect. I know from listening to the girls talk that baby clothes get food and poop and spit up on them and that the babies grow out of them almost faster than you can buy them. That doesn't mean that the outfits aren't absolutely adorable. I snuck a couple unisex outfits into my basket to buy for Carly and Nicky's baby; they weren't finding out the sex so I had to pick gender-neutral things.

I was walking through the section displaying what

seemed to be thousands of different blankets. A multi-colored one caught my attention; I loved the different splashes of colors. It stuck out from the rest of the blankets in that section; I liked that it was unique. My hand caressed the silky softness of it and I swallowed a lump in my throat. Someday a baby would be wrapped in the blanket and clasped to a mother or father's chest as it was rocked to sleep. It wouldn't be MY baby, but this blanket would bring comfort to a special baby one day. Tears splashed down my cheeks as I thought of that baby. Then I thought of Addyson Rose; the baby girl lost to Kyle and Izzy. I lost it completely. I had to leave the blanket section.

Go back and buy that blanket, Josie.

I whipped my head around, looking for who had spoken to me. I knew who it was but my brain didn't want to admit that Izzy was speaking to me again. "I can't just buy a random baby blanket when I won't ever need it, Izzy."

Josie, just listen to me. Go get the blanket, buy it, and take it home. It's big enough to use as a lap blanket if you want. Or put it away in a closet and forget about it. I can't explain why I want you to buy that baby blanket, but I really need you to get it.

Shaking my head, wondering how I'd explain the purchase if the girls saw it or Kyle noticed me come home with it. I grabbed the multicolored baby blanket and headed to check out. Once I had my purchases safely in a big bag, I whispered, "There, Izzy, happy now?" and headed to find my friends.

Yes. Thank you Josie. That blanket will mean a lot one day. Hey, be super patient with Kyle tonight; he's having a rough day with Dr. Xander.

I immediately felt my heart begin to pound at the mention of Kyle. Finding my friends and seeing they were almost ready to checkout as well, I felt relief. I'd head home soon and Kyle and I could spend some time together. I wondered what talking with Dr. Xander had stirred up.

CHAPTER 17

Kyle

*"If you bury the pain deep down it will stay with you indefinitely, but if you open yourself to it, experience it, and deal with it head-on, you'll find it begins to move on after a while." ~**Greg Behrendt***

It's not that I didn't like Dr. Xander; he seemed like a very knowledgeable and caring man. I simply didn't like the emotions he was messing with. I had carefully guarded my heart since Izzy died; I knew how to keep the feelings away. I let little bits of happy mix in with the sad, but overall I kept them all locked away. The guilt was too much, the sad was overwhelming, the happy memories led to sadness; it was easier to just keep it locked away.

But, Dr. Xander said I needed to feel; he said the numb heart I was trying to function with would eventually be the death of me, both literally and figuratively.

On the way to see the doctor, Izzy had bombarded me as I drove my motorcycle through the streets of Torey Hope.

Kyle, I'm not going to stop bothering you about this. I can't explain it, this is just something I have to do; I need to see you happy. I want you to know that I love Josie and I love you with her; it's a little strange I'm sure to have your dead wife supporting you in moving on with a new woman, but I've watched the hurt in your eyes for too long, Kyle. I need to see you smiling and happy; you have so much to offer to Josie and your friends. Please, stop fighting this you stubborn ass and just admit that you love her.

"Damn it, Izzy-bel, it's not that easy!" I revved the engine of my Harley and took a turn a bit too sharply in my frustration with her, with this voice in my head.

Yes, it IS that easy, Kyle! I'm dead; there's nothing we can do about that. Believe me, if there were a way to change that, I would do it in a heartbeat. I'd come back to you and we'd love Addyson Rose for the rest of our lives. But, we can't, I can't. So, instead of sulking about it, I'm here to be sure you're happy. You were my best friend from the day we met, I can't leave knowing my best friend isn't happy.

"So, what, once I'm with her, you'll leave for good?" I wasn't sure if that was something I wanted or feared.

Ah-ha! See, you're not denying you want to be with her! I knew it! Gotcha! I can give you a little more time, but I don't know how long I have. I don't know if I'll be able to come back. That's why I need to know you're happy before I'm gone. I want to think I could talk to you whenever I want, but I don't have an answer to that. Now, would you PLEASE just admit that you love Josie and stop being stupid about it?

"I've got to go now, Iz. I have an appointment." I felt a little bad ignoring her and walking away, but she was really getting to me. I didn't want to admit my feelings; I wanted to hide and keep the pain at bay. If I admitted things, the pain and the tough situations were going to arise.

"Kyle, when was the last time you laughed?" His piercing eyes watched me carefully, gauging my reaction.

"Josie and I watched a movie just recently. It was her first time watching a movie in a theater. I hadn't seen a comedy in quite a while. I laughed a lot." I recalled watching Josie laugh during that movie and my gut clenched.

"Close your eyes, please." When I rolled my eyes and hesitated, Dr. X just waited patiently. "Ok, picture the last time you were happy. Tell me about it." He gave me a direction and then just waited.

My mind filled with images of being happy. I tried to sort them all out, but they were floating around; too jumbled, too intertwined. "My wedding day. Grabbing coffee with Josie. The day we found 'the' house we'd been searching for. The day Josie and I set up her studio. When Josie and I decorated my shop. Dancing with Josie at the house the other night. Walking up the steps to take Josie on our first date. I don't know Doc, there are a lot of happy times running through my mind." I sighed and leaned back into the couch cushion.

"Kyle, which parent do you love more? Your mom or your dad?" His question caught me completely off-guard.

"I don't love one more than the other. They are both very special to me. They are different, but I could never pick one over another." I spoke in a way that I hoped showed him how ridiculous his question was. I couldn't tell what he thought because he just wrote on his little notepad.

Nodding his head as he finished writing he spoke again, "Name your favorite teacher in school, stick to grades Kindergarten to third." Confused by his line of questioning, I switched gears and named Mrs. Price, my first grade teacher. I had loved that woman. She was strict but fair and always let us have fun while learning.

"Ok, same question, but this time fourth grade through eighth grade." He just kept writing as he made his inquiry.

"Easy, fourth grade, Mr. Ramey. That man was wonderful. He was funny, but we learned a lot too." I still didn't see where these questions were going, but thinking about some of my favorite people was nice so I just let him do his thing.

"Ok, what about in high school?" He tapped his pen on his notepad momentarily while he waited again for me to answer.

"Well, I guess I'd have to say Mrs. Ready. She made English and Literature fun, even while reading those terribly long poems which made no sense until she explained them." I hadn't been the greatest student in high school, but Mrs. Ready had gotten me through four years of Language Arts, and I was grateful for that.

"Okay, Kyle, I just have a few more questions. Did you have pets growing up?"

Man, the guy switched topics like someone with ADHD. Did he do this to all of his patients? I was starting to get a little annoyed with it to tell the truth.

"Um, pets? Yeah, sure. We had this great dog. His name was Duke. I loved that dog. He got sick and had to be put down. We got another dog, Molly. She was my best friend through high school. Doc, I don't mean to be rude, but where are all of these questions going?" I was anxious to get out of the office but I knew we still had about 30 minutes in the appointment.

"Kyle, I need you to think about your answers to the questions I asked you. You've already told me you don't love one parent more than the other. What about those teachers; could you pick one over another?" He cocked his head to the side and gave me time to think.

"I don't think I could. I loved them all for different reasons, they were all very different people, and I learned something from each of them. I don't think I could pick." I wasn't sure if he was looking for a right or wrong answer, so I just answered as honestly as I could.

"Good, good. What about Duke and Molly? Which dog was better?" His eyes held an intensity that I didn't understand, almost as if he was making a point, but I hadn't picked up on it yet.

"Doc, I couldn't pick one dog over the other. They were both perfect dogs. Completely different, but completely perfect. Duke was a small black dog and liked to take walks and play ball. Molly was bigger, completely white, and loved to run with me. I'd love to have them both back, they were truly my best friends during the time we had them." Maybe I should look into getting a dog again; I really did miss having one.

"So, Kyle, what I'm hearing you say is that you're able to love more than just one thing at a time, is that correct?" He didn't wait for me to answer, he just went on speaking, leaving me to think about what he'd said. "Something I need you to hear and understand and accept is that the human heart is capable of loving in many different ways. It can love various people, pets, places, cars, foods, etc. I bet you could easily list at least one hundred people or foods or places you love. That's because the heart can handle loving more than just one thing at a time."

I rolled my eyes and sighed deeply. "Okay, Doc, you got me. I sure didn't see where you were going with all of those questions. I get it now. You're saying I could love Josie even though I loved Izzy more than life itself. Right? Okay, let's say I agree with you on that one. How do I let go of the guilt and the feeling like I'm leaving Izzy behind if I move on with Josie?"

"Well, that guilt isn't coming from Izzy or anyone else in your life. I know your friends here in Torey Hope. None of them are judging or laying on the guilt. I'm sure your parents and Izzy's parents just want you to be happy. You didn't leave Izzy, you didn't cause her death. A bad thing happened and you dealt with it; you'll deal with it the rest of your life. But those words 'the rest of your life' are key. You still have a long life ahead of you; you need to live it the way Izzy would have wanted you to live it. From what you've told me about the dear girl, I'm guessing she would want you happy, right? She's gone, Kyle. She's not coming back. She can't make you feel guilty. It's ok to move on. You two shared a love that won't soon be forgotten. Just like the heart, the human mind can handle a lot. You can keep your memories and love in your heart and in your mind while still building new memories and letting in new loves. Do it slowly; work at your own pace. But let the guilt go. You have no reason to feel guilty." His eyes and words were sincere. How many people had told me these same things over the past few months? Why did hearing the words from a man with the word Doctor in front of his name make it easier to accept?

"Our time is up for today. I'll see you next week. Be kind to yourself. My last thought for today? When I asked about laughter and happiness, did you notice a theme?" He waited for a moment, but when I didn't offer an answer he continued. "I can tell by your face that you know what theme I'm talking about. Since you don't seem to want to admit it, I'll share it with you. Josie. Josie was the theme in your answers about being happy and laughing. Sure, you mentioned your wedding day, but other than that you focused on Josie. I've not met her, but this girl seems to be good for you. You face lit up when you spoke about her. Spend time with Josie this week. Let yourself be happy; be happy together." He stood and waited for me by the door. "That's your assignment for this week, Kyle. Don't overthink things, just be happy." He shook my hand, and I walked out of his office.

My head was swimming.

Having a medical professional tell me that it was okay to move along was more freeing than I had anticipated. I think I had sort of hoped he would tell me that hanging onto the numbness and not moving on was exactly what I needed. It would have been easier and less painful. But, I guess I knew in my heart that he was going to say what everyone had been telling me for months; it was ok to move along. I didn't have to forget Izzy; I would never forget her. But, loving Josie didn't mean I had never loved Izzy; it didn't mean I'd ever stop loving Izzy. It just meant that I was capable of loving more than one person. My heart fluttered with the thought of loving Josie; of admitting to myself and her that I could love her. But, I'd been telling her for a long time that I could never give her my whole heart; how would I convince her otherwise?

I checked my watch, I had about 10 minutes before I was meeting up with the guys. I laughed at the term 'the guys' because it would be the grandpas, the dads, and the little boys; we were quite the group. Luckily today was fairly warm for the season, and the guys had decided to meet at the park so the kids could play.

I parked my motorcycle and stowed my helmet. Walking towards my friends I watched them play football with their sons. From the oldest man down to the youngest boy, the joy on their faces was contagious and I couldn't help but smile. I wanted that, I wanted to play with my child. A fleeting image of a little girl all dolled up in a dress and Converse flitted through my mind, but then it was replaced with an image of a little boy; rough and tough and tumble, my little boy would fit in perfectly with the guys. I stopped short; in a heartbreaking moment I remembered that Josie couldn't have children. Would I be able to live life with her without filling our home with our children? Would she be open to adoption? I pictured her in my mind; no matter what, I could love her. We would figure out our family situation later.

"Hey, Martin! Glad you made it. Come on over, let's show these guys how we used to play." Jeremiah spoke to me, and I smiled at the memories of the two of us playing high school football. We had four great years together on the team; neither of us had planned on taking it further than high school, but we'd been pretty good.

After a good half hour of play, the littlest boys were wearing down. Nate suggested they go rest on the playground swings. Beckett went with them to keep an eye on them and push their swings if needed.

The rest of us ambled toward the picnic area. Breaking out bottles of water, we sat and caught our breath for a moment. "Did you go see Dr. Xander today, Kyle?" Nicky never held back what he was thinking; I appreciated that in the man.

"Yeah, I did. Jeremiah, you and Audrey were right; he's good." I smirked at Jeremiah's look; it was as if his face was saying 'you doubted me?'

"So, did he tell you it's ok to love Josie?" Nicky looked at me expectantly. I saw Nate smile and shake his head at his brother's question, but I also saw all the men were waiting to see what my answer was.

"Actually, yeah, he did. I know you all have been telling me the same thing, but for some reason hearing it from him made it easier to take." I shook my head, I still couldn't believe how much better I felt after talking to the doctor.

"So are you going to marry Josie now?" Nicky always

wanted people married and having babies. I hated to disappoint him.

"Well, Nicky, I'm thinking marrying Josie may be jumping the gun a little bit. I think I'd like to date her. Listen, man, I know you always want people to have babies after they get married, but I need you to not mention that to Josie. She can't have babies and it makes her sad; can you be sure not to mention having babies around her?" I hoped to save Josie the pain of explaining her situation to Nicky.

"That makes me sad; I know how much fun babies can be. But you can still try to make babies after you're married, right? Because trying to make the baby is just as much fun, actually probably MORE fun, than the baby itself." We all laughed at Nicky. Beckett arrived about that time.

"What's so funny? Never mind, your cheeks are red, it must be something I'm not supposed to hear about yet. Dad, one day you're going to have to tell me about the red cheek talks. I'm not getting any younger, you know?" Beckett spoke to his dad and Jeremiah's cheeks flushed a little more.

"Yeah, Beck, we probably should have a sit down discussion sometime soon." Beckett was happy with that answer.

He turned to me, "Kyle, did Dr. Xander tell you it's ok to love Josie?" Everyone around me snickered; I guess they all knew my feelings for her before I was ready to admit them.

"Yeah, Beck, he did. Seriously though, guys, I'm a little worried. Now that I've accepted it's ok to move along and that I can love her without forgetting about Izzy, I'm afraid that

I've told her too many times that I'd never be able to give her my whole heart, and she won't ever believe that I can love her completely." Why had I pushed her away so much; now I was going to pay for it, would she ever believe that I loved her? Her parents didn't love her, her husband didn't love her; hell, I didn't think she even knew how to love herself. I kept telling her I'd never be able to love her but now I wanted her to accept my love? Fuck, I hoped I hadn't messed this up too much. And, how exactly was I supposed to go about this now? Just walk in the front door and tell her I loved her now?

"Well, you definitely need to show her that you love her. Probably take it pretty slowly at first; don't make it seem like it's just about the ssss….um, make her know it's about her, nothing else." The men laughed and Beckett looked confused as his dad spoke to me. "Audrey had a really hard time accepting that I could love her, she thought she had ruined things with her past. I had to show her that I loved her for her and nothing else."

"Take her out on real dates. No more of this practice date crap." I smiled ruefully at Jack Jordan as he spoke.

By the time we finished shootin' the shit, the boys were getting restless with the playground and were ready to walk to the Captain's house. I excused myself from the group, saying I had some things to do at home. I don't think I fooled anyone, but they were all nice enough to not give me any grief; they all knew as much as I did that I just wanted to get home to spend time with Josie.

CHAPTER 18

Josie

"Let go. Why do you cling to pain? There is nothing you can do about the wrongs of yesterday. It is not yours to judge. Why hold on to the very thing which keeps you from hope and love?" ~**Leo Buscaglia**

As I walked into the house, I heard my cell phone ringing. Grabbing it, secretly hoping it was Kyle, I breathlessly said hello.

"Hi, is this Josie?" A male voice I didn't recognize inquired of me.

"This is Josie," I replied hesitantly.

"Hi, I'm Eric, I work at the school with Nate Morgan. I

think his wife is your cousin. Anyway, I know this is a little crazy since we've never met, but I was wondering if you'd be up to a coffee date sometime. It wouldn't have to be an actual date, I've just seen you around town and I'm fairly new to Torey Hope, so I thought maybe we could get to know each other. If you want to talk to Nate first, get the lowdown on me, that's okay." Eric sounded nice and I could tell he was nervous asking me to get coffee with him. Having no experience with this type of thing, I took the out he graciously provided.

"I'm pretty new to the dating scene, Eric, so I think I better talk to Nate before I agree to coffee. If I feel up to it, I'll ask him for your number, okay?" I hated turning him down, but I wasn't really in the right frame of mind to be dating anyone. Well, anyone but the unattainable man I lived with.

Eric took the rejection good-naturedly and I thought, for just a moment, that maybe I *should* date other people. Waiting around for Kyle to come to his senses and *possibly* choose me over the memory of his dead wife could be completely pointless. But, would I just be fooling myself if I tried dating other people?

I heard Kyle coming in the house as I was hanging up the phone.

Pretend you're still on the phone, Josie. Let him hear you talking to that guy who just called. Let him think you're planning a date with him. I know it's a little white lie, but Kyle needs a swift kick to the balls to get his ass in gear and this will do it.

I didn't have much time to think about Izzy's words; I just picked up the phone and put it to my ear and pretended to be having a conversation.

"Yeah, Eric, that's a great idea. I've not been there before. What night did you have in mind? Yeah, I don't think I have any plans then so that should work great. Ok, sounds good. Alright, I'll see you at 6:00 then. Thanks for calling. You too. Bye." I had kept my back to the doorway the whole time so Kyle couldn't see my face. I knew I'd not be able to pull the charade off if I looked him in the eyes. I felt bad trying to trick him, but when your love interest's dead wife speaks to you and offers a way to get him to realize he's into you, you don't question it. Well, that's not true, you question the hell out of it; you question the hell out of yourself; you convince yourself you've gone insane. But, I still followed Izzy's instructions.

I hung up and turned around, wondering if Kyle had even heard my play acting. He was directly behind me and his eyes were intense. "Hey, Jo-Jo. How was your day? Good time with the girls?"

"Yeah, it was a lot of fun, just what we all needed I think." I shuffled my feet, not really looking at him, feeling guilty for the lie I was letting him believe. *It's ok, Josie, I'll take the blame if this goes south. Give it a little time, he's processing it.*

Kyle walked toward me, stopping right before his body was flush with mine. My heartbeat doubled and my body tingled. The slight touch of his fingertips running down the back of my arms brought shivers to my skin. Having no way to control my racing heartbeat, I gave into the feelings racing through me; my breathing increased, but I noticed that his did too. Looking up into those deep brown eyes, I wanted nothing more than to wrap my arms around his neck and bury my face in his chest. Instead, he brushed a strand of hair from my face and leaned in to quickly kiss my cheek. Working hard to overcome his racing pulse and his heavy breathing, he spoke, "I'm glad you had a good day, Jose. I'm going to shower, then let's get dinner and watch a movie. You up for that?"

Swallowing my disappointment that he didn't kiss me while rejoicing that we had the evening together, I smiled at him and agreed. "Sure, KJ, I'll order something. What do we want? Mexican? Chinese? Pizza? Italian?"

We decided on Chinese; I placed the order while he took his shower. I'm not proud of it, but I stood outside of the bathroom and just imagined what he looked like. I visualized the water running down his perfectly taut, perfectly tatted, perfectly toned body. I had no clue what I was doing in that department, but I wanted to run my hands down his body and lick the water from his skin. My fantasies were interrupted when I heard him talking.

"Fuck it, Izzy, I'm too late. She was making a DATE when I walked in. I knew I'd ruined it and today proves it. You were right, I was being stubborn and stupid and now I've lost her." His voice was anguished and low, my heart broke for him while it fluttered for what this meant for us.

I couldn't actually hear Izzy, maybe because the door was closed or maybe because she wasn't speaking directly to me; but I could hear a low whispery buzz and I took that to be Izzy as she spoke to him. He was quiet while the whispery buzz floated through the air then I heard him laugh and speak sarcastically.

"Yeah, sure, Iz. I'll just go out there and say, 'Listen, I heard you making a date. Well, after talking to the shrink today, I've realized I *can* love you and I'm pretty sure I *do* love you. So forget all that shit I told you about never being able to give you my whole heart, cancel your date, and love me.' Yeah, that will work just great." He was quiet again while he listened to the whispery buzz.

"I was kidding Izzy, just being a smartass. I can't just say that to her." He paused as the whispery buzz was heard. "No, I won't. I won't put her in that situation." Pause. "So, what do you suggest I do then?" Pause. "Yeah. Yeah, I could do that. Thanks, Izzy. I'm really glad you're here. I mean, I know you're not *here,* but I'm glad you're helping me. I guess I was being pretty stupid, huh?" The whispery buzz faded away and Kyle finished his shower.

Heading to my room to change into something more comfortable for the movie, I felt a breeze against the back of my neck. Turning to close the window I stopped short when I realized the window wasn't open. I felt the soft kiss of breeze against my cheek as I turned around slowly. A paper on my nightstand fluttered to the ground. "Izzy, is that you? If it is, could you talk to me? You're sort of creeping me out." I knew Izzy wasn't going to hurt me or cause problems but her "presence" in the room was a little unnerving.

It's me, Josie. I'm learning what I can and can't do. Talking to you and Kyle is easier, although it took me a while to learn how to do it. Moving things is much harder. Touching you or him is near impossible. I touch, but you don't really feel it.

Listen, Kyle fell for the fake date thing. I'm not sure if he'll bring it up or not; just let him think you're going out on Saturday night. He's going to ask you out on a real date before that. Make him work for it, but cut him some slack. Talk to him, make him explain how he knows he can love you now; believe him when he tells you he CAN love you now. Once you two get your shit together I'm not sure how long I'll be around; love him, be happy, live life.

I started to reply to her, but I felt her absence before I could. She had left. Putting on my pajama bottoms and a tank, I headed to the door to pay for the Chinese food. I had just set it all up on the coffee table when Kyle came into the room. His hair was still damp and flopping in his eyes with the lack of styling products he usually used to keep it in place. My mouth went dry at the sight of him with no shirt on; his perfect abs gave way to the most delicious V surrounded by colorful tattoos. All too quickly he pulled on a black t-shirt, but I noticed the fire in his eyes as he took in my white tank and flannel pants.

We quickly doused the fire building between us by settling in to eat our dinner. Talking with Kyle came so naturally; we never ran out of topics to discuss, from random to important. I loved nothing more than laughing with him and being around him.

"You want to watch a movie, Jo?" His eyes told me that he'd rather do something else, but he was keeping things casual. I was anticipating how he was going to bring up his appointment with Dr. Xander and how he was going to ask me out. Maybe Izzy was wrong, maybe he wasn't planning on that. We could keep it safe and watch a movie for now.

Kyle and I had a game we played called Movie Roulette. We'd made up a list of numbers corresponding with movie genres. A roll of some dice would pick our genre. A second roll of the dice took us to the list of movies available to watch on television at that time and we'd pick the movie that corresponded with the numbers on the dice. Sometimes we got some great movies, sometimes it backfired terribly and we ended up talking through most of the show.

I picked up the dice. "Come on, baby, bring me something good!" I giggled as I tossed the dice. I watched in complete disbelief and amusement as the dice floated in the air for a bit, spun around, and landed on two. Two was the romance genre. I had no doubt that Izzy had made those dice land on two. I glanced quickly at Kyle to see if he'd noticed.

He was frowning a bit; I got the idea that he noticed and wasn't amused. He didn't know at that moment that I'd spoken to Izzy so he was probably worried she'd blow her cover.

"Nice roll, Jo-Jo", he said as he cleared his throat. He picked up the dice and tossed them. Again, the dice took on a life of their own, stopped in midair, looked to be spinning around, and landed softly on the coffee table. Kyle's head jerked up to find me looking at him; I shrugged and smiled at him. I didn't want him to think I was freaked out by Izzy's antics.

The movie we, um, *Izzy* landed on was Message in a Bottle. It was an older movie but one neither of us had seen. I wondered briefly why Izzy had picked this particular movie out of all the movies out there.

We settled in, comfy cozy on the couch. Kyle was in the corner and he held his arm out to me so that I could settle into his side. If Izzy hadn't told me that he was going to ask me out; if I didn't know that he knew now that this could go somewhere, it wouldn't have been smart to cuddle into his side. But, because I knew all of that, I let myself curl my body into his and revel in his scent.

The movie was a strong message to both Kyle and me. Some of the coincidences were scary. The main character had lost his wife and didn't want to or know how to move on. Throughout the movie I kept glancing up at Kyle or I'd feel his gaze on me. The ending of the movie had me crying; all that they missed out on and then it was too late. I understood in that instant why Izzy had picked this movie for us. I think it was a movie more for Kyle than for me; the message of loving each other and living in the now before it becomes too late was apparent and very clear to me. I glanced towards Kyle to see if the message had resonated with him as well.

We both chuckled nervously and spoke simultaneously.

"Well played, Izzy."

"Well, she got her point across didn't she?"

The words came out at the same time and we sort of just looked at each other as if waiting for the other to explain the statement.

Kyle spoke first, "Who got her point across, Jo? The woman in the movie?" His hand caressed my cheek.

"No, um, I'm referring to another woman. I don't think you know this, but Izzy has been talking to me as well as talking to you. I know she manipulated those dice so that we'd watch that movie. I think she wanted us to see the message in that movie." I spoke hesitantly, not sure how Kyle would react to my words.

He ran his hand over his face and blew out a laughing breath. "So, Izzy's been talking to you, too, huh? Well, I should have known when you didn't seem freaked out by what those dice did." He glanced around the room, "Are you here Izzy-bel? We get the message loud and clear. I get the message." We both sat waiting in silence to hear Izzy or see something to indicate she was in the room.

"I don't think she's here, KJ. I think we'd feel her. She's probably really tired. She said talking to us was easier than moving things; I bet moving those dice took a lot of her energy." I turned to speak to the room in case Izzy could hear us, "Thank you for the message, Izzy. I think it was one we both needed. We'll take it to heart."

"Let's get this mess cleaned up and then spend some time talking, Jo. Whatdya say? I think we've got a lot to talk about." He pulled me close to him and kissed my head.

After cleaning up our dinner we naturally made our way up to Kyle's studio. He spent a lot of time in this room; drawing his artwork for tattoo designs and listening to his eclectic collection of music was something I could almost always find him doing. When we entered the room, he automatically flipped on some music.

A random song started playing but within seconds the music skipped ahead two or three songs and landed on "Say Goodnight" by Bullet for my Valentine. This wasn't a song I had ever heard, it was a bit too hard for my taste, but Kyle and I stood in his studio riveted by the lyrics. Living in misery, sacrificing to hold someone, no breath left, seeing love reflected in a baby's eyes, being there until the end, saying farewell....the words hit close to home.

There was no doubt in either of our minds that Izzy had chosen this song. The song was harsh and dark and haunting; the words causing us both to catch our breath. It was as if Izzy was letting Kyle know she was never leaving him, she was with him forever, but she had to move on with Addyson Rose just like he needed to move on with me. When the song ended, Kyle reached for my hand and pulled me close to him.

"Well, that's another score 1 for Izzy on her selections and messages," Kyle laughed after a moment. "Ok, Iz, I get it. No need to beat a dead horse."

I smiled sadly; I was grateful for Izzy being on our side, cheering us on. But, part of me felt guilty; if I could have given him back his wife and baby, I would have in a heartbeat.

Moving away from the dark, haunting lyrics we'd just heard, Kyle pulled me over to his workspace. "Jose, I wanted to play a song for you. I think it's going to come across terribly cheesy, but it's got to be done. That movie we watched wasn't the best movie ever, but it had a powerful message of acting on something before it's too late. Being the music fan that I am, I immediately thought of the song 'Message in a Bottle' by The Police. I want you to hear a couple of the lyrics." He flipped through some files on his computer and pulled up the song, complete with lyrics. The song was one I had heard before, but I'd never focused on the words.

Kyle pulled two stools over to his computer station, placing mine in front of his. Sitting behind me, wrapping his arms around me to mess with the computer, he paused the music on one part. "'*Another lonely day with no one here but me, more loneliness than any man could bear, rescue me before I fall into despair*'. Jo, even though I was doing it because I didn't want to lose Izzy's memory, my days were so terribly lonely until I met you; you've rescued me from the despair I had fallen into." He spoke softly into my ear as the song played on. My heart caught on the words, "*A year has passed...*" knowing that he'd been without Izzy for over a year.

Pausing the music again, he let me read the lyrics to myself, '*Only hope can keep me together, love can mend your life, but love can break your heart.*' I looked at him, hoping he'd elaborate more on the message in those words.

"Josie, you're my hope, you're what's been keeping me together. Your love is mending my life. But I'm scared of all of this too; I'm scared because love can break my heart. I don't know if I would survive the pain again." He hugged me close to his chest, and I felt the raw honesty of his words.

He stood and walked to the light switch to dim the lights in the room. I felt my breathing increase and stood facing him, waiting for what was next.

Walking towards me slowly, he turned me around and caressed his thumbs along my shoulders. With achingly slow movements he moved the straps of my shirt slowly off my shoulders and down my shoulders. Leaning in, he feathered kisses along the nape of my neck and along my shoulders. My breathing stopped. My body ached for his touch.

"We need to get those wild horses drawn up, Jose. I want to get it on you; I want to see my work on you." His hands ran seductively down my sides and then back up to return the straps of my shirt to their original position.

Turning me around he tipped my chin up, "We need to

talk, Jo. Some things have changed. No more practice dating. No more stopping kisses and pretending they shouldn't happen. I want to see more than my ink on you; I want to see me on you." With that final comment he brought his mouth down on mine. This kiss was different than all of the others had been. This kiss was all Kyle, he was holding nothing back.

CHAPTER 19

Kyle

"Don't let yesterday use up too much of today."
~Cherokee Indian Proverb

I knew this had to go slow; I couldn't move too fast when I'd not even told her about my session with Dr. Xander. Hell, I'd not even asked her out on a date; she still had a date with some other guy. We needed to clear some things up, but I couldn't stop just yet.

My hand curled around the back of her neck so that I could position her head in such a way that I could deepen the kiss. We had kissed before, but this time was different. This one wasn't about testing forbidden waters, this one wasn't about tasting what we couldn't have. This kiss was about hope and heat and us, just us.

I pulled her close to me knowing that she would feel the evidence of just how much I wanted her pressing into her belly. The gasp that escaped her was my undoing. My hands traveled up her torso and I hovered dangerously close to her breasts. She must have sensed my question because she strained her chest in such a way that my hands were on her before I knew it; she was perfect. "I'm sorry they are so small, I know there's nothing arousing about them." Her voice caught, and I pulled back slightly; I knew we needed to slow down, but I couldn't stop right now, not when she needed to hear what I had to say.

"Josie, I don't want to hear you put yourself down like that again. I know your parents and Wayne did a number on your confidence, but you're with me now and you're absolutely perfect." As she scoffed, I kissed her to stop her doubt and brought my thumbs to her breasts, groaning as her nipples strained against the fabric of her shirt. "Jo, you fit in my hands perfectly and your body responds to mine just right. Feel that? Feel how your body is straining to meet mine? Whatever you've believed about yourself in the past, let it all go and believe only what I tell you. Your body is alive for me, and we're going to have a damn good time finding out all about what your body wants from me and what mine wants from you." I kissed her one last time and pulled her close to press myself against her soft belly once more. "But, until I take you out on a proper date, our bodies are going to have to just deal with some longing." I laughed at her pouty little face, I could sense her discomfort and sexual tension. I knew she didn't have experience with feeling this way, so I offered her a compromise.

"Tell you what, Jo-Jo, let's talk. Then we can experiment with some of the great 'not sex' things available for us to do." At her questioning look I chuckled, "Oh, Jose, there's so much we can do without actually having sex; I think this is going to be a lot of fun."

She sadly shook her head, "Ky, that sounds great, but I don't want you to get your hopes up; I'm just no good..." I put a finger to her lips and tipped her chin up to kiss away her words.

"What did I say, Jo? No more of that. I guarantee you'll be good at anything we do together. Your nipples are so hard I can feel them through my shirt. I'd place money that you'll have to change your panties because they are so wet. It's not even remotely a possibility that you won't be good at sex or the acts leading up to it." I kissed her again, biting at her lip, wishing like hell that we'd already had our talk so we could move on to some of the more fun stuff. But, I let her go. "Ok, let's meet in your room in five minutes. We'll talk. Talk first, play second." I smiled at her blush and felt myself grow harder at the sight.

As she walked out of my studio, I ran my hands through my messy, unstyled hair. I wasn't worried about things with

Josie; I was just feeling terribly guilty about my responses to her. My body had never felt this much sexual tension around Izzy; I'd never been this hard and anxious to touch her. Making love to Izzy had been beautiful and real and perfect; but, in all honesty, it had never been breathtaking and my body was already feeling like my breath was being stolen away by Josie, and I'd barely touched her. I needed to focus on the now, the present, the girl I was moving on with. I wasn't hurting Izzy, she wanted this for me, she wanted us to be happy. I sighed into my hands and willed my body to calm down. I needed to be able to talk to Josie, not jump her as soon as we laid on her bed. These primal urges I was feeling were beyond what I'd felt in the past. I wanted her with a hunger I'd never known. I had a feeling that what was already sizzling between Josie and me was going to be explosive once we reached that point.

I pulled a chair from the corner of my room, dragged it through the bathroom, and set it up next to Josie's bed so I could sit near her but keep some distance between us.

Josie came walking in from the kitchen carrying two cups of hot tea. Libby Morgan had gotten Jo hooked on hot tea, and she always made some when she felt the situation called for it. Libby had taught her that hot tea was good for most every situation. I took a steaming mug from her hand and sat it on her nightstand. She spied the chair I'd brought in and smiled at me, "Don't trust the bed, huh? Well, me neither, so good call." She climbed into her bed and pulled the blankets up around her as she leaned against the headboard. "Okay, so let's talk, KJ."

I took a deep breath; where should I start? I decided to get the thing that was bothering most off my chest first; like the band-aid Nicky had suggested, just rip it off. "Um, listen, I overheard you making a date on the phone when I came in. I won't try to stop you from dating if that's what you want to do, but I was sort of hoping that we could give this thing with us a chance first. I'd never ask you to cancel a date for me. Um, but, I was just thinking maybe you and I could have a *real* first date earlier in the week; before you go out with whatever-his-name-is on Saturday." I felt like a complete douche, but I needed her to know I wasn't thrilled with this other guy.

Josie hung her head for a moment, and I feared I'd made her mad with my request. I wasn't going to apologize for asking her out on a real date; I didn't demand she cancel her other date, so I didn't know why she seemed miffed.

"Ky, I've got to be honest with you; that's what we need between us from here on out, right? Honesty?" Her gorgeous blue eyes looked at me with such sincerity that my heart almost stopped out of fear of what she was going to tell me.

"Yeah, Jo, we've got to be honest with each other. Always." I reached out and took her hand. "What is it?" Whatever it was, we'd deal with it. Izzy had convinced me to take this step, and I wasn't going to give up on her. Maybe she was more excited about this guy taking her on a date than I thought she was; was she going to tell me she was falling for someone, and I was too late? I thought back to the way her lips tasted, the way her breathing increased, her moans as my hard length pressed against her, her nipples pebbling under my touch; no, she wasn't falling for anyone other than me. I felt it.

"Well, Izzy convinced me to do a little role-playing on the phone when you walked in. I don't really have a date on Saturday; Eric works at Nate's school and called to ask me out, but I turned him down, telling him I wasn't ready and if I decided wanted to go out, I'd ask Nate for his number. But Izzy made me pretend to still be on the phone when you walked in. She said you needed a kick in the balls to get your ass in gear and that thinking I was going on a date with another guy would be just the thing. She didn't give me much time to think it over, so I sort of panicked and just went with it. I'm so sorry, KJ, I shouldn't have lied to you. Izzy said if this all went south she'd take the blame for it." She winced slightly as she lifted her head to look at me, as if afraid I was going to be mad.

I threw my head back and laughed; it felt good to just let loose with a big hearty laugh. I loved the feeling of the laugh rumbling from my stomach to my chest and reverberating off the walls. "A kick to balls, huh? Yeah, that sounds like Izzy." As I wiped some happy tears from my eyes, I spoke, "Well played again, Izzy-bel. Well played."

"Listen, Jose, I'm not mad at you. In fact, hearing that you don't have a date on Saturday is some of the best news I've heard all day. Means you and I can get a couple dates in this week rather than just one." I rubbed my thumb across the back of her hand and noticed how she shivered at my touch. My mind flitted to how my touch would affect her later. Shaking my head to clear my thoughts, I came back to the present.

"Okay then, next topic. I met with Dr. Xander today. I'm not sure what I was expecting going in. I had Izzy badgering me the whole way there; I think I really wanted him to say it was a good idea to protect myself and my heart by holding the memories of Izzy close and not opening myself up to moving along. But, from the moment I sat down, he told me the exact opposite. Told me that the way I was trying to keep my heart numb would eventually be the figurative and literal death of me. He did some exercises with me which pointed out the ability humans have to love more than one thing at a time. Nothing he said was earth-shattering; he said mostly the same type of things all of my friends and family have been saying all along. But, hearing it from a medical professional seemed to break through something in my head and heart. He made me see that YOU are what makes me happy. He made me see that I can love Izzy forever and never lose memories with her, but I can also move on and build new love and new memories. He gave me an assignment between now and my next appointment; I'm supposed to let go of the guilt, be happy, spend time with you, and just live life. I think if Izzy could have smacked me upside the head, she would have. She all but did as she told me, 'See, Punk Boy, it's the same thing I've been telling you this whole time!'" I smiled at the thought of Izzy being so irritated with me. I let out a deep breath as I finished my recap of my session with Dr. X.

"So, what does all of that mean, Ky?" Josie seemed anxious and hesitant as she looked at her tiny hand in my larger one.

"What it means, Jo, is that I've been wrong all this time. I kept telling you I could never give you my whole heart, but that's not true. I can give my heart to more than one at a time. I was so scared of the hurt that might come from loving again, it was just easier to convince myself and you that I couldn't love you the way you deserve than take the chance and risk the pain. It means that I want to give us a chance; I can't stand the thought of losing you but what's that saying? 'It's better to have loved and lost than to have never loved at all'? Well, it's true. Pain and hurt are an ugly part of life; but without those emotions, we wouldn't know the emotions on the opposite spectrum. I'd rather have loved Izzy and lost her than to have never loved her at all. I'd rather take a chance on us and find love between us than to keep hiding from some-thing that could be amazing." As I spoke, I realized for the umpteenth time that day that I meant every word I was saying, and I really did have room in my heart for Josie. I grasped her hand tighter and looked at her. "Are you on board with this, Josie? Can we give us a chance?"

"Kyle, I want that more than anything. But..." She shut her eyes tight, and I saw her jaw tighten.

"But, nothing, baby. I told you, no more thinking you're not good enough. You are perfect, just the way you are. You're my best friend, you brought me out of darkness, you are what makes me happy; nothing about you is wrong. You are beautiful, smart, caring, and sexy as hell. Over time I'll show you just how sexy you are. Just because Limp Dick couldn't get it up to pleasure you doesn't mean you're not good at sexual things, Jose. I want more than anything to show you just how good you are at those things, but not tonight. Whatdya say we draw up your tattoo before bed? I don't want to ink it on you just yet because I have plans that involve you laying on your back, but let's get it drawn up so it's ready." My body warred with me; it wanted to climb in bed with Josie and love on her until the sun came up. But my head and heart knew that we needed to move slowly. So we climbed to her studio and laid out plans for her tattoo.

Once we had the plan laid, I told her I'd work on the design for the next week or so to get it perfect. Then I'd show it to her for approval and we'd set a date to get it started. I planned on doing it in three separate sessions to save her the pain and sitting for 6+ hours. We had a great plan for three wild horses running; a black, a brown, a white. It was going to be stunning. The script would read "Reckless Abandon". I couldn't wait to get my design on her body.

"Jo, I think it's time to head to bed. Let's go out tomorrow night. Mexican sounds good. We'll come back here and see where the night leads. Sound ok?" I drew her to me and wrapped my arms around her. Leaning down, I kissed her head and groaned a bit as she turned her face to look up at me. The desire in her eyes almost did me in. "God, Jose, I want to come to bed with you, but it would make me seem like today was just about getting in your pants and that's not what it's about at all. So I'm going to kiss you and send you to bed. We'll see where we're comfortable letting this go tomorrow." I kissed her mouth; she surprised me by sliding her tongue against my lips, seeking entry. I pulled her tighter against me and let our tongues dance together. When our breathing was coming in heavy pants, I pulled away. "Good night, Jo. Check your phone in a bit. I'm going to send you a song I want you to listen to before you go to sleep."

As she went to her room and I headed to mine, I grabbed my phone and pulled up the song I was looking for.

Me: Goodnight, Jo. Sleep tight. This song makes me think of you. Sweet dreams. I'll be dreaming of you so my dreams will be beyond sweet. THE MIDDLE by Jimmy Eat World

CHAPTER 20

Josie

"It sounds like a cliché, but I also learnt that you're not going to fall for the right person until you really love yourself and feel good about how you are." ~**Emma Watson**

I clicked the link Kyle sent me and listened to the song. "The Middle" by Jimmy Eat World sounded like a strange title and group, but I knew that Kyle liked a mix of all kinds of music and I wanted to hear the song he thought of for me.

I laughed and got teary eyed when I listened to the upbeat, fun, encouraging song. I liked that this song was what Kyle thought of for me. I was proud that I wasn't writing myself off any longer. I would keep trying my best and not worrying about what others thought. I didn't need to be good enough for others anymore, I just needed to be good enough for me.

I woke up the next day with a smile on my face. I wasn't 100% sure what was going to happen between Kyle and me, but the fact that we were going to give it a chance made me happy. A niggling little thought ate at me; what if we didn't work out and I lost my best friend? But, what Kyle said the night before came to mind, "I'd rather have loved and lost than to never have loved at all." I knew, deep down, after all the time we'd spent together that I already loved Kyle. I feared losing him in my life if things didn't work out, but I didn't want to hide from what we could have just because I was afraid.

I padded into the kitchen and turned on water for tea. I knew that Kyle would be at the shop most of the day and I had plans to get some new paintings finished and get started on some custom scrapbooks. We planned to go out that night; I was glad I had work to keep me busy because I was beyond excited to get to go on a real date with Kyle.

I noticed a bottle of lotion sitting on the counter. Why in the world was my lotion in the kitchen? My first thought was Izzy; was she practicing moving things? But why my lotion?

Upon closer inspection, I noticed a rolled up paper sticking out of the bottle. Without even reading a word on the paper, I was smiling like a loon. Kyle had left me a "message in a bottle" like the movie we had watched. I started giggling uncontrollably at the fact that he'd used a lotion bottle.

Grabbing the bottle and removing the paper roll, I settled in at the table and unrolled the note.

My dearest Josie,

So, our house is sorely lacking in beautiful glass bottles, but not to worry, I'm a resourceful man and I will woo you with messages in other types of bottles. Hence, the lotion bottle.

Josie, I am scared to death of what's ahead of us. But I'm also so excited I can hardly stand it. Allowing myself to move on is painful but also freeing in a way.

I'm looking forward to our date tonight. I challenge you to wear something that makes you feel sexy. You don't even have to tell me what it is, I may not even see it, but wear something that makes you feel good.

I'll pick you up at 6:00 p.m.

Kyle

P.S. Your lotion bottle wasn't completely empty so the lid is still the bathroom. I didn't want you to think I wasted a whole bottle.

～

I immediately called the girls; if I was going to wear something sexy, I needed a little guidance. We agreed to meet up for lunch, a little shopping, and girl time. That meant I had about 3 hours to paint and work on scrapbooks. I was glad for the distraction.

Three hours later I was hopping out of the shower and rushing to get my hair and makeup finished. I had gotten a little wrapped up in my painting. More and more I was finding myself lost in music and art, no longer searching for who I was, but just enjoying the person I was becoming.

I rushed into the little deli where the girls and I were meeting. I was greeted with three smiles and raised brows. Breathlessly, I slid into the booth next to Audrey. "What? I'm not that late, am I?" I looked at my watch.

The girls just smirked at me for a bit. Carly spoke first, "Maybe this is the hormones speaking but I get the feeling that things are good for you and Kyle. You're glowing, Josie."

"Oh my God! Did you have sex with him!?!" Audrey practically shrieked her question.

"Audrey, good grief, how about you not announce it for the whole place to hear?!" Libby smiled apologetically to me.

"Sorry, sorry. But, you ARE glowing. Did you have sex with Kyle?" Audrey took her voice down to a whisper.

"No. Not yet. But he's admitted that he has feelings for me, and he's ready to see where something between us could go. We're going out on a real date tonight. He said we'd see where things went after the date. He keeps talking about 'other stuff' we can do without moving to sex too soon. I don't know what he's talking about; I want to tell him that we don't have to do other stuff because I was never very good at foreplay, but he's forbid me to say I'm not good at something. He says that the way I respond to him already shows him that things between us will be perfect." I sighed with a big goofy grin on my face and the girls waited on me to continue. "We watched that movie, *Message in a Bottle,* and this morning he started leaving me messages in bottles. But he's so flippin' cute because he couldn't find a pretty glass bottle so he used a half empty lotion bottle. He challenged me to wear something that makes me feel sexy for our date tonight. So, that's why I called you girls. I knew you'd help calm my nerves and find me something sexy. Now, before we do that, let's eat, I'm starving!" I smiled a genuinely happy smile at them and they all got a little teary-eyed when they smiled back.

"Wow, Josie, all of that sounds great. We are so happy for you. I remember that movie, how did you guys end up on a movie that was so closely related to your own situations?" Libby spoke quietly.

Our waitress came before I could answer. After placing our orders, I took a drink and the girls waited. I wasn't going to hide things from them and they already knew that Izzy was speaking to us, but would the dice thing be too much?

"Well, I'm going to need you all to have a very open mind here." I waited to see that they were willing. "Izzy picked the movie for us." Not a single one of my friends scoffed, so I went on to explain our Movie Roulette game and the whole scene with the dice and how we ended up on that certain movie. I shared about Izzy making the song play, too. "Girls, it's not a song I would have ever picked to listen to, but the lyrics are perfect. It was like her own little message to us that she'd always be with us but she needed to move on and so did we."

As we finished our lunches, Audrey gave me a big cheesy grin. "So, Josie, what exactly did you have in mind for feeling sexy?" I know my face turned bright red and my sputtering answer just made the girls smile.

Jumping in to save me, Libby spoke. "Audrey, leave her alone. We're here to help, Josie. I think you should start with some sexy underwear. You'll know they are there, but Kyle may never even see them. Or maybe he will, who knows? Let's get you a matching bra and panty set, that always makes me feel sexy and Nate loves them."

"Oh! And let's get pedicures! I'm not sure it will make you feel sexy, but it will feel wonderful, so let's do it!" Carly smiled at me. I knew calling my friends would be the perfect distraction for me.

Shopping for undergarments with the girls was interesting to say the least. They all decided it was a good time to get some sexy underthings for themselves so we all spent time giggling and trying things on. If I was nervous about being naked in front of them before, all of that disappeared in front of the 3-way mirrors. I envied their confidence and enjoyed just being one of the girls while we tried on thongs and cheekies and bikini panties plus bras. One thing I realized is that all four of us were beautiful in our own sizes and shapes. I found all of them attractive in different ways and I came to understand that our unique sizes and shapes and coloring were what made us beautiful. We were four very different women with four very different bodies; slim hips, fuller hips, small breasts, larger breasts, flat tummies, rounder tummies. But all beautiful. Standing in that fitting room with all of them, laughing and talking and sharing, I had an epiphany that I was beautiful just being me. No matter what my parents said, no matter what Wayne said. Not even what Kyle said. I was me, and I was beautiful just the way I was.

It was emotionally difficult watching Carly with her round, protruding belly. She caught my eye once or twice and grabbed my hand to let me touch her, so I could feel the movement. Tears welled in my eyes, but I was grateful for her sharing that with me. Her pregnant belly and full breasts, preparing for the birth of her and Nicky's baby, were a miracle that I would never tired of seeing and I was so blessed to get to share it with her.

"Josie, no matter what, always dress sexy for yourself. If you feel sexy you'll feel good for YOU. Don't just dress sexy for Kyle or anyone else. You don't need to feel good for them, you do it for you. Now, once you feel good and sexy, Kyle will be so turned on by your confidence that he won't be able to stop himself. But don't ever do it just for him, always do it for you first." Libby smiled at me and nodded as Audrey gave me her advice.

"Oh! And I'm going to email you a recipe for some cookies you should make for him. Nate loves them and so does Nicky. I just recently found the recipe, but they are so delicious that I'm claiming them as my own and calling them 'Libby's Little Butter Cookies.' You should be pulling them out of the oven just as Kyle comes to get you tonight. And wear an apron; Nate goes all gaga when I'm baking and wearing an apron. Seriously, these cookies are so good; Nate calls them 'sex cookies'." Libby giggled as she told me about these cookies; I had a feeling she'd be doing some baking soon herself.

Once I was home, I realized I had just enough time to mix up the cookies that Libby wanted me to bake. While the dough was chilling, I'd have time to take a quick bath and make sure all was nice and smooth just in case things progressed after our date.

Before I dried my hair, I slid on a pair of emerald green silk thong panties and a matching silk and lace bra. It was the favorite of the three sets I'd purchased that day. I loved the feel of my skinny black pants sliding up my legs and the freedom the thong gave me. My small breasts stood up proudly with help from the bra and looked beyond hot in the V-neck sweater I pulled over my head. I donned a pair of peep-toe heels and the perfect necklace before heading to the kitchen. Apron in place, I scooped up cookie dough and began the baking process. Before long the entire house had a warm, sweet, buttery scent. I mixed up some of the 'optional' icing because, in my mind, icing is never optional, it's a must.

I heard the doorbell ring as the last batch had 2 minutes left to bake. Rushing to the door, trying my best to wipe the flour off my face, I swung the door open to find Kyle standing there looking like the tatted, pierced god that he was.

We stared at each other, and I saw him swallow hard. He gritted his teeth and moaned a bit.

"Fuck, Jo. What are you doing to me?"

CHAPTER 21

Kyle

"Letting go doesn't mean that you don't care about someone anymore. It's just realizing that the only person you really have control over is yourself."
~Deborah Reber

"Fuck, Jo. What are you doing to me?" She was wearing figure-hugging jeans, a low-cut sweater, 'fuck-me' heels, and an apron. A freakin' apron. Did she know the types of fantasies I'd had about women in aprons and shoes like the ones she was wearing? Something about the way the apron hugged her waist and curves went straight to my quickly lengthening manly parts.

Just when I thought I was going to be able to control myself, she brought her finger to her mouth and sucked it. "Sorry, I still had some icing on my finger." She said it innocently enough, but I saw a gleam in her eyes as if she realized it was affecting me. The sexy confidence in her eyes warred with her sheltered innocence; I'd never seen anything hotter.

I'll blame it on the hypnotically heady scent of something delicious wafting through the air, but I grabbed her around the waist and crushed her mouth with mine. The growl that echoed around us was proof of how much this girl got to me. I wanted to spend every moment with her talking and laughing and, yes, getting to know her body.

Backing away from her as a piercing beep reached through my hazy brain, I let her go as her slightly swollen mouth formed a surprised 'Oh' and she ran off to the kitchen. I followed only to be punched in the gut as I watched her perfect ass bend over to remove small, golden cookies from the oven. I observed her in silent satisfaction as she removed the cookies from the sheet to a cooling rack. I noticed a bowl of icing on the counter. I slowly made my way to the bowl without her realizing it, taking a small swipe of icing with my thumb. Walking behind her quietly, I grasped her waist and leaned down to whisper into her ear. "We're going to need to save some of this icing for a little later, but right now I want to taste it on your lips. Turn around, Jo."

I felt her breathing increase and her heart beat was palpable under my lips on her neck. She turned around and her gorgeous eyes traveled up to mine. The hooded, sexy look she gave me was almost too much. I slowly spread the icing onto her full bottom lip with my thumb and groaned as she slipped her tongue out. Pinning her against the counter, I lifted her off her feet so that I could wrap her legs around my waist. Pulling her bottom across the counter so that her center was flush with me, I brought my head down and sucked her bottom lip into my mouth, biting and soothing with my tongue. I lost myself into the sweet taste of her mouth and the dance our tongues were quickly learning. My hands crept up her torso, and I stopped breathing as she ground herself against my hard length.

If we didn't stop now, we'd never get to dinner, and I didn't want that. Actually, that's a lie; I DID want that, very much, but I wanted this to be more. So, with great effort, I backed away from her. I'd never had sex just to have sex; it just wasn't me. I wanted the whole deal with Josie; my traitorous body wasn't happy with me, but sex with Josie was going to be real, not just a physical release.

"Hi, Jo." I gave her a quick kiss with a rueful smile. "Um, I'm not sure that's how most first dates begin, but I think we've got a little history on our side, so we can be excused for our faux pas. You look gorgeous; you taste even better." I smirked at her blushing cheeks, loving the fact that I had this type of effect on her. "Go freshen up if you need to, then let's go get dinner. I'm going to save some of this icing for later." She blushed even harder, but I noticed a spark of interest in her eyes that gave me a shiver of anticipation. I was going to enjoy teaching Josie about what could really go on between a man and a woman.

I laughed at Josie's pouty lip over not taking the Harley; I knew she loved riding the bike, but winter had come back a bit this week in Torey Hope, and I didn't want her to be too cold. "I promise you all the rides you want when the weather warms a bit, Jo." My heart felt full when I walked around to her side of the car and opened her door; grasping her hand in mine, I felt damn near unbeatable as we walked into our favorite Mexican restaurant.

"¡Holá, amigos!" The host greeted us with a smile; it was safe to say we ate here quite often.

"Nos gustaría una mesa tranquila por favor," I spoke quietly to the host. Josie's head whipped around so quickly I feared she'd get whiplash. I just winked at her and let her lead the way as we followed the man to the far corner of the restaurant. We were the only people in that area and our host quickly lit the tall candles on the table.

"I am happy to see you both smiling. You are good together. Be happy." The man smiled broadly as he left us at the table.

"What did you tell him? When did you learn Spanish?" Josie asked incredulously.

"I told him we wanted a quiet table," I spoke with a smile. "I didn't exactly learn Spanish, I simply memorized that one request just for tonight." I laughed as she rolled her eyes and giggled.

"Well, it was very sexy, Señor." She grinned at me and opened her menu. The only thing I wanted to feast on at that moment was her, but I checked myself and decided on an actual entrée.

Once we'd ordered, we enjoyed our chips and salsa. How the hell did the girl make chips and salsa look sexy? I had no idea, but I had to stop watching her eat before I busted a nut.

We talked about our days. I made her laugh telling her of the grown man who almost passed out in my chair when I did his "Mom" tattoo. Her eyes mesmerized me as she told of getting lost in her painting and the music she turned on across the hall in my studio.

When she told me about her little shopping excursion and the undergarments she may or may not have purchased, I could do nothing but stare at her and imagine what she may have on underneath her clothes. The mention of the four women being in sexy panties and bras all together in one big dressing room did nothing to help the hard-on I was sporting under the table. Never would I hit on Nate or Jeremiah or Nicky's wives, but the thought of my girl almost naked with three other gorgeous women was a little too much to take.

My girl. I had just referred to Josie as my girl. I let it float around in my head for a bit as I took her hand across the table. My girl. I liked it.

"So, Jo-Jo, you want to go to the mall? A movie? Bowling?" I knew what I really wanted to do, but I didn't want to make it obvious, so I figured I'd put the ball in her court.

"How about a quick stroll around the mall to walk off dinner and then we can head home for dessert." I smirked and raised my eyebrows at her. Ducking her head to hide her quickly reddening cheeks, she laughed, "I meant the cookies I made, you pervert." Laughing together, I paid the bill and held her hand as we walked outside into the bitingly cold air.

The mall was just a block from the restaurant so we walked briskly to beat the cold. As we strolled through the mall, Victoria's Secret came into view. "Want to play a guessing game, Ky?" The sexy challenge in Josie's voice went straight to my gut. She wanted me to walk around a lingerie store and play a game with her? Anything to please my girl.

"Wow, you're quite the eye candy in a place like this, Ky. I may have to fight the drooling women off of you with sticks. 'Back, bitches, he's mine!'" Her eyes snapped to me in surprise, as if fearful of my reaction to her claiming me as hers.

"That's right, baby, I am yours. You claiming me, calling other women bitches, and us standing in a sexy lingerie store is almost more than I can deal with right now; if we didn't have an audience I'd show you just how much I'm yours." I leaned down and kissed her a bit more possessively than I meant to. "What's this game you want to play, Jo?"

"Well, I may or may not have shopped in here today. I may or may not have bought three sets of matching panties and bras that made me feel super sexy. I thought you could try to guess which ones I bought; if you see things you like, I'll be sure to make a mental note that maybe I should pick them up next time I'm here." The sparkle in her eyes intensified as she swept her arm around the store. "So, what do you think I may have bought?"

Not being one to care if people stared at me, I made a big show out of picking up various garments and debating, out loud, if I thought she would like that particular set. She was embarrassed, but I could tell she was also having fun. There were some extremely sexy pieces, but I assumed that her first foray into lingerie would have been a bit tamer. Although, she was with Audrey, so maybe she went with the sexiest she could find.

In the end, I guessed a deep purple lacey set, a silky black set, and a breathtaking emerald green silk and lace set. She didn't confirm or deny if my guesses were correct, but I was anxious to get back to the house to see if I had guessed anything correctly.

Walking into the old Victorian, I was struck with how perfect my life was right now. I had a heap of sadness and a passel of great memories, but I also had a perfect woman in my arms and in my life. Watching Josie learn to love herself as

I fell in love with her was a miraculous thing. My heart constricted a bit at the thought that we'd never have children, but I clung to the hope that our love and friendship would bring us through that painful reality. One thing that made it somewhat easier was that we KNEW she couldn't have children, so it wouldn't be like the painful years of trying and failing with Izzy. Also, part of me wondered how I would react to Josie having my child. Part of me wanted it more than anything, but part of me felt like I would be betraying my little Addyson Rose by having another child. While these thoughts flittered through my mind, I decided it was all a moot point since Josie knew she couldn't have children.

"Here, try this cookie. Libby says Nate loves them and calls them 'sex cookies.' I'm not exactly sure why, but they are definitely tasty." Josie held a cookie at my lips. I bit into the iced confection and immediately had a new favorite cookie. The crisp buttery texture balanced perfectly with the smooth sweetness of the icing.

"Mmmm, Nate calls these sex cookies because they are almost as good as sex. Either that or they always lead to sex." I grabbed Josie and kissed her long and hard. "Now, woman, are we watching a movie or TV or spending our evening on other activities?" She giggled at my feigned demanding question.

"I think I'd like to spend it on other activities if that's okay with you." She blushed and leaned in to kiss me again.

"Yeah, Jo, that's okay with me. More than okay." After

retrieving the left over icing from the fridge and smiling wickedly at her surprised look, I grabbed her hand pulled her to the bedroom. "Which room?" I questioned.

"Mine for tonight." Hearing her qualify 'for tonight' did strange things inside of me; knowing that she planned on there being more than one night brought on many feelings inside of me, all of them good.

Walking into her room, she paused and turned to me. "Can we do something I've never done?" I chuckled and raised my eyebrows. Giggling, she gave me a little shove. "Not that, not yet. Can we dance?" Hearing that my girl had never danced with a man made me sad, but it also had me feeling like a strutting peacock knowing that I was the first to dance with her.

"Sure we can, Jo. Here, I'll pull up some music. How is it you've never danced? Not even at your wedding?" How did a man marry this beautiful girl and not dance with her?

"No, Wayne was too busy hob-knobbing with business associates. He didn't want our wedding to be too common-place so there was no dancing." She hung her head as if this had been her fault.

"Jo, baby, look at me. None of his lame-ass shit is your fault. I'm sorry you've never danced, but I'm also feeling pretty damn proud that I get to be your first. Come here." I swept her into my arms as a song started on my phone. I hadn't chosen a song, I'd just chosen *romantic* on the little concierge and hoped that something good came up.

"Wanted" by Hunter Hayes came on and I smiled at how perfect this song was for this moment. Was Izzy messing with my phone? I didn't feel her presence, so I had to chalk this one up to fate.

Josie wrapped her arms around my neck and gazed up at me as I sang the words to her. I sang about her beauty both inside and out; of no matter how good she made me feel, I wanted to make her feel more; of how I wanted to hold her forever and make her feel wanted. As she settled her cheek against my chest, I didn't know if I'd ever felt more satisfied. A shadow in the corner of the room caught my attention, and I stopped breathing for a split second when I realized it was Izzy. She smiled, blew me a small kiss, and offered a small wave before she was gone. I smiled sadly, but not too sadly. I missed her, and I was sad she was taken from me, but I had this great girl in my arms and no amount of missing Izzy was going to bring her back. It hit me like a ton of bricks at that moment: if given the chance, at this exact moment, what would I choose if given the chance? Bring Izzy back or move on with Josie? I thanked God that I wasn't given that choice because I think it would have killed me to make that call. But, what I realized in that moment, for the first time, I wasn't sure what I would choose. In the past I would have chosen Izzy in a heartbeat every single time. But, now, with my sweet Josie in my arms, I was grateful to not have that choice to make because I wasn't sure I could turn her away.

The song ended and Josie roused herself from her content

placement on my chest, looking up at me she smiled. "Thank you for the dance. We should do that more often, I like dancing with you."

I laughed and kissed her lips quickly, "I like dancing with you as well, Jo. Another song?" At her nod, I clicked play on my phone again and smiled into her hair as Mr. Big's "To Be With You" came through the speakers. Again, fate was playing some pretty perfect songs tonight.

As the song played, Josie's hands began roaming up and down my back and then moved to my chest. When her fingernails trailed over my nipples, I let out a hiss and her eyes snapped to mine. In a split second she realized that her actions had caused that sound to escape from me and I saw a power-hungry glint in her eyes.

When the song ended, her fingers danced over my chest again and a low rumble sounded from my chest. "Are you trying to get yourself in trouble, Jo? Because if you keep making those innocent little moves you may find yourself on the receiving end of some trouble." I smiled as I said it to let her know that she was perfectly safe, and I had no intention of moving any faster than she wanted to move.

Her tiny fingers began to slowly lift the hem of my shirt so that her hands could freely explore under the cloth. Trying to be patient, but failing, I reached behind my head and pulled the shirt over my head. The quick catch of her breath and the way her tongue wet her lips tried my patience even further. "I need to kiss you now, Jo." Clasping the sides of her face, I crushed my lips against hers and swallowed her whimpers as I nipped at her full bottom lip. Taking cues from me, her teeth nipped at my lip and then she brought her sweet tongue to sooth the sting.

"What's next, Jose? Your call here, baby." I knew what I wanted her to decide, but I had to let this be up to her. I smoothed my thumb over her bottom lip and groaned when she took it into her mouth and bit it.

"Can we get naked and see where things go? I'm not saying we will or won't have sex tonight, Kyle, but I want you to know that I'm not going to think less of you if we end up making that decision. I think I want you as much, if not more, than you want me. Now, before you strip me, last chance to guess what color I bought." I loved that, in the middle of this heat and passion and the unknown, my girl could still joke around.

"Um, ahhh, the pressure! Okay, okay, I'm going with... green!" I waited to see what her answer would be, but she just stepped closer to me and put my hands on the bottom of her sweater.

"I guess you'll just have to find out." My hands made quick work of her sweater and I groaned when I saw her perfect breasts wrapped in shiny emerald green against her creamy white skin. My hands, having minds of their own, took their fill of her breasts. "Perfect choice, Jo. Perfect." I reveled in the hard peaks under my fingertips; grasping her waist, I undid the button on her jeans and let my hands sneak under the material at her backside to find that she was wearing very little back there. "Damn, Jo, are you trying to kill me? A thong? It's a good thing I didn't know about this until now, or I would have been trying to get your pants off at dinner." She giggled and shimmied her jeans off, stopping to take her shoes off.

"Jo, baby, can you put the shoes back on? Please?" She furrowed her brows in confusion but slid them back on. I walked her to the full-length mirror on her closet door. "Look at yourself. Perfect. Beautiful. Mine." I punctuated each word with a kiss to her neck.

"Ky, look at *us*. We are gorgeous together. Our skin, our height, our hair color; we are so different but we fit together so beautifully." Her voice became a mere whisper, "Take it all off and touch me, please."

Without another word, I removed her bra and her thong. I started to move her to the bed, but she stopped me and kept us at the mirror. "I want to watch your hands on me."

"No problem, baby. Reach up and clasp your hands behind my neck." As she did this, her whole body was on display for me, nothing hidden. My hands roamed down her waist to her hips, letting my fingers feather over her core before traveling back up and settling in on her breasts. The moans and whimpers coming from her as she watched my hands on her made for a very uncomfortable party behind my zipper. "What do you want, Jo? Tell me what you want me to do."

Frustrated, she whimpered helplessly, "I don't know. I want but I don't know what I want. Just, just... God, Ky, just make it feel good." Her legs began to tremble so I picked her up and laid her on the bed. "I'm leaving my pants on for now, Jo. I'm afraid if I take them off I'll bust out of the starting gate before the signal is even given." I picked up her foot and removed first one shoe then the other. Trailing kisses up her leg, I stopped where I most wanted to be and spoke softly. "You okay with this, Jo? Can I taste you?" The thrust of her hips against my mouth was answer enough for me; I placed my lips against her and tasted with my tongue. Holding her hips down, I continued an assault on her core. Within seconds, she was moaning my name and shattering; the sounds she was making were building my anticipation ten-fold.

"Oh, my God, Kyle. What was that?!" She asked breathlessly as she rode the wave back down and returned to earth. I moved up her body, laid on my side, and pulled her to my chest.

Kissing her, I laughed, "That, Jo, was what I'm guessing was your very first orgasm. A pretty damn great one if I do say so myself." I smugly kissed her again, and she snuggled into me.

"Wait! What about you? You didn't get to do anything. I'm so sorry." She started to panic as if I was mad that I hadn't gotten off.

"Jo, baby, I'm so close to coming in my pants it's not even

funny. Don't ever think that watching you come means I didn't get to do anything. I'll never get tired of watching that and knowing that I'm the one bringing you that pleasure." I kissed her again, "Plus, I'm not done with you yet. Rest up for a bit, then we've got more to explore." Her raised eyebrows showed me that she didn't think there could be more, and I happily accepted the challenge to prove her wrong.

CHAPTER 22

Josie

"It took me a long time not to judge myself through someone else's eyes." **~Sally Field**

I never knew that a body could do that. I'd never found sex with Wayne enjoyable at all, but I never knew all that I'd been missing out on. I just thought good sex wouldn't hurt, I had no clue it would feel so spectacular. And we hadn't even had sex yet.

Recalling his mouth and hands on me, I started to feel that tingly feeling again. Feeling greedy, I wanted more. "I think I'm ready for Round Two if you are." I felt shy but curious as to what we could do next.

Kyle rolled me under him and lit me on fire with his kiss; I knew that he was holding himself back for me and I appreciated it, but I was also anxious to see what he'd do if he let loose. I guessed I'd have to wait for that until the situation we were in wasn't so new to me.

His hot mouth and tongue and teeth on my breasts had me arching off the bed in an attempt to get closer to him. My body was on fire as he slowly trailed kisses down my stomach; he found the place he seemed to like the best and had me thrusting my hips against his tongue before I knew what had happened. "Touch me, Kyle." Without another word he slowly slid one then two fingers inside and I strained against the feeling of fullness.

"Relax, Jo. You're so damn tight, I don't know how I'll hold myself back. Just let go and let me do all the work for now." His fingers continued the in and out motion, bringing me back to that trembling, shaking state I had been in before. A single flick of his tongue and a curl of his fingers had me screaming his name and exploding.

His mouth was quickly back on mine. "I will never get tired of hearing you scream my name, Jo. That was beautiful." The hard length of him pressed into my hip and I was suddenly curious.

"Can I touch you now?" I asked as my hand began to travel down toward my intended destination. I watched as he closed his eyes and gritted his teeth when I reached him. "God, Jo. I don't know how long I can let you do that." He hissed as I tightened my hand around him. Removing his pants and reaching under the waistband of his underwear, I looked into his eyes.

"Can I taste you too? I don't know what to do, Wayne said..." The growl that came from him stopped me short.

"Never talk about that asshole when we're together like this. You can touch and taste anything you want, and you'll be perfect at it." Before he was completely done with this speech, I had dipped my finger into the bowl of icing, rubbed a bit on him, and flicked my tongue out to taste the tip before I took him completely in my mouth. "Fuck, Josie!" His hips bucked under my mouth, and I felt an extreme sense of power that I had such an effect on him. Adding my hand to the motion had him swelling and groaning more; I was surprised to find myself being pushed away. "Jo, you've got to stop, I can't take anymore, and I'm not letting loose in your mouth this first time. Just use your hand if you want to see where this was heading."

I kissed his mouth and continued the motion with my hand and watched in fascination as pleasure ripped through his body and he shouted my name. Grabbing his shirt to clean himself up, he wrapped me in his arms, and we settled into a comfortable position.

"Jo, I'm a greedy bastard, and I want more of you. I thought that taking it slow would be good, but now all I can think about is being inside of you. Let's sleep a little and see what happens when we wake up. Before that, though, we should talk about protection. Are you on the pill? Do you want me to wear a condom?" He was so sweet and sincere in his question, I smiled into the dark and felt his arms tighten around me. I made note of the caring way he didn't mention "birth control" knowing that birth control wasn't something I needed to concern myself with.

"I had the doctor run STD tests at my last annual exam and they were all clear. I'm just guessing here but I'd assume you've not been sleeping around, right?" At the slight nod of his head and the kiss of his lips on the back of my neck I continued. "Since I can't get pregnant and we're both free of diseases, I don't think anything will be necessary as long as that's okay with you as well." He turned my head towards his mouth and kissed me long and slow; I felt him harden behind me.

"That's more than okay with me, Jo. Sleep now, babe, we've got some fun stuff to take care of in a little bit." I cuddled into him and fell asleep wondering just what we'd find to occupy ourselves with once we woke.

I blinked and looked at the clock. We'd been asleep about 2 hours. Well, I'd been asleep, I could feel the evidence of Kyle NOT sleeping poking into my backside.

"Sorry, baby, I couldn't keep my mind off of you." His arms tightened around me, and I'd never felt so content and wanted and, yes, loved. The words hadn't been spoken, but the feelings between Kyle and me were right there, floating on the surface.

Rolling myself to face him, I smiled. "Hmmm, you've been thinking of me, huh? What exactly have you been thinking, Ky?" I lightly ran my hand along the length of him and grinned as he groaned.

"You little minx." He laughed almost painfully and kissed me. Whispering softly in my ear he spoke, "I'll tell you what I've been thinking. I've been thinking about the sounds you made when I touched you and tasted you. I've been thinking of the look of pure pleasure on your face when you shattered from my touch. I've been thinking about what it's going to be like when I finally have you under me; how beautiful it's going to be when I show you just how perfectly we fit together." The words he spoke brought goosebumps and had me shivering.

"I want to feel that, Kyle; I want to see how perfectly we fit. Show me, please." I leaned in to kiss him and found myself quickly rolled onto my back. The sensations between our bodies were overwhelming. The heat rising from where our skin touched, the contradiction of his hard body against my soft curves, the contrast between his olive colored and tattooed skin against my pale alabaster hued skin; it was a feast for the senses.

"Josie, before we go any further, I want to you to know that I love you." At the look of surprise on my face, he kissed me to punctuate each word. "I," a kiss to the head. "Love," a kiss to the nose. "You," a kiss to my lips that lingered. Pulling back slightly, he spoke in a raw, emotional voice. "Jo, you're my light, my hope, my future. Before you, I looked toward the future and saw only blackness; now I look at the future, and I see promise. A promise of you, of us. I had accepted that my life was to consist of just existing, but finding you brought me out of just existing to start living again. Thank you for that. Thank you for being you, for needing me, for saving me." He laid his forehead against mine when he finished speaking. Closing my eyes, I let the tears run down my face. Kyle noticed my sniffle and pulled back, "I didn't mean to make you cry, Jo." He spoke with a smile and kissed away my tears.

"I'm not crying because I'm sad, Ky. I'm crying because what you said was beautiful. I never thought I'd love anyone, let alone find someone who would love me. My goal was to start loving myself, I would have been happy with just that. But then I found myself here in Torey Hope surrounded by family and friends. You saved me from my past, you helped me learn to let go and just be me, you showed me how to love myself, you loved me." Reaching up and cupping my hands around his face, I whispered, "Kyle Martin, I love you. I hate the hand you were dealt, but I am grateful that our paths crossed; I want that hope and that promise you see when you look toward the future. When I look at the future the details are a blur, but you and I together is a sure thing." We held each other for a moment, savoring the words spoken between us.

"No more talking, Jo." His mouth trailed down my neck, and I gasped as he took a nipple in his mouth. His kisses were hot along my stomach and then all-too-quickly he was gone. I shivered at the loss of his heat and watched as he stood to remove his underwear. I smirked at his red briefs, hiding nothing of his desire for me; I knew that Kyle was a commando or briefs guy. At this moment I was a fan of the briefs outlining his glorious body, but seeing him commando was something I needed soon. My body tingled in anticipation as he crawled back onto the bed and fit himself perfectly between my legs.

"I love you, Josie." His lips settled against mine as he filled me, and I reveled in the completeness of it all. Holding himself still for a moment, he gave me time to adjust to his size. Then, with small thrusts, he began to move, and I started to lose myself in it all. "Don't close your eyes, Jo, stay here with me; look at us, watch us together." My heart sped, and I watched as he slid in and out, over and over. I couldn't help it, I gave into the feeling and closed my eyes, sinking into the sensations he was giving me.

Within moments I felt that now familiar tightening in my belly indicating that I was about to lose control. "Kyle..." I panted as his thrusts increased.

"Jo, baby, I'm so close. Come with me, let me feel you, come now, baby." He gritted his teeth as he spoke and drove into me harder and faster. The deep groan I heard matched perfectly with the swelling sensation I felt as he let go; with a final thrust he buried his face in my neck, breathing heavily. "Fuck, Jo. That was amazing. You were amazing." Kissing me, he shuddered as our bodies lost the connection, but he gathered me in his arms and sighed deeply. "We'll clean up in a minute, baby. I just want to hold you for a while. I love you, Josie."

I woke to a cold bed and a dark room. My body ached in a delicious way that reminded me what Kyle and I had shared. Padding to the bathroom, I took care of business and cleaned myself up a bit. It was very, very early, and I wondered where Kyle was. Cocking my ear, I listened to the silence of the house. The strains of music coming from his studio reached me, and I climbed the stairs. Rounding the doorway, I found him sitting on a stool haphazardly placed in the middle of the room. His naked back made my breath catch and I eyed the colorful tattoos with awe and appreciation. I watched as his body trembled and I heard him sniff his nose. Kyle was crying. His tall, lean, taut body was slumped over and shaking. I walked slightly farther into the room and my heart stopped when I saw what he was holding. A photo.

A photo of Izzy.

CHAPTER 23

Kyle

"It's true that we don't know what we've got until we've lost it, but it's also true that we don't know what we've been missing until it arrives." **~Author Unknown**

My body shook as the tears left me. "God, Izzy, I'm so, so sorry. I loved you in the only way I knew how, and it was perfect for us at the time." I paused, trying to gather my thoughts and words. "I know you can't come back, and I've accepted that. I know that you never doubted my love. I no longer feel guilty moving on. But, after what I just shared with Josie, I feel guilty that you and I never had that. I feel bad that I never gave you that earth-shattering experience. Making love to you was beautiful, but it never made the earth move for either of us and for that I am sorry. Thank you for being my friend and loving me and for encouraging me to love Josie. I know I'll see you some day; until then, please be happy. I love you, Izzy. Bye." I took a deep breath as I let go of Izzy for the final time.

I felt Josie behind me and I stiffened, fearful of how this would look to her. Laying the picture on the table to my left, I turned to her and gathered her in my arms. "That was beautiful, Kyle. I think you just gave yourself and Izzy some real closure." She held me in her arms, running her fingers up and down my back. We stood like that for a short time, just breathing in the moment. "So, earth-shattering, huh?" She spoke with a smile in her voice.

"Yeah, Jo, earth-shattering. You have no idea. Now, before we move the earth again, I think we need some breakfast. I'm going to make you my famous blueberry pancakes and watch your earth shatter again." I smiled and kissed her as she laughed.

"Mmmmm, famous blueberry pancakes, huh? Sounds promising. Can I request you make them in just your underwear?" She blushed as she asked, but I knew there was nothing she asked that I wouldn't try to give her.

Two hours later, stomachs full of delicious blueberry pancakes, desires sated again, water saved by sharing a sensual shower, and dishes done, I kissed her goodbye and headed to the shop. I had a client coming in and needed to get things set up. Josie planned on working on her paintings today so I knew there would be a good three or four hours where she was immersed into her own little world.

After filling in my client's outline for over an hour, I stated it was time to take a break. I texted Josie, hoping to catch her on a break of her own. When I didn't hear from her for ten minutes, I headed back to finish the last hour on my client. A niggling thought was eating at my brain, though. Josie was just caught up in her painting, right? There wasn't any reason to worry about her; I was just feeling more connected and protective because of last night. Right?

CHAPTER 24

Josie

"It's all about falling in love with yourself and sharing that love with someone who appreciates you, rather than looking for love to compensate for a self-love deficit." ~**Eartha Kitt**

Josie. Josie! Please listen to me. Damn it, Josie, turn the flippin' music down and listen to me. Please, JOSIE!!

Startled, I broke free from the trance of colors I was in. Between the music and the colors and the emotions of last night, I'd totally lost myself in the painting; I was anxious when I recognized the panic in Izzy's voice.

Turning the music off and wiping my hands, I paused to listen.

Josie, get to the shop now. Don't clean up, don't change your clothes, just go now.

"Izzy, you've never scared me before, but you're scaring me now. What the hell is going on?" I spoke in a panicked voice and headed down the stairs, breathlessly anticipating what Izzy was trying to tell me.

I think someone is here. I don't know who it is, but I sense he's not a good person. You need to get to Kyle now. I'll follow the best I can.

I saw a black car blocking our driveway when I peeked out the window. Turning on my heel, I snuck out the back door and ran through some backyards and empty lots until I reached the middle school. Fate was on my side because Nate and Jeremiah were there playing basketball; if they'd had their children with them, I never would have stopped to ask them for help, but since it was just the men, I ran over to them and breathlessly explained the situation the best I could.

"Nate! Jeremiah! Hi, um, I'm sorry to interrupt your game but I think my ex-husband is in town and I think he's following me. Izzy told me to get to the shop, but a black car was blocking our driveway so I started to run. Can you guys walk me the rest of the way to Kyle's shop?" Once I was finished talking, I stopped to catch my breath and was hit with the reality that my ex-husband was most likely here. Here in my safe place. Here where I'd hidden myself in the safety of my family and friends. Wayne had found me and now my safe place was no longer secret or safe. Tears welled in my eyes.

Nate and Jeremiah immediately dropped what they were doing. "No problem, Josie, we've got you. Jeremiah, call Audrey and tell her to call the police. If it's the ex, he's breaking the restraining order. Tell her to let them know we'll be at the shop. Come on, Josie, let's walk. We'll take the short cut, that way there's no hidden areas for him to trap us into." Nate spoke quickly and efficiently as he and Jeremiah flanked and we started toward the shop. I wasn't relaxed, but I felt as protected as I could be at that moment. I tried not to worry, I tried not to look around frantically, but I failed at both.

Jeremiah hung up with Audrey, smirking even though the situation was tense. "Well, if it's the ex, he better hope that the police get to him before Audrey gets to the shop. She's a bit pissed off." We all smiled ruefully in an attempt to lighten the atmosphere.

I glanced behind me and recognized the figure following us; he was about two blocks behind us but there was no doubt who it was. Wayne Erickson, my ex-husband, had found me.

We reached the shop and I ran toward the back to find Kyle while Nate and Jeremiah guarded the door to keep Wayne out.

"Kyle!" I shrieked and realized too late that he may have a client here. The look of sheer terror on Kyle's face when he rounded the corner almost brought me to my knees. Luckily it looked like the shop was empty; I rushed to his arms and began to sob hysterically.

"Josie, baby, what's wrong. Damn, I knew something was off. When I couldn't get a response from you I should have come straight home. Josie, talk to me. Why are Nate and Jeremiah here?" He held me as I cried, but I could tell he was anxious and wanted some answers.

Composing myself the best I could, I began to speak. "I was painting, totally in a zone, when Izzy started yelling at me. She told me to get out of the house and get here, to you, now. She didn't know who it was, but she felt someone bad was at the house. A black car was blocking the driveway so I cut through backyards and empty lots until I got to the middle school and found Jeremiah and Nate. Jeremiah called Audrey to have her call the police and they walked me here. It's Wayne, Kyle. He found me."

At that moment, a voice from my past boomed through the front of the shop. "Step back, I'm not here to cause trouble, I just need to speak to Josephine Erickson." Kyle kept me behind him as we walked toward the front. I saw Nate and Jeremiah, arms crossed over their chests, standing in front of Wayne. He looked scrawny and pale compared to the tall, solid, strong men standing in front of him. "Josephine, come here. This has gone on long enough. It's time for you to come home." Wayne spoke with derision, and the look of disgust on his face was almost comical.

I stepped out from behind Kyle but kept hold of his hand.

"My name isn't Josie Erickson anymore, Wayne. I'm Josie Decker and this IS my home." I spoke with force and held my chin high with a confidence I didn't realize until that exact moment that I had.

"Josephine, I've known where you were the whole time. I've had a crew watching you the entire time you've been here. I've just been biding my time while you got this little trashy side out of your system. But now it's time to return to who you really are." He tried to take a step toward me and all three men moved to shield me at the same time.

"Wayne, there's a restraining order against you, and you're breaking it. The police will be here soon. I am where I want to be; you and I are divorced; I'm not going back to that life. This is my life now." Kyle stepped in front of me when he saw the anger form on Wayne's face.

"Wayne, you need to listen to her and leave. The police are on their way. Just let it go and save yourself some trouble. Josie's made her decision, and she's staying here." Kyle spoke with authority; the "fuck'em" attitude coming out, he was not the least bit afraid of Wayne. I knew there was more he wanted to say, but he held himself in check in hopes of this ending quickly and easily.

"Fuck off, you piece of trash. You may think that because you've had a piece of her she's yours now, but one *lousy* lay doesn't mean anything. I had every inch of her first, and I need her back on my team. Josephine, I'm running for state senator, and I need you to complete the 'perfect family' picture. My media people are going to spin a story about your mental breakdown and my trying to find peace; they will portray our reunion as true love, and we'll move up the social and political ladders together. You've not done anything yet that we can't cover up or hide or spin. You need to do this for me and for your parents, for all that we did for you." Wayne was speaking forcefully, his desperation and anger becoming more and more apparent.

"I'm not going to say this again. I. AM. HOME. I'm not coming back to you. What you and my parents did to me is unforgivable; the only thing you deserve for all you 'did for me' is a swift kick to the nuts and a bad case of crabs." I felt Kyle chuckle next to me as he tightened his arm around me. "Now, the police just pulled up; too bad you didn't leave when you had the chance. I'm sure your connections will have you out before too long, but have fun wherever they take you. Don't come back here." I spoke with disgust and conviction and finality. Wayne was not going to ruin my new life.

"Josephine, I can't have my ex-wife causing me issues during this campaign. I will have people watching you; I swear, if you do anything that could be used against me or deemed unacceptable in the eyes of voters, there will be hell to pay for both you and your new family." He sputtered his threat through gritted teeth and squinted eyes. My stomach revolted as I recalled the pain from his fists; would he hurt me again? Would he hurt my family and friends?

"Wayne Erickson, you are under arrest for violating a

protective order. You have the right to remain silent. Anything you say can and will be used against you in a court of law. You have the right to speak to an attorney, and to have an attorney present during any questioning. If you cannot afford a lawyer, one will be provided for you at government expense. Do you understand these rights?" I watched in satisfaction as the officer placed the cuffs on Wayne's wrists. As childish as it sounds, I found comfort in the fact that he grimaced when the cuffs were tightened; he deserved to feel some pain.

"Yes, I understand my rights. My attorney is in the car, he'll follow us to the station." Wayne spoke dismissively to the officer, as if this arrest was less than a blip on the radar of his important life. He was probably right, his lawyers and PR people would have this erased within minutes. "Josephine, I meant what I said. Don't do anything to tarnish my reputation. I'll find out about it."

I smirked when the officer jerked on the cuffs a little harder than probably necessary as Wayne made his threat. "I suggest you keep your mouth shut, *Mister* Erickson." The officer spoke in a condescending way and led Wayne to the patrol car.

The officer who remained explained to me that since this was the first violation of the protective order, no physical harm was done, and no children were involved, then it would be classified as a class 2 misdemeanor. Unfortunately, with Wayne's status and lawyers and PR, he'd be out and back home being Mr. Running-for-Public-Office by the end of the day.

Kyle was pissed. "So, he can violate this 'protective order' but nothing happens because he didn't get a chance to HURT her?! In order for him to be in more trouble she has to get HURT? Are you fucking kidding me?!" I tried to calm him as he ran his hands through his hair.

"Kyle, I don't think he'll come back. He doesn't want any bad publicity. He's trying to get elected, he's not going to take any chances with that." For the most part, I believed what I was saying. I really didn't think Wayne would want any negative publicity, and if he violated the restraining order, or protective order, again he'd be in more trouble. I didn't think he'd risk it. But, a small part of me worried about his threats.

"Yeah, Jo? What about his threat that he'll have people watching you and that you better not step out of line or make him look bad? What about that?" Kyle turned to the officer. "Is there anything that can be done about that?" My heart hurt for Kyle because I knew he was scared and worried and just trying to protect me and our families.

"We will put an extra patrol around your house to watch for suspicious activity, but unless the people he has watching you actually DO something, we can't really do much." The officer spoke in an almost defeated manner, as if he'd dealt with this type of scenario before.

"Thank you, Officer. We'd appreciate any extra protection you could offer. Is there anything else that needs to be taken care of or are we done here?" After giving the officer my statement, we were allowed to leave. Kyle locked up the shop and we walked, hand-in-hand, towards home. A car pulled up beside us and Audrey waved.

"Come over to our house at 6:00 pm! Everyone is coming over and we're going to do a pizza feast! You can't say no; you guys need your friends and family tonight. Be there!" She laughed and drove off. Kyle and I could do nothing but smile at her retreating car.

"She's right, we need to spend time with family and friends tonight. But do you know who I want to spend my time with this afternoon?" I teased at Kyle, bumping his shoulder as we walked. His expression was grim, but he took the distraction and played along.

"Hmmm, I don't know. Who would you like to spend time with this afternoon? Libby? Your uncle?" I laughed out loud and stopped walking so I could hug him. I didn't care that we were on the sidewalk in the middle of town, I pulled his face towards mine and kissed his lips.

"I want to spend my afternoon with you. Maybe a bath or shower and a nap before Pizza Feast? Or maybe something else to while away our time?" We smiled at each other, and the cool air around us seemed to disappear as our gazes heated.

~

After a snack of Libby's Little Butter Cookies, we spent the rest of our afternoon in the bedroom. It was safe to say that Kyle kept my mind off of Wayne, multiple times. A quick nap refreshed us. We woke in time to take a shower before heading to Audrey's. Well, we had time to take a shower. We didn't have time to play in the shower, but Kyle thought the day wouldn't be complete if I didn't get to learn about shower sex. We were fashionably late to the Pizza Feast.

"You're late! But since you're both glowing and grinning like idiots, I'm going to assume you have a legitimate reason for your tardiness and let it go this one time." Audrey grinned and hugged me to her chest. "You will give me details later understand?" Her feigned whisper was heard by everyone around us and chuckles abounded.

Jeremiah clapped Kyle on the back, "You will NEVER give me details understand?" That broke the embarrassing tension and everyone laughed. Except Beckett; he just rolled his eyes and shook his head, walking away he mumbled, "I'll never understand the red-cheeks and jokes you guys make."

"You still haven't talked to him about making babies, have you?" Nicky piped up from his position behind Carly. He was rubbing her belly and kissing on her neck.

"No, no I haven't. I know I need to do it soon. But I get all flustered. Maybe I could have his uncles help me with it some day? Whatdya say, Nate? Nick? Want to help me explain it to him?" Jeremiah looked at the men hopefully

Nate looked like a deer caught in headlights, but Nicky readily agreed. "Sure! We can tell him something simple about it, nothing too detailed. Then we'll go get ice cream. Nate, you better get ready now so you can tell Sawyer and Decker about it one day." Nicky always looked at things in such a simple manner.

"Um, sure, we'll make a day of it. Guess I better figure out the best way to do it before my own kids are old enough to need 'the talk.' Man, I'm trained to talk to kids about issues every day at school, but the thought of talking to my nephew or my own kids about 'making babies' is overwhelming." Nate ran a hand over his face.

"It will be fine. Nicky's right, they don't need a lot of details. Tell Beck the basics and then don't elaborate unless he asks something requiring specifics." Libby spoke soothingly to her husband and kissed him chastely on the cheek.

Kyle must have sensed I was getting a little melancholy with all of this talk of 'making babies' because he clapped his hands together, "Okay, where's this Pizza Feast taking place? I'm starving." The distraction was taken and everyone headed to the kitchen. I hung back just long enough to speak quietly to him.

"Thanks, KJ. As much as I love the 'making babies' process with you, it hurts a little to know we'll never be successful in that department." I leaned in to kiss him. He surprised me by spinning me around and down a dark hallway.

"Mmmmm, I will make it my mission to be 'successful' in that department every single day. My success is based on how many times I make you scream my name. So far, I'm batting a thousand. Pretty successful in my opinion." He bit my smiling lip and then ran his tongue across it sucking it gently into his mouth. "I think I may be successful again tonight, and tomorrow, and the next day." Now my gloomy attitude was changed to one of lustful desire, and I wanted nothing to do with pizza; I only wanted Kyle, in bed, with me. He reached up and tweaked a nipple while whispering in my ear. "Think of all the ways we can be successful while you're enjoying your dinner, Jo. Just know that the entire time we are here, I'll be thinking of the next time I get to bury myself in you. You just let me know when you're ready to leave, babe."

I groaned into his mouth, "Now, let's leave now."

Laughing he kissed me quickly, "That would be rude, now wouldn't it. You'll just have to be a little hot and bothered for a while."

We both jumped at the sound of Beckett hollering down the hallway. "Mom! Can you turn down the heat? Kyle said Josie is hot and it's bothering her." Stifling a laugh so as not to embarrass the child, we composed ourselves and headed into the kitchen only to be met with smirks and grins from the adults gathered around the table.

The rest of the evening was perfect. Laughing with

friends and family, enjoying our favorite pizza, and playing a rousing game of Euchre was just what I needed.

Later that night, Kyle was exactly what I needed. Several 'successes' later, we fell into a sweet slumber. I refused to let Wayne ruin my happiness. I was a wild horse, recklessly abandoning the corral he was trying to lock me in again. I would live my life and love Kyle. Wayne wouldn't ruin it.

The next morning I woke to the glorious scent of hot tea and pancakes delivered by an even more glorious man in tight black briefs and an impressive outline under said briefs.

Eyeing my breakfast momentarily, I turned my hungry gaze to him and smiled seductively. "Mmmm, I'm hungry, and I think I know what I've got a taste for." I watched Kyle take a deep breath as he sat the tray down and then adjusted himself.

"I'll be waiting right here, but you don't want your tea and pancakes to get cold." He leaned down to kiss me quickly, but I grabbed him and pulled him on top of me.

"Tea and pancakes can be warmed back up. I'm already hot and ready to go, don't make me wait, Ky." I kissed him hungrily as I freed him from the confines of his briefs. Within seconds he was right where I wanted him. It was a very successful morning and we learned that Kyle's famous blueberry pancakes are delicious even warmed up.

Over the next several weeks the weather warmed slightly, and I found myself smiling more than I'd smiled in my whole life. Kyle brought sunshine to my world, and I enjoyed every second I spent with him. He left me little messages in various bottles all over the house. My favorites were an A-1 steak sauce bottle, a shampoo bottle, a ranch dressing bottle, and an empty bottle of hair color from one of his many dye jobs. Every note started the same, *My light, my hope, my future,* every note spoke of his love for me and his plans for our future, and every note was signed the same, *Your promise, Kyle.* No question about it, I had found my happily ever after; I was head-over-heels, madly in love with the man.

After about two months of planning and setting things up, I started my first group at The Center. The group would meet one night a week. Titled "Let's Chat," it was advertised as a group to listen to anything you wanted to talk about. We had rules, or guidelines, to keep us within time limits, not be offensive to others, keep things within legal limits, and we'd set up procedures if the person speaking needed more help than what we could offer. The group had met three times so far and it was going wonderfully. Members were meeting new friends, finding things they had in common with others, seeing that some of their problems weren't as bad as they once thought, and just getting things off of their chest. I appreciated when Nate or Libby would come with me to help enforce our guidelines; overall, I'd call "Let's Chat" a thriving and rewarding venture. I felt like we were truly helping others and it felt good to do that; we'd had one person so far who needed more help than just talking could help and Dr. Xander had graciously stepped in to offer some free sessions to that person.

~

Kyle had been chomping at the bit to get my tattoo started; the outline had been inked and healed, the color was next.

"You ready, Jo? We'll work for about an hour then take a break. We can split it up or get it all done today. Your call." He leaned in and kissed me and I was reminded why I wanted to get it all done at once. Laying on my back was going to be off limits for a while; I wanted to keep my healing time as short as possible. I had many things I liked to do with Kyle while I was on my back.

"I want it all done today please." I smiled as he narrowed his eyes knowingly at me.

"You dirty little girl, you're thinking about how you can't lay on your back for a while, aren't you?" What can I say? He knew me well.

"Maybe, maybe not. Let's just get it done. We can figure out alternatives while it heals." I pulled my shirt over my head and made eye contact with him before walking to the table and laying down. "Mmmmm, I wish I could sleep while this is going on, I'm so tired. You do a good job of keeping the needle light on the skin, but it's still not enough to allow me a nap." I winked at him as he prepared his ink and gun.

"Have you been staying up too late painting? Are our late night rendezvous getting to be too much for you?" He spoke mostly in jest, but I could tell that he was truly concerned for me.

"Nah, I'm good. I just need a nap here or there to get all caught up on some sleep. Ok, Ink Master, work your magic." I took a deep breath and willed myself to ignore the pain and just focus on the continual buzz of the machine.

Three hours and two breaks later, I was done. We had changed our original design somewhat, alternating from three different colored horses to three horses of the same shade. It was a silhouette of the three horses, and they were almost bronze in color. They ran across the middle of my upper back and the words 'Reckless Abandon' graced the bottom of the design. It was truly a work of art, and I was so very proud of it. It represented so much for me; since my arrival in Torey Hope, I'd grown into the person I'd always wanted to be, into the person I'd always felt was inside trying to escape.

That night I'd had every intention of showing Kyle my alternative positions since I couldn't lay on my back, but fell fast asleep as soon as my head hit the pillow and didn't wake until the sun rose the next morning. Smiling as I rolled over to find Kyle, my hand instead touched something round and smooth. Cracking an eye I recognized a syrup bottle and I had to laugh. Sitting up, I removed the rolled up note from the bottle. The sweet smell of syrup assaulted my nose, and I immediately bolted from the bed, making it to the toilet just seconds before it was too late.

Kyle jerked the shower curtain open to find me hunched over the toilet, panting as if I'd just run a race. "Jo, baby, what's wrong?" He immediately ended his shower and jumped out to help me.

"Oh, God, I don't know. I was fine, but then I smelled that syrup, and I barely made it to the bathroom. Do you think the chicken we had last night was bad?" I knew I'd eaten more of the chicken than he had, maybe that's why I was sick but he wasn't.

"I don't know, babe. Climb back in bed and rest a bit. Want some Sprite to settle your stomach?" The thought of the Sprite appealed to me, and I was able to keep it down. By mid-morning, I was still tired, but I felt better so we chalked it up to something I had eaten and went on about our business.

When Libby, Audrey, and Carly came over later to eat lunch, I told them of the bad chicken. I didn't notice the quick glances made back and forth between them as I told my story of woe.

CHAPTER 25

Kyle

"Life is not about waiting for the storms to pass...It's about learning how to dance in the rain." ~**Vivian Greene**

Two things were worrying me. The first was the damn black car that showed up in town 2-4 times a week. I knew it was Wayne or, more likely, one of his cronies. Josie knew it as well. The police knew it, but the car and person inside had done nothing wrong, so there was nothing they could do but make note of it. The Captain and I had spoken about this issue at length; he and some of his military buddies were doing what they could to keep an eye on Wayne. Captain

Decker couldn't be sure, but he had a feeling that some of those same buddies had roughed Wayne up a bit the last time he'd been seen in Torey Hope. It wasn't much and it wasn't close to what I wanted to have happen to Wayne, but it was all we could do until he made another move.

The second thing that was worrying me was Josie. She had lost weight, she was always tired, and she couldn't seem to kick this stomach thing. She'd been feeling bad for over a week; just when it would seem she was better, she'd get hit with it again.

We had to bail on a family get together about ten days into her illness; she wasn't up for it, and we decided she shouldn't be alone with Wayne prowling town, and we also didn't want me to inadvertently give her germs to the kids. So, I ran over to John and Cindy Morgan's house to get a couple plates of food for Josie and me since we couldn't make the gathering.

Libby, Audrey, and Carly met me outside before I could even ring the bell. They asked after Josie; their questions seemed weird to me. When Cindy and Judy came outside, the girls reiterated Josie's illness to the older women and many furtive glances were exchanged. I began to worry that the women thought something more serious was going on with Josie. If she wasn't better in a few days, I was going to have to convince her to see a doctor.

I entered the house, unsure of which Josie I'd find. Would she be sleepy and weepy and sick or happy and upbeat and hungry? The strange thing about her illness was that she was always hungry, but then she'd be sick as a dog the next day.

"Mmmmm, what did you bring?" She literally attacked me before I even had the food down on the counter. "Oh, thank you so much for going to pick this up. I don't want to get anyone sick, but I'm sooo hungry. I don't think I could have stayed awake long enough to fix food tonight though." I watched as she devoured the meal I'd brought her; I was happy to see her eat, but still so worried about her.

Later that night, when she woke from a late evening nap, I took her in my arms and made love to her; she cried. I was scared I had pushed things too far since she wasn't feeling well, but she told me it was "the most beautiful thing she'd ever experienced" and they were happy tears.

The next day, knowing that the girls were all coming over to put finishing touches on Carly's baby shower, I headed to the shop while Josie was still sleeping. Usually, out of fear of her being alone, I'd wait until she was up and could come with me to the shop or I'd work at home until she went to one of the girls' houses or The Center.

I wrote her a little note, rolling it up and placing it in an empty mouthwash bottle; I'd already found out earlier that using bottles that had food smells turned her stomach, so I was sticking with safer bottles.

My light, my hope, my future,
Good morning, Jo-Jo. I didn't want to wake you because I

know you're still not feeling well. Enjoy your day with the girls. I'm giving you until the end of the week to get better and then we are going to the doctor. I can't keep worrying about my girl.

    Your promise,

    Kyle

Heading to work, I tried my best to shake the niggling fear of how I would handle it if something was seriously wrong with her. I didn't think I'd survive losing someone I loved again. As I leaned my bike into the curves, I fought off the worry that tried to take over.

CHAPTER 26

Josie

"No one can make you feel inferior without your consent." ~***Eleanor Roosevelt***

I was so very sick and tired of being sick and tired. I'd never dealt with an illness that lasted this long, and I was totally over it. Most of the time the mornings and evenings were the worst, so I was glad the girls were coming over around 11:00 am. I knew I'd be feeling better by that point. I really hoped they brought something yummy for lunch, I knew I'd be starving by that point too.

I spent an hour or so painting; I had some orders I needed to get sent out, and I was also working on a painting of my tattoo. I wanted to hang a replica of Kyle's design in my studio. After finishing up some work, I headed to the closet to grab a new towel for a shower. When I pulled a towel out, I shrieked as a package fell out at me. Laughing and rolling my eyes at my jumpiness, I picked the package up and started to return it to the shelf. Before I got it put away, I realized it was the colorful baby blanket that Izzy had convinced me to buy months ago. With no actual thought, I removed the blanket from the packaging and held it to my face. Tears began to fall and in moments I had completely lost it. I slid to the ground, crying into the blanket. I was so happy with Kyle, so why was I crying like a fool over a baby blanket? We had a happy life, we had both resigned ourselves to loving our nieces and nephews instead of children of our own. None of these thoughts comforted me at that point; I continued crying.

I cried for so long that I was embarrassed to still be in that exact position when the girls arrived. I hadn't heard them ringing the bell or knocking incessantly so they had used their key to get in. After much fussing and coddling, they finally convinced me to take a quick shower while they set up lunch. My stomach growled loudly at that suggestion, and we all giggled. I didn't notice the "I told you so" looks that passed between the three of them.

By the time I emerged from the shower, Cindy and Judy had arrived with Janie, my uncle's girlfriend. I was surprised to see the older women, but it made me smile tearfully to see them all gathered together. "To what do I owe the pleasure of getting to see all six of you today?" I joked with them and then got distracted when I saw the deli sandwiches and desserts they had brought. I knew that the butterscotch pie was one of Janie's specialties, and I predicted I could have eaten that entire pie in one sitting.

"Let's grab some food and sit down." Carly suggested, and I practically knocked people over to get my plate. I guess since I was still feeling ill in the mornings and evenings, my body knew it had to get food when it could.

"Slow down there, Cujo." Audrey laughed as I stepped in front of her to take a slice of pie along with my lunch. "Dang, girl, we brought plenty, no need to growl."

I should have laughed at her joke, I knew I was being an animal about getting food into my mouth, but instead I burst into tears. "I....I...I'm so...so...sor...sorry," I wailed. All of the women put their plates down and gathered around me which made me feel loved and that led to more tears.

"Oh, dear, I see what you mean, girls. Come on, Josie, let's get you some food and drink and settle down to talk." Cindy gave me a tissue and guided me to the couch while Judy brought my food. I humbly ate my lunch, purposely not scarfing it down, and felt myself settle down a bit.

"I'm so sorry, ladies, I have been so sick and so tired, and I just can't stop crying over the silliest things. And hungry; if I'm not puking, I'm eating. Kyle's worried sick about me; I have to say I'm starting to worry a bit too. I've never been sick this long, but I just can't seem to kick this bug." I took a deep breath and forced myself to pause before starting in on the butterscotch pie.

"Well, I think you'll start feeling better soon. In my experience with this type of bug, it shouldn't last much longer." Libby spoke quietly and patted my leg.

"Speak for yourself, sister dear! When I had that particular 'bug' it lasted a whole nine months!" Audrey joked, but I only heard nine months.

"Nine months?? I can't do this for nine months. It's only been just over a week and I'm about ready to go insane. Libby, why did you get over it so much quicker? Is there medicine? If so, I'll let Kyle take me to the doctor first thing in the morning." I seriously thought I'd start crying again when I thought about feeling this way for nine months.

"Josie, you don't have a bug honey. The girls are dropping hints, but I don't think your mind is tracking well right now, so I'm just going to spell it out for you. Josie, honey, we think you may be pregnant." Cindy spoke slowly and softly, gauging my reaction to her words.

I sat stock still, mouth opening and closing, like a dying fish. My brain attempted to comprehend what she had just said but her words were beyond comprehension.

"I can't get pregnant." I spoke resolutely, fighting off the increasing feeling of anger. How dare these women come into my home and bring up the one thing that broke my heart more than anything in this world.

"Fact: You're sick in the morning and the evening. Fact:

You're exhausted all the time. Fact: You can't stand certain smells. Fact: You cry at the drop of a hat. Fact: If you're not puking, you're attacking any food that's placed in front of you." Audrey ticked these points off on her fingers.

"Josie, hon, we know you and Kyle have been intimate. Have you been using protection?" Judy asked quietly, and I fought the urge to roll my eyes at her.

"We've had no reason to use protection. There's no need to protect me from something that I can't do. And we've both been tested so protection wasn't an issue." I gritted out, in hopes of not being rude.

"When was your last period?" Carly softly prompted me.

"It was...um, wait...it was....oh, God, I don't remember. They've never been consistent so I've never paid a whole lot of attention to it." I shook my head, still trying to recall my last period.

"Well, in my not-professional-but-almost-always-right opinion, you and Kyle have probably been bumping uglies like rabbits so add that to the fact that there's been no protection and all of your symptoms....yeah, 99.9% sure you're pregnant. Listen, Josie, we debated on speaking to you about this for days. We didn't want to bring up something that could potentially hurt your feelings, but almost every single one of us has been pregnant at least once and we recognize the signs." Audrey stopped to let her words sink in.

"I'd have to agree with Audrey. I know this is extremely hard for you to wrap your head around, and we will be devastated if our prediction isn't correct, but I really do think you're pregnant, Josie." Libby smiled slightly at me.

"Josie, why do you believe you can't get pregnant?" Janie inquired.

"Um, well, when I tried to get pregnant with Wayne and couldn't, he took me to the doctor and they sent me a letter later stating that I only had a 1% chance of conceiving." I recalled the day I got that letter in the mail and the way my heart had shattered.

"Just a letter? No follow up from the doctor for further testing or other options?" Audrey questioned.

"Um, no, just the letter. I was so devastated that I just put the letter in the trash and tried to forget about it. Wayne asked about it later; it was strange that he brought it up since I knew he didn't want kids. 'So, hear anything from the doctor?' When I told him what the letter said he laughed and said, 'Just one more thing you can't do right, huh?' I knew he wouldn't approve of pursuing it further, so I just let it go." Tears had started to stream down my cheeks again.

"Well, this may be a bit presumptuous, but I brought a couple pregnancy tests. You can tell me to shove them up my ass if you want. Or, you could take one to the bathroom and pee on the freakin' stick!" Audrey was barely able to restrain herself. "I brought a couple so if the one right now isn't positive yet, you can take a few more over the next couple days. But, based on your symptoms, I'd say you could probably just breathe on the darn thing and a positive would pop up. I'm placing money, Josie, you are so totally knocked up." I started to giggle anxiously at Audrey's words as the realization of what could be happening began to sink in.

Oh my God! Could I actually be pregnant? How did I never get pregnant with Wayne but with Kyle it happened almost immediately? I needed to calm myself down; I would be devastated if I took the tests and found them all to be negative. I needed to prepare myself for disappointment; but my heart swelled at the possibility that my dream was maybe within my reach.

"Well, I guess I better go pee on a stick." I said with a tearfully happy smile as Audrey handed me the package.

After the longest three minutes of my life, I had the answer in my hand and tears streamed unchecked down my face.

"Thank you all for coming over and being here for me." I hugged the ladies as they filed out the door to head home.

"Are you sure you're going to be okay? I feel terrible about leaving you like this." Audrey held me a little longer than usual. "We can hang out until Kyle is home; he'd probably be pissed if he knew we were leaving you without him being home."

"No, it's okay. I'm just going to lay down, I don't need a babysitter. Thank you again for being here." I smiled shakily.

"We love you, Josie. Let us know if you need anything." Carly and Libby each gave me a hug and I was so very grateful for this group of women, my family, who I knew would support me through anything.

Locking the door, I headed to the kitchen to get a drink before I laid down; I was exhausted both physically and mentally. Within minutes, I was sound asleep. My nap wasn't peaceful though; Izzy kept trying to talk to me. *Josie, go see Kyle; you need to be with him right now.*

"Izzy, I'm tired, please just let me sleep. I'll talk to Kyle when he gets home." I rolled over and tried to sleep.

Josie, please. You two need to be together right now; you need him and he needs you. Go to him or have someone take him to you or call him to come home.

"Dang it, Izzy, I love you, but I feel like crap and I just want to sleep. Kyle will be home soon and we can talk then. I haven't even been able to let today sink into my head yet, I just need to sleep." I sat up, irritated with being so tired yet not being able to sleep because Izzy kept pestering me. I knew I shouldn't have felt that way, she had been our biggest supporter and I owed a lot to her for bringing Kyle and me together. That didn't mean that I was thrilled that she kept interrupting my nap.

"I'm sorry, Izzy. If I call Kyle will that make you happy?" I thought maybe if I could placate her then maybe I could sleep. Kyle had about an hour before he'd be home.

Call him, Josie. Ask him to come home to you. You two

should be together right now. I feel like something is wrong, but I can't figure out what it is.

"It's just from all of the emotions from today and the fact I've been so sick. It's okay, Izzy, I'll call him." I picked up my phone and called Kyle. It went straight to voicemail which meant he was still with a client finishing up a design. I left him a message.

"Hey, KJ, I'm going to try to finish taking a nap. If you get a chance within the next five minutes, you can call me. If not, I'll just see you when you're home. I love you. Um, we should probably talk tonight." I hung up and went to the restroom hoping he'd call back before I fell back to sleep; now that I'd left him the message, I really just wanted him with me right now.

As my eyes were drifting shut, I heard my phone ring. "Hello?" I should have glanced at the screen; if it wasn't Kyle, I was going to be irritated that I'd answered instead of falling to sleep.

"Hey, Jo, I just saw you left a message; I didn't listen to it, just called you back. Everything okay, baby? How are you feeling? Are you and the girls having a good day?" The love and concern in his voice reached to my heart and made me smile a warm, gooey smile.

"Yeah, I'm fine. I'm really tired so I'm going to finish a late afternoon nap. I made the girls leave a bit ago; I just wasn't up for company. I've not gotten it all figured out just yet, but I think I may have a surprise for you tonight." I yawned as I spoke.

"I don't like that you're there by yourself. I've got to finish this piece, but I'm going to have either Nate or Jeremiah come over to check on you. Hang on, I'm texting them both right now." He disappeared for a moment and then his soothing voice was back. "Okay, hopefully one of them can run right over. I'll keep you on the line until they get there. So, a surprise, huh? Does it involve lingerie? If so, I think I already like this surprise. Jo? Jo, baby? Are you still there?"

As Kyle's voice broke through my slumber, I realized I'd fallen asleep while he was talking. A knock at the door brought a groan from me. "Ugh, I think one of the guys is here. Hang on, I'll go let them in. This seems really silly, they shouldn't have to babysit me; you'll be home within the hour." I trudged myself to the front door, feeling bad that Nate or Jeremiah was having to give up their time to "watch me".

As I reached for the door, I heard two voices. Kyle was shouting, "Wait, Josie! Check to be sure it's Nate or Jeremiah first." Izzy was right at my side, her voice commanding, *No, Josie! Don't open it!*

Both of their voices registered in my brain as I swung the door open. Expecting to see Nate or Jeremiah, the words of Kyle and Izzy sunk in simultaneously with the panic that seized my heart and my phone clattered from my grasp. Too late, I realized that I shouldn't have opened the door without asking who it was. Wayne was standing in front of me, reeking of alcohol, bloodshot eyes, clothes and hair is disarray. I immediately knew that a drunk Wayne was a mean and unpredictable problem.

"Hello, Josephine, you little tramp. I've come to take you back home. You've made enough of a mess for me; we need to start sweeping certain things under the rug and piecing our love story back together before you can ruin everything." He staggered into the door, pushing past me. Jumping out of his way, my stomach revolted at the stench of his breath and sweat.

"Wayne, I'm not going with you. I've done nothing wrong and I don't want to be your wife or help you run for office. I need you to leave; if you leave now, the police won't have to know about this." I instinctively glanced toward the street, hoping the patrol car would miraculously drive by.

"You stupid, whore. Don't you think I know you've got police watching you? I've been sitting here for a week watching you. I had my people doing it for a while, but they weren't telling me enough, so I came to do it myself. I know all about your disgusting tattoo; don't worry, I've got an in with a dermatologist who will laser it right off. You're a real little slut, aren't you Josephine? Spreading your legs for that piece of trash, you better hope you don't have any diseases from him; I don't plan on making it a habit to fuck you, but you definitely won't be getting off on my cock if you've picked up something from him."

Blanching at his harsh words, I protectively rubbed my

stomach. In a split second, with no warning, Wayne's fist struck out and crashed into my temple. The intense pain washed through me at the same time the contents of my stomach threatened to erupt. I crumpled to the ground, instinctively rolling myself into a protective ball.

A large, clammy hand stroked my cheek and then fisted in my hair, causing screaming pain to shoot through my scalp. "You fucking little whore, did you think you could hide your dirty little secret from me? I had an inkling it might be true when I saw that blonde bitch making her little purchase at the drugstore; but now, watching you try to protect yourself, I know the truth. No worries, we'll get that taken care of right away, even before we remove the tattoo." I whimpered as he deliberately twisted his fist in my hair, causing even more searing pain.

"Wayne, stop. You don't need this type of bad press; if the media finds out what you're doing right now, you'll never get elected. If you let me go, I'll go home with you and help you get elected. Please Wayne, just don't hurt me." I stopped myself before saying anything about the baby. The precious life growing inside of me was barely a reality to me just yet, I was scared to believe it was even true, but I wanted to protect it with everything I had in me. I didn't know if Wayne was bluffing about knowing my secret; perhaps he was hoping I'd reveal the answer if he pretended to know.

"Ahh, Josephine, you're more stupid than I thought you were. I won't be placated; I know you have no intentions of

going home with me. I'm not going to fall for your little ploy."
He shifted our bodies on the ground so that he was pressing
himself between my legs; I swallowed as bile threatened up
the back of my throat when I realized he was hard against me.
The thought of him being turned on by hurting me didn't give
me a lot of hope in this situation.

"Mmm, feel that? Little dirty slut like you, my cock hard
against you probably gets you all wet. Think that piece of
trash would care to share you with me? He didn't seem to
care that I'd had you first, maybe he won't care if I have you
last." At my sob, Wayne laughed cruelly. "You see, Josephine,
the media already got wind of your torrid little relationship
and life here in Torey Hope; my opponents are having a field
day running my name in the mud because of you. 'Ex-wife',
'live-in boyfriend', 'out-of-wedlock', 'tattoos', all of those words
are being slung against me and used to show me as unfit to
run our state. ALL BECAUSE OF YOU!! So my supporters
are bailing ship, my campaign is over. FUCKING
BECAUSE OF YOU!" His spit spattered against my face as
his hips thrust against me.

"So, you and I are going to go away for a while. My career
is already ruined, might as well go all out. At least I'll get the
pleasure of watching you suffer and knowing that your filthy
little boyfriend will suffer too. Or suffer again I guess I should
say. Really is a shame about all that he's already been through
and now he's going to lose someone again. Does he know
about the baby?" He narrowed his eyes and sneered as he

spoke to me. "Ahh, I can see that he *doesn't* know yet; how sweet. Did you have a big plan to surprise him with the news?" I could tell he was still fishing; he wasn't 100% sure I was pregnant. I knew I couldn't give anything away.

"Wayne, I don't know what you're talking about. You and I both know that I can't get pregnant. Why would you come here and rub something in my face that you know hurts me." I spoke as calmly as I could. I prayed that he bought my act.

"Oh stop fucking around with me, Josephine. The little letter that arrived for you saying you couldn't get pregnant was a total fabrication. Being in the same social circles with a doctor who would do anything to make sure his sweet little wife didn't know he was banging his nurses left and right has its advantages. All I had to do was promise to keep his little secret and he wrote down whatever I wanted him to; I felt like the 1% was a nice touch, don't you think? I figured it would keep you just desperate enough and clinging to that slight chance." He chuckled as he seemed to reminisce over his deceit.

"So, if the letter was a lie, why did I never get pregnant?" I was in pain and scared, but I needed to know. In my gut, I already knew, but I needed to hear it from him; I needed to hear him confess his complete and total deceit of me.

"Ah, that. Well, that's another secret I can't have getting out. The public would have a ball knowing that I couldn't keep a wife, I couldn't get it up, and I couldn't father children. I had some tests run and it appears I'm completely sterile; I couldn't let that get out, so I made you think it was your fault. And now, all of this is your fault again. Blame yourself for the pain your man is going to suffer." His hips ground into me again. "Damn, I could never get hard for you before, but knowing you're scared and trying to protect your precious little baby, that's got me all turned on; I think I may fuck you once more, right here in his living room, before I take you away. We'll leave enough evidence so that he'll know I was the last one in you before you were lost to him forever." His fisted hand let loose long enough to reach down and attempt to get my pants off. "Stop fighting, bitch; the more you fight, the more I want you."

I stilled momentarily; trying to gather my wits and devise a plan. Physically, I couldn't fight him off; I needed something to hit him with. In my mind I spoke to Izzy. "Izzy, I'm sorry I didn't listen to you. I need your help and then I need you to go get Kyle. Izzy, please, can you hear me. I need you to move something close to me so I can hit him. Then get Kyle as quickly as you can. Izzy?" I didn't know if she could hear me; she had been around less and less since Kyle and I had gotten together for good. It was almost as if she'd done what she needed to do and then it was her time to move on. What if she couldn't hear me? I began to furtively glance around the room, trying to think of something I could reach to hit Wayne.

"Stop looking around, bitch!" I gritted my teeth and swallowed a sob as he roughly shoved his hand down my pants.

"Mmmm, still dry as a desert; no worries, I'll be happy to shove myself in there and make you scream." Grabbing my hand he forced me to feel his erection and I battled the vomit threatening to escape. If letting him do what he was planning would protect me and the baby long enough for Kyle to get to me, so be it; I would suffer through sex with Wayne once more if it meant I could save the baby and stay with Kyle.

The next several minutes played out perfectly yet so horribly. A knock sounded at the locked door just as the flower vase sitting in the middle of the coffee table fell over, rolled to the edge, and dropped to the floor. As I stretched my fingers toward the vase, I felt the cold glass fill my hand. "Josie! Josie! Open the door! Are you okay? JOSIE!" I heard both Nate and Jeremiah pounding on the door just as I brought the vase up to connect with the side of Wayne's head.

"You stupid bitch! Now you've gone and fucked it all up. You're dead if I'm not walking out of here with you." I watched his fist come at me, almost as if I were in a dream and it was moving in slow motion. My only thought was that if he hit me in the head, maybe the baby could still be okay. My head jerked violently when his fist pounded into the side of my face; the pain throbbed through me and the light began to fade. "You did this, bitch. All you had to do was help me out, but instead you've gotten yourself and your baby killed. Think about the pain you're causing your friends and family. You never could do anything right." He punched the side of my head again and stood up. Fighting to keep my eyes open, I fought against the blackness that threatened to sweep me under. "Say goodbye, baby." And with that, my world shattered in heartbreak and pain as his foot connected over and over with my chest and midsection.

CHAPTER 27

Kyle

"Today is the first day of the rest of your life."
~Author Unknown

Talking to Josie on the phone made me feel a little better, especially since I knew that Nate and Jeremiah were both on their way to the house to stay with her until I got there. My heart clenched in my chest to know that she was still so tired that she was falling asleep on the phone with me. Tomorrow, no question, I was taking her to the doctor to find out what was wrong. Her sweet sleepy voice came back to me as she woke up, "Ugh, I think one of the guys is here. Hang on, I'll go let them in. This seems really silly, they shouldn't have to babysit me; you'll be home within the hour."

How did the guys get there so soon? They weren't that close to our house, there was no way they'd be there yet. Panic seized me, "Wait, Josie! Check to be sure it's Nate or Jeremiah first." My heart sank and I immediately called the police after I heard the sickening words, "Hello, Josephine, you little tramp" and Josie's phone clattered to the floor.

The extra patrol car had been called out to a wreck on the interstate so it wasn't nearby. It wouldn't take me long, but I feared it would be longer than Josie had. My only hope was Nate and Jeremiah. And Izzy. Her voice came to me, softer and further away than it had in the past. *Kyle, get to her quickly. Wayne isn't planning on either of them coming out of this alive. She needs you, get to her, please.* Hearing the sob in Izzy's voice broke my heart and filled me with such anxious fear I didn't know if I was going to be able to drive. "I'm trying, Iz, I'm going as fast as I can. Can you go back to her? Help her in any way you can. Please, Izzy, help her, I can't lose her too." I choked down tears as I started my bike and screamed the tires down the road.

Pulling up less than fifteen minutes from the last words I heard from Josie, I found the front door wide open. As if in a nightmare, not wanting to know what lay ahead of me, but needing to know, I dragged my legs up the stairs. Jeremiah was on the ground, holding my sweet Josie; she looked to just be sleeping but I saw tears in Jeremiah's eyes and I knew she was hurt badly. Nate had a bloody and barely moving Wayne pinned to the ground.

Walking to Josie, I dropped to my knees, "Josie, baby, I'm here. I'm so, so sorry, Jo. I should have been here. Please, Jo, open your eyes, don't leave me." I took her hand and lightly ran my finger down the side of her face which was already black and blue and swelling up. "God, baby, I'm so sorry." Without taking my eyes off of her, I spoke harshly to the other men, "Where the fuck are the police and ambulance?" As I spoke, Josie groaned and doubled over in pain; tears ran down her face and she gasped for breath.

"Nooooo, please, nooooo! Baby....can't breathe....hurts...," with a final gasp for breath she was out again. Knowing she was in such severe pain was killing me. Wayne began to stir and I was on my feet before I even knew I'd made the decision.

"You fucking bastard! If she dies I will spend the rest of my life making sure you suffer for it." I watched in sick satisfaction as my foot connected first with his face, then his head, then his stomach, over and over.

"Alright, man, that's enough; Josie needs you. The ambulance is here." Nate pulled me away from Wayne's once again still form.

Rushing to Josie, I held her hand and listened in horror as Jeremiah told the paramedics what Wayne was doing when they busted open the door. I had never felt so close to killing someone as I did when I listened to Jeremiah describe how

Wayne had kicked her repeatedly. No wonder she was doubled over in pain, he had battered her entire midsection and chest multiple times. The paramedic explained that her difficulty breathing was most likely due to one or more broken ribs. They immediately put oxygen on her to help with her breathing. My sweet girl moaned in pain and continued trying to ball herself up to lessen the pain. "Give her something for the pain, damn it!"

"We can give her a low dose to take the edge off; they will be better able to assess and treat once we're to the hospital. Sir, do you know if she's allergic to any medicines?" The paramedic worked efficiently to assess Josie's injuries and began preparing the pain medication.

"She's never mentioned being allergic to anything." What if she was allergic and I just didn't know it? She would have mentioned it in all of our talks, right?

"Could she be pregnant? Does she have any previous injuries, illnesses, or conditions?" The man was quick, professional, and very calming in his proficient manner.

"No, she can't have children. I don't know about previous injuries. She's been sick to her stomach and really tired for over a week. She has no conditions that I'm aware of." I rattled off the answers to his questions as I held her hand and prayed for her to be okay.

"Okay, we're going to get some low-dose morphine into her to help with the pain. Then we'll get her loaded up. You're welcome to ride with her or meet us at the emergency room." As he injected the pain medication, Josie stirred; moaning and grabbing at her belly, she whispered, "Baby...," before succumbing to the pain and head injury again.

"It's okay, Jo, I'm right here." I hated that she was scared, in pain, and calling for me. Could she not tell that I was there with her?

"Alright, let's get her loaded." She was on a stretcher and loaded into the ambulance quickly. I trusted that Nate and Jeremiah could handle Wayne until the police took over; they were pulling up as we drove away.

Josie's vitals were taken and recorded on the way to the hospital. She struggled to breathe and was in obvious pain. As a breath caught in her throat, she began coughing and the moans of pain that escaped from her were more than I could handle. "Fuck! Help her, give her something!" Leaning down, I whispered in her ear, "It's okay, Jo, I'm here. We're almost to the hospital; we'll get you all taken care of. Just rest, baby. I love you, I'm here, I'm not leaving."

I had called Captain Decker so that he could grab her insurance information and meet us at the emergency room. Leaving him to deal with the details of checking her in, I followed the stretcher as far as they would let me go.

"Sir, I'll have to ask you to wait here. Once the doctor assesses the patient, we'll be able to give you more information. I'll grab you a chair; there's coffee down the hall. Someone will be out to give you information as quickly as possible." While I knew the nurse was just doing her job, I felt angry and helpless as I stood there watching my light, my hope, my future be wheeled away from me.

Dropping into the chair, I fisted my hands in my hair and tried to fight off the tears that threatened. Feeling hands on my shoulders, I looked up to find Nate and Jeremiah. Nicky and Captain Decker stood to the side. I stood, needing to do something other than just sit there. I started to speak to the men, but my voice broke and all I could do was hug first one then the other. "Thank you...," was all I got out before my body began to tremble and I had to sit back down as the sobs shook me to the core.

"Man, I'm so sorry we didn't get there sooner. I'm sorry we didn't stop him in time." Jeremiah ran a hand down his face.

"Mr. Martin?" I found myself speaking to a police officer when the only thing I wanted was to hold Josie in my arms and hear that she was going to be okay. "I'm very sorry for what you're going through, but we needed to touch base with you about the situation involving Ms. Decker. First, it appears from witnesses that the offender physically assaulted Ms. Decker but, from evidence at the scene and what these men saw, there was no sexual assault. The hospital will be able to verify that for us." I breathed a sigh of relief; Josie was hurt and away from me, but at least she hadn't been hurt worse.

"Mr. Erickson is under arrest and is being booked right now. Because of his previous violation of a protective order and the fact that he physically assaulted Ms. Decker today, he's being held without bond for now. Some other evidence has come to our attention which will likely keep him held longer. When Ms. Decker is able, we need to get a statement from her." The officers shook my hand and gave me a card before walking away. Part of me vaguely wondered what other evidence had come to light, but my main concern at that moment was Josie.

"Son, all of the family is here. I'm going to go out and update them the best I can. Once you see her and she's settled in, please come let us know how she is." I accepted the hug that Captain Decker gave me and watched in numbness as all of the men, except my best friend, walked away.

"J, thanks man. You saved her from something much worse." I believed it with everything I had that the two men had stopped Wayne from raping her.

"No thanks needed; I just wish we could have stopped him from kicking her. I wanted to kill the fucker, he just kicked her over and over, even after she had stopped moving. It probably only took us 30 seconds to bust the door open and reach her, but it played out in slow motion and all I can see is his foot connecting with her again and again. Damn it! Man, I'm so sorry. Do you need anything?" Jeremiah looked at me expectantly.

"No, I just need to hear that she's going to be okay. J, I don't know that I'd survive losing her too." I broke down again and gave into the tears as Jeremiah wrapped an arm around my shoulders.

"You're not going to lose her, Kyle. Izzy worked too hard to get the two of you together, she's not going to let Josie leave you yet." We chuckled, knowing that Izzy would be pissed if all of her work was for naught.

"Mr. Martin? We've got Ms. Decker stabilized and settled into a room; you can come with me to see her." As I walked with the nurse down the hall, I steeled myself for what I was going to see. "Now, Mr. Martin, I need to warn you, Ms. Decker is in and out of consciousness due to the head injury; this is something we are monitoring closely. Her face is swollen from the blows she took, she has an IV so that we could get some fluids into her since she was slightly dehydrated, we've given her some more pain medication so even when she comes to for a bit she's very groggy. I'll give you a moment with her and then have the doctor come speak to you." The nurse was very professional and I appreciated the information she had given me.

I stood outside the door, frozen in fear; the last time I walked into a hospital room I found the love of my life cold and still; the sheer horror I faced in entering that room was enough to bring me to my knees. *Kyle, go to her. She needs you. You two aren't over, not by a long shot. Get in there and hold her. She's scared.*

Izzy's words came to me, from far away, but they penetrated the terrified state I was in and I walked into the room.

My heart stopped to see my Josie lying there. The left side of her face was black and blue; even with the oxygen on she struggled to breathe; she was pale and lifeless, just lying there.

Gathering courage I didn't know I had, I took a deep breath and pulled a chair over. I fought away the memories of sitting exactly like this as I watched Izzy fade away from me. Grasping her hand, I spoke, "Josie, baby, I'm here. Can you hear me, Jo? Wake up for a bit and talk to me or just squeeze my hand so I know you can hear me." I was desperate for any type of communication from her; my heart warmed with slight relief when she gently squeezed my hand. It wasn't much, but for now I'd take it.

Sitting silently, I battled the demons in my head telling me that I was losing her the same way I lost Izzy. I forced myself to acknowledge that Josie had squeezed my hand. She was breathing on her own, although it was labored. And her skin was warm, she was injured but she was still with me.

"Mr. Martin, I'm Doctor Ramirez. We've run some tests on Ms. Decker and it appears that she has a concussion which we will monitor. The pain she's experiencing is from two broken ribs; she lucked out that neither of those broken ribs punctured a lung. She's struggling to breathe a bit because of the pain from the broken ribs. Our plan is to keep her comfortable and monitor her to be sure nothing else pops up." I listened to the doctor speak. With each word, my body relaxed a bit more. Unlike with Izzy, the doctor was indicating that Josie was going to be okay.

"Sir, I've checked in with her next-of-kin and they've all

indicated that you are to be the one with Ms. Decker and receiving any information about her. I need to ask, are you aware that Ms. Decker is pregnant?" The doctor's words floated around in the air, my brain attempting to make sense of them as it warred with memories of the past when another doctor spoke those words to me.

"Josie can't have children, she can't be pregnant." I shook my head as I delivered that information.

With a slight chuckle, Dr. Ramirez spoke again, "Son, we've run enough tests on her blood to determine with 100% accuracy that she is most definitely pregnant. Now, whether this is good news or unwanted news, I need you to be very aware that her injuries are very serious in regards to the health of the fetus. It appears her attacker was inebriated enough that more of his kicks landed on her chest than her lower abdomen; this is good for the protection of the baby. I've had OB in to do an ultrasound to confirm a heartbeat and rule out any bleeds in the uterus. At this point in time the baby's heartbeat is strong and there are no concerning issues regarding the pregnancy; the fetus is measuring approximately two months along. However, the health of the fetus could change at any moment. So, in all honesty, Josie's prognosis looks fairly good; the baby's prognosis is a little more hit and miss, all of it will be contingent upon the mother's health." Dr. Ramirez shook my hand and left me staring, dumbstruck, as he walked out the door.

Josie is pregnant. Two months pregnant. For now. My

baby's heart is beating inside of Josie. My head began to spin and the emotions of the day overtook me. I sunk back down into the chair.

Taking her hand in mine, I whispered as if speaking aloud would make it not true. "We're having a baby, Jo-Jo. A baby, Jo!" I drew her hand to my lips and placed a kiss against her soft skin. Her other arm, fighting to lift through tubing and wires, slowly moved to her stomach and protectively settled there.

"Knock, knock....hey there. I'm here to check on you both and return to the clan with a report. How is she? How are you?" I looked blankly at Carly as she spoke from the doorway. "Kyle? What's wrong?" She entered the room slowly and came to face me.

Shaking my head to clear the emotional drainage and shock, I gathered myself and relayed information in regards to Josie's injuries so Carly could share with the family. Laying a hand on my shoulder, Carly spoke hesitantly, "Is there any other information you'd like me to share?"

"She's pregnant, Carly. I don't know how and I don't know when, but the tests they ran prove that she's definitely pregnant. At this point the baby is strong and doing well." When Carly didn't gasp or even look the least bit surprised, I realized she already knew. "You knew? So Josie knows too? Why didn't she tell me?" My heart sank at the thought of her knowing this and not sharing it with me.

"I can't speak directly for her, but I can speak based on

my experience if you'd like." Carly's offer was soft, and I knew she'd battled infertility in the past. I nodded my head indicating I wanted her to continue. As I held Josie's hand, I listened to Carly's words and tried to make sense of them.

"All of the women in the family started suspecting Josie was pregnant when her 'bug' didn't go away and it was mainly affecting her in the morning and evenings. We didn't want to press the issue without knowing for sure out of fear we'd hurt her feelings if we were wrong. But today, Audrey insisted on buying some pregnancy tests. Josie was a crying mess when we got to the house, so we went ahead and spelled out what we thought she was experiencing. Long story short, she took the test and it was immediately positive. I understood her reserved attitude about the results. I knew, in her heart, she was rejoicing and wanted to shout to the world; in her head, she was doubting and cynical and terrified that it wouldn't last, that it was just a fluke." Carly's eyes widened, and she stopped speaking; my gaze followed hers and saw that Josie's eyes were open. Without a word, Carly stood and kissed Josie's cheek and then patted me on the back. "I'll go let people know what's going on."

"Kyle, the baby? Did they tell you there was a baby? Did I lose the baby?" She spoke in a breathless whisper, struggling to breathe even with the oxygen on her face. Tears welled in her eyes as she anticipated my answer.

"The baby is safe. They checked the heartbeat, and it's strong. They want to monitor you both for a while just to be sure. Josie, why didn't you call me as soon as you found out you were pregnant?" I understood what Carly had explained, but I was hurt that Josie didn't let me know about the baby right away.

"I'm sorry, Kyle. Oh, God, it hurts so bad to breathe; my chest hurts, it's like it's being squeezed in a vice." She stopped speaking to take some shallow breaths.

"Jo, you've got broken ribs; he kicked you in the stomach but mostly in the chest. I'll get the nurse, but they said your whole chest and midsection will be terribly painful for a while." I rubbed her hand as I pushed the call button and waited for her to go on.

"I wanted to call you, but it seemed so unreal; I didn't want to get your hopes up for something I was sure was a mistake or would end before it even got started. And I was sort of worried you'd think I'd lied to you or was trying to replace Addyson Rose." Josie's eyes implored mine for assurance.

Our ICU nurse arrived. Assuring Josie that the pain medication wouldn't harm the baby and reiterating what I told her about the pain in her chest being normal, the nurse took a moment to record some vitals and left us alone again.

"Josie, baby, I would have never thought you lied to me. If I had to guess, I'd assume it was that douchebag Wayne who lied." When Josie's eyes closed at the sound of his name, I knew I'd hit the jackpot on my guess.

"He blackmailed the doctor into writing the letter. I

guess Wayne was sterile but didn't want that information getting out to his adoring public, so he let me believe it was a problem with me. Somehow he knew I was pregnant, that's why he kicked my stomach. I'm sorry, Kyle, I should have insisted on protection with you; I just never thought it was an issue. I didn't mean to trap you with a baby." Tears fell from her eyes, and I stood to wipe them gently from her cheeks.

"Josie, stop. You didn't trap me. I'm not mad or upset, baby. I'm thrilled. I have always wanted kids and having a baby with you is a miracle, a dream-come-true." I kissed her mouth carefully and whispered against her lips, "We're having a baby, Jo!" Her tearful giggle made my heart stop. Resting my forehead against hers, I breathed deeply and let myself relax enough to believe things were going to be okay.

"Kyle, my chest hurts so badly. I can't get a full breath. Kyle?" I watched as Josie began to restlessly move her position in bed then the pain medication took over, and she fell into a groggy sleep.

"Just rest, Jo. I'm right here." I leaned in to kiss her cheek and noticed she was clammy and her skin had lost about four shades of color. As I ran my hand across her forehead to wipe away perspiration, I heard the monitors begin to make an intrusive noise in the room. "Jo? Josie? Can you wake up, baby?" I pushed the call button right as a nurse appeared at the doorway and bustled into the room. "She was complaining of her chest hurting and not being able to breathe. Then she got all sweaty and clammy and fell asleep right as the monitors started chiming."

The nurse checked a few things on the chart, took her blood pressure, listened to her heartbeat. Another nurse came into the room, and they spoke while they assessed. "Chest pain, high heart rate, low blood pressure, sweaty and pale, muffled heart tones. Call the rapid response team." As one nurse made the call, the other ushered me out the door.

I heard her words, "Sir, we'll come for you in the waiting room as soon as we've got some answers" just as the announcement "Rapid Response Team to ICU 214" boomed across the hospital's speaker system. I rounded the corner to the waiting room, heart shattering, fear coursing through my veins, as members of the rapid response team flew by. I was met with wide eyes and concern when I walked into the waiting room.

Collapsing into a chair, I sobbed, no longer able to hold it in. "It's Josie, she was talking and then her alarms were ringing and she fell asleep or passed out, she couldn't breathe, they made me leave so the rapid response team could figure out what's wrong. God, please don't take her from me, don't take our baby from us." I sobbed into my hands, but gratefully stood into the arms waiting to engulf me.

Many tears, tense minutes, and prayers later, a doctor came to find me. "I'm Dr. Roberts, I'm with the rapid response team. It appears after initial assessment that Ms. Decker had a pericardial effusion which led to a cardiac tamponade." At the clueless looks he was receiving he went on, "What that means is that the blows she took to her chest caused a slow bleed around her heart. It's been slowly filling with blood and now it's gotten so full that it's putting pressure on her heart which is what's causing her chest pain and the high heart rate and low blood pressure."

Without waiting for him to continue, I gruffly spoke, "How do you fix it? Is it going to hurt the baby?"

"We have two options in reducing the pressure on her heart. The first is the best choice regarding the baby. We will use a needle inserted to aspirate the blood from her chest. Our hope would be that the bleed will stop and nothing more will need to happen." He stopped as if he didn't want to speak about the other option.

"What if that doesn't work?" I choked out.

"If the needle aspiration doesn't work, we'd need to take her into surgery which would put the baby at a much higher risk." He spoke matter-of-factly; I both appreciated his bluntness and hated it at the same time. "Now, I need to get back in there to assist with the needle aspiration. I will send someone out to let you know if it's successful when we're finished."

"Thank you. Doctor? If it comes down to Josie or the baby, save Josie first and foremost." My heart broke speaking those words, but I knew they were straight from my soul. I'd be haunted forever if I lost another child. But I'd cease to exist if I lost Josie before we even got the chance to live our lives.

CHAPTER 28

Josie

*"How do geese know when to fly to the sun? Who tells them the seasons? How do we, humans know when it is time to move on? As with the migrant birds, so surely with us, there is a voice within if only we would listen to it, that tells us certainly when to go forth into the unknown." ~**Elisabeth Kubler-Ross***

My heart was pounding, my chest was a vice around my lungs, and the pain in my ribs took my breath away. I felt Kyle's hand slip away and my world went black. Not a cold, scary black; more of a soft, calming black. Nothing hurt, I could breathe easily again, my ribs weren't screaming in pain, and my head wasn't throbbing. I looked around, looking for something familiar. "Kyle? Izzy?"

The black that started as soft and calming began to constrict around me and I wanted nothing more than to escape it. In a panic, I frantically began running toward the pinpoint of light I saw in front of me. I heard Kyle's voice behind me, but the light pulled at me more forcefully than his broken timbre. I ran to escape the pain that was behind me; I ran to escape the uncertainty; I ran to escape the sheer exhaustion. As I got closer to the light, the incessant beeping behind me became a steady buzz until it disappeared altogether as I reached the light.

Opening a door, the blackness was filled with light and I gasped at the gorgeous scene in front of me. I immediately felt drawn to stay here; I wanted to be here, it was so comforting and beautiful. Searching for someone I recognized, my gaze fell on Izzy. Sweet Izzy.

Josie, you shouldn't be here. You need to go back to Kyle and your baby.

Yes, yes....I should go back to them, right? But I was so relaxed and happy here in the light place. I loved it here. I wanted to stay. Maybe Kyle and our baby could come to this place with me.

Josie, I'm serious. You can't stay here right now. Kyle and the baby need you. It's not time for you to come here yet.

When I continued walking around this light place in a daze, Izzy moved in front of me, and I stopped short.

Reaching out, I touched her cheek; my whole body filled with warmth. "Izzy, I want to stay here. It's beautiful, and you're here. Please, just let me stay for a while. I'm not ready to go back." I gestured behind me to the darkness, "Back there I'm in pain, and I don't know if our baby is going to survive. Can't I just stay here until the pain back there is better?" I pleaded with her; I was so very tired of the exhaustion and the pain. If I could just rest here, for a short time, everything would be better.

Feeling a strong hand on my arm, I watched as I was forcefully turned back toward the door. *No, Josie, you can't just stay here, not even for a little bit. This place isn't for you yet. You have a lifetime of happiness ahead of you. You belong with Kyle; he's back there waiting on you, and he's so very scared. I know things hurt right now, but be strong and go back. For Kyle. For you. For your future.*

Without warning, Izzy shoved me back through the door and into the blackness. I sobbed as the door closed and I was completely alone. *Head back to Kyle. Walk toward the voices, Josie.*

With no other choice, I followed her instructions and walked toward the buzzing. As I got closer, the buzzing became a more distinct beep and within the sea of voices, I was able to discern familiar ones.

"So, did the needle aspiration work? Is she okay? What about our baby?" The panic in Kyle's voice broke my heart. How could I have wanted to leave him?

"We feel, for the time being, that the procedure was successful. We will keep her moderately sedated to allow her body to heal before we begin waking her up. During that time, she can most likely hear you, so talk to her. We'll be monitoring the baby as well as Ms. Decker's heart, ribs, and head. If all goes well, we'll keep her in ICU for 48-72 hours before moving her to a monitored floor. I can't be 100% sure, but I'd say she'll be here about a week. Mr. Martin, you can go in to see her. Everyone else can go in one at a time, but you need to be done visiting by 9:00 p.m." I heard the doctor's footsteps walking away and a heavy sigh from Kyle. I wanted to touch him, to hold him, to tell him I loved him.

The blackness around me began to swirl softly, and I felt like I was floating. It wasn't as peaceful as the place of light, but the pain was bearable and the beeping and voices were only slightly irritating. I don't know how long I floated like that, but too quickly my body was slammed with pain, and I felt as if I was thrown down onto the hospital bed. Dizziness threatened to overtake me; keeping my eyes closed, I waited for the spinning to stop. Taking deep breaths, I willed myself to assess the level of pain. Surprisingly, I was very sore, but the throbbing head and screaming ribs had dulled significantly. My mouth was cottony, and I longed for a drink.

Moving my hands, I felt the sheets and wires and IV tubing, but I also recognized the soft silkiness of Kyle's hair under my fingertips. "Ky...Ky..." My voice was scratchy, but I tried again. "Kyle?" I pulled gently on his hair and choked out a giggle when his head popped up in surprise and confusion.

"Josie, baby, you're back." He leaned in to cup my face with his hands, "You don't even know how much I've prayed for you to come back to us. I love you, Josie. Let me get the nurse." He kissed my head and began to pull away.

"Wait, Kyle." He stilled and sat down, waiting patiently for me to continue. "Can I get a drink?" He allowed me a small cup of water but no more until the nurse came in.

"Before you get the nurse, can you tell me what happened? I just want to talk to you before anyone else comes in." I reached my hand out to him and breathed a small sigh of relief when he took my hand and settled on the edge of my bed.

My eyes filled with tears as I tried to gauge the expression on his face; I needed to know, but I was afraid to ask. Tears spilled over my cheeks, and a sob caught in my throat.

"Oh, Josie, baby..." His thumbs brushed away my tears.

"What about the baby?" I spoke in an unsure, shaky voice, petrified of what Kyle would tell me.

CHAPTER 29

Kyle

*"You gain strength, courage and confidence by every experience in which you really stop to look fear in the face. You are able to say to yourself 'I have lived through this horror. I can take the next thing that comes along.' You must do the thing you think you cannot do." ~**Eleanor Roosevelt***

"What about the baby?" Her voice was shaky, and I sensed her fear and anxiety.

"Jo, the baby is fine. It was you we were the most worried about. You've been in and out of consciousness for three solid days; they started trying to wake you up after 12 hours, but you were being stubborn and just wouldn't come back to us. We've been worried sick waiting on you to wake up." I gave her another sip of water and kissed her mouth.

"Eeew, Kyle, I've been out of it for three days, I'm sure my breath is atrocious." I smiled as she covered her mouth.

"I'd kiss rot-mouth for the rest of my life if it meant I'd have you next to me. Listen, I'm going to get the nurse and let everyone know you're awake. They'll probably be ready to move you to another floor pretty soon, so you can have more visitors. Rest a bit, and I'll be back." I smoothed her hair away from her face. "I love you, Josie. And I love our baby. Thank you for not leaving me." Leaning down, I kissed that precious mouth I'd become so fond of and then went to find a nurse and tell our family that she was awake.

Josie spent close to a week in the hospital. By the end of that time, she was up and moving around under doctor's orders. We had follow-up appointments scheduled with her primary care physician, a cardiologist, and weekly appointments set up with our new OB for at least the next month or so since Josie was considered a high-risk pregnancy for the time being.

It turned out Wayne had been up to his eyeballs in illegal activity; his issues with Josie were just the icing on his cake. His public image had started to tarnish with the prostitutes and gambling, but it completely fell apart when it was leaked that he was embezzling money. Once this information started to get around, the doctor Wayne had blackmailed came forward admitting to writing the letter and Wayne bribing him. Between the assault on Josie, the drunk driving, the embezzlement, the bribes, and the prostitutes, even Wayne's team of lawyers couldn't save him, and he was spending at least the next 6 years in prison. Last we heard, he was on suicide watch.

Josie was feeling completely healed and had returned to painting and scrapbooking. Watching as her belly popped out and expanded, seemingly before my very eyes, was something I would cherish forever. The swell of her belly against my body and the fullness of her breasts as they changed in preparation for our baby, well, I didn't think there was anything sexier.

The day had come that I had been planning since she'd come home from the hospital. The girls had helped me with the details, and I could only hope that Josie would be open to it.

"Hey, Josie, can you come down here for a minute please?" I hollered up the stairs, hoping my voice didn't sound as nervous as I felt.

"Can you wait 15 minutes, so I can finish this piece?" Not the answer I had been planning on. So, I hung out in the kitchen, flipping through pages on my phone, trying not to let my anxiety win out. When I heard the music she was playing switch off, I knew she'd head to the kitchen to wash her hands. I quickly placed the bottle on the counter and snuck out of the room. I waited in my bedroom, knowing that was where the trail of bottles would lead her.

I had left 3 wine bottles, all with different clues leading to the next bottle throughout the house. The fourth and final bottle would be in my bedroom. I sat on the bed and waited for her to find all the clues.

Listening to her laugh and comment on my clues as she scavenger-hunted her way through the house was music to my ears. "There better be a big treat waiting for me when I find the end of this game, KJ!" I stifled a laugh so that she wouldn't know where I, or the final bottle, was located.

"You're crazy, you know that? Where did you find all of the actual glass bottles? Are we moving up in the world?" She smiled that gorgeous, heart-melting smile of hers as she sauntered into my bedroom. I rolled the final bottle toward her feet and watched silently as she bent over to pick it up.

"How did you know to look for the final bottle here, Jo?" I was teasing her, but I wanted to hear her say it.

"Well, your clue said 'the one room you'd be happy to spend the rest of your life in if I was with you,' and I automatically thought of your bedroom." She blushed as she admitted it to me, but I had known that my clue would lead her straight to my bed.

"Read the message, Jo." As she opened the roll of paper, I stood and walked slowly toward her. With trembling hands and tears rolling down her face, she read the note. Right as she finished reading and looked up at me with a tearful smile, I dropped to one knee and took her hand.

"Josie, you are my light, my hope, my future. You saved me from darkness, but more than that you brought the light back to my life. I want you in my life forever. Josie Marie Decker, will you marry me?" I waited until she nodded her head before retrieving the ring box I'd shoved in my pocket.

"The girls helped me out, but the final decision was mine. I already asked the Captain and he gave us his blessing. Josie, wear this ring and be my wife." I slid the understated diamond ring onto her finger and stood up, gathering her into a fierce hug and then dropping my lips to hers in an even fiercer kiss. Coming up for air, I leaned back slightly. "Um, one more thing. Do you think you'd like to marry me today?" Her eyes widened in complete disbelief, and I had to laugh at my sweet girl gaping at me like a fish.

CHAPTER 30

Josie

"Love yourself first and everything else falls into line. You really have to love yourself to get anything done in this world." ~**Lucille Ball**

Mrs. Josie Martin. It had a nice ring to it. Kyle and I had been married a week, and I still hadn't tired of hearing my new name or writing it on forms. I rolled over in bed to watch my gorgeous, magnificent husband sleeping. I would never tired of waking up in his bed, now *our* bed. Glancing down at my ever-growing belly, I thought back to our simple yet beautifully perfect wedding.

After I finally picked my jaw up off the floor, I realized that Kyle was serious about getting married the exact day he proposed to me. How he knew that I wouldn't want another huge wedding, I don't know, but it proved to me yet again how perfect we were for each other.

When I laughed and agreed that I could marry him that day, he made a quick text and all the family swooped in within twenty minutes. By 4:00 that afternoon, I was manicured and pedicured, massaged and exfoliated, face made up and hair swept up, and stepping into the most gorgeously simple white dress. I adored that my friends had picked something simple yet elegant; I also appreciated the fact that the empire waist was very forgiving and hid my small baby bump quite nicely.

At 4:30 p.m., in my uncle's springtime backyard, I walked down the aisle. I was on the arm of the only man I would ever consider as a dad; Uncle Robert squeezed my hand gently and kissed my cheek. Whispering in my ear he spoke, "Josie, I'm sorry for all that brought you to Torey Hope, but I'm so very glad you came here. I love you and I want nothing more than for you to be happy." Tears glistening in his eyes, he placed my hand in Kyle's and took his place next to Janie in the front row.

Kyle and I said "I do" in front of our small group of family and friends. I cried when he read what he had written on the final note I found during the scavenger hunt just that morning.

Josie, my light, my hope, my future:

We were brought to Torey Hope to find the love of our family and friends, but we also found love in each other. Just when I thought I'd never escape the blackness, your smile and your heart and your spirit brought sunshine and warmth back to my life. We have both suffered heartache, but out of that heartache we have learned to love again. You are my hope, I am your promise, and our baby is our future.

My eyes welled with tears again as he read those words and we spoke our vows; vows which would bind us together forever. When I escaped my former marriage, I had no plans on ever marrying again or being with a man again, but the love that grew between Kyle and me was too much and too beautiful to ignore.

Our wedding celebration took place in the Captain's home, and I wouldn't have had it any other way. Audrey was in her element and had planned a fabulous little feast and party to celebrate our nuptials. We spent the evening eating and drinking and talking and laughing; for a girl who grew up unloved and unwanted, I couldn't have asked for a more perfect wedding celebration.

"Since I planned our honeymoon to the mountains to see the wild horses for after the baby arrives, I guess we'll just have to spend the next couple of days honeymooning in our bed, Jo. You okay with that?" My husband kissed me and, true to his word, kept me in our bed for the next couple days.

~

I couldn't keep my roaming hands off of him any longer. Reaching out, I ran my palms down his back and listened with satisfaction as he moaned slightly in his sleep. Wanting more than he was providing at that moment, I ran my hand over his hip, up his obliques, and back down to the front of his briefs. Taking hold of exactly what I was looking for, I leaned in and dotted kisses along his back, taking pleasure in knowing that the hardening taking place in my hand was all for me.

"Jo, you can play for about thirty more seconds and then I'm going to roll you over and claim your body as mine. And I'll keep claiming you as mine until neither of our bodies can move anymore. So, enjoy your game, Mrs. Martin...." His voice trailed off, and I felt him stiffen in my hand. "Time's up, Jo." And with that I found myself rolled to my back, clothing stripped, and a very hot, very hard man nestled between my legs. "Good morning, wife."

I grinned like a fool at his words. Before I could speak, his mouth consumed mine. My body, on fire from the touch of his hands roaming in all the right places, writhed underneath his. Breaking the kiss, I smiled, "Good morning to you, husband."

Kyle spent several sweet moments in which he spoke to our baby, whispering his "I love you's" to my tummy. I laughed out loud when he whispered, "Soon those beautiful breasts will be yours, but until then, Daddy is going to enjoy them. Now, go put on some headphones so you don't hear me making your mommy scream." A final kiss to my belly and all baby talk was put on hold.

"Jo, I loved your body before, but you're killing me with all of these swells and curves you've got now. I think I want to keep you pregnant all the time." He nipped at my breast and then kissed away my whimper, "Or at least have fun trying to keep you pregnant all the time."

Audrey, Libby, Carly and I *may* have spent several hours together earlier in the week and we *may* have discussed several sexual positions that *may or may not* supposedly be sensational during pregnancy. Gathering my sexual prowess, I pushed at Kyle's chest to make him move from on top of me. "What's wrong, Jo?" His confusion and poutiness was cute.

"I want to do it this way," I positioned myself on all fours and turned my head to look at him over my shoulder, "If you're okay with it?"

With a primal gleam in his eyes, he positioned himself behind me. Leaning forward to capture my lips he all but growled, "I'll take you in any and every position I can get you, but having you like this in front of me is fucking perfect." He filled me then and all talking ceased. My belly burned as his hands caressed its swollen form; my breasts, already so sensitive to the touch, ached as he toyed with them. His hands held me in place as he thrust over and over. Reaching around, he found my core and rubbed his thumb until I was about to shatter.

I cried out when he removed his hand and whimpered in frustration as he quickly moved our position. He worried about being on top of me too much with my belly getting in the way, so he laid me carefully on my side and I found myself facing him with my leg being drawn up over his hip. Filling me in one smooth motion, one arm holding me and one hand cupping my face, he rested his forehead against mine, "Sorry, Jo, that position was hot, but I just needed to make love to my wife." And with that, no other words were needed as he proceeded to make love to his wife.

I was drifting into a sweet slumber when I heard him whisper the words that would warm me and fill my heart and soul for the rest of my life.

"I will spend the rest of my life loving you, Josie."

EPILOGUE

Kyle

As yet another family member walked out of our tiny hospital room, I looked at my wife and smiled wearily. "I think they've all been in, we can rest a little now." I settled into the double-wide bed and gathered my sweet girl to my chest. Gazing down at our beautiful daughter, wrapped in a gorgeous multi-colored baby blanket, I was mesmerized as the baby instinctively rooted around and latched on to nurse. "I don't think I'll ever see anything more beautiful than that." I lightly rubbed my hand on my daughter's head and let my finger trace the swell of Josie's breast.

"Hey now, you know there's none of that for six weeks. Doctor's orders." Josie joked.

Leaning in to kiss her, I whispered, "I'm just going to have to come up with six weeks of foreplay then." I smiled at the shiver that ran through her body.

"You know, the nurse will be in any moment and we haven't done it yet." I continued to whisper seductively in her ear.

"I know, I know, we need to do it, but I just don't want to screw it up. I want it to be perfect." She sighed, exasperated at a topic of discussion we'd been having for weeks. The name.

"Jo, baby, I think you've got the one you want in your head. I think I've got the one I want in my head. Let's both write them down and see what we come up with." We'd been trying to narrow down a first name forever. We'd quickly agreed on Belle for the middle name in honor of Isabella; the first name, though, had been more of a struggle. We'd narrowed it down to a final three but neither of us seemed to want to make a decision.

I looked one last time at my precious baby girl and wrote down the name I felt was perfect for her. I watched as Josie held the baby out in front of her, inspecting her carefully, before writing down the name she wanted. I handed her my paper and she handed me hers. Opening them at the same time, we both laughed in relief; we'd picked the same name.

After signing all of the paperwork once we'd finally settled on the name, I texted the family to let them know what we had decided on. Then, gathering my wife and our baby in my arms, I cozied us all up in the big bed and took a deep breath, relishing the peace that I felt in my life.

Had it not been so quiet in the room, I may have missed it; Izzy's voice came to me from very far away. *I'm so very happy for you, Punk Boy. Just be happy, loving Josie.*

I pictured my sweet Izzy-bel, holding our little Addyson Rose. In my mind, Addyson had her mother's huge violet eyes and naturally pink lips. I watched that picture in my mind and saw them moving further away from me. "Thank you, Izzy. Thank you for making me see what was right in front of me. Because of you, my love, my friend, I will spend the rest of my life loving Josie." I was speaking low so as not to wake my girls, but Josie heard me anyway. She turned a questioning look to me.

Kissing her nose, I spoke softly, "I was just saying goodbye and thanks to Izzy. I told her that, thanks in part to her, I will be happy to spend the rest of my life loving you."

Tears welled in Josie's eyes. "I had the same conversation with her recently. I got the feeling that she won't be coming back to us anymore." I nodded my head in agreement to her assessment of Izzy's situation. It seemed that Izzy had reached her goal and was moving on.

"Kyle, thank you for loving me. Thank you for teaching me how to be Josie and how to love myself. You helped me find my spirit again." She leaned up to kiss me. The movement jostled the baby between us, and she made a cry of agitation.

Taking the baby from my wife's arms, I stared at her perfect little face and imagined her life as she grew up in Torey Hope. This was the place that Josie and I would live and love, surrounded by friends and family. "Welcome to Torey Hope, Zoey Belle; welcome home."

A NOTE FROM THE AUTHOR

When I started writing my very first book, I had one goal in mind and that was to see if I could write a book. About halfway through that book, I realized that one of the other characters needed her own story so the second book was born. When I finished the second book, I was crushed that the stories were over. My readers asked for more stories from Torey Hope; I let my imagination do some running and came up with the stories in the Christmas novella along with Kyle and Josie's story.

If Loving Josie is your first time visiting Torey Hope, I'd like to invite you to go back to where it all began and read For Nicky, A Torey Hope Novel Book 1 which is Nate and Nicky Morgan's story along with Libby and Audrey Decker. The story continues in Because of Beckett, A Torey Hope Novel Book 2. You can round out your Torey Hope reading (until the next books release!) with Christmas in Torey Hope, A Novella.

While writing Loving Josie, I was again feeling blue to be leaving these families behind. One day, in the shower (where else do great ideas come from!?!) I was hit with the idea to take the young boys in the first four books and write their stories. So, in the next books, you'll fall in love with Decker and Sawyer Morgan (Nate and Libby's twins), Zach Morgan (Nicky and Carly's son), and Kendrick (Jeremiah and Audrey's son). The boys grew up as cousins and best friends, went to college together, and now they are home to settle in to the only true home they've ever known...Torey Hope. Look for these stories in 2015.

If you'd like to read the first books in A Torey Hope Novel Series, please visit my Amazon author page to see all of the books available. www.amazon.com/author/adellis

OTHER TOREY HOPE NOVELS

Excerpts from other Torey Hope Novel Series books

A *Torey Hope Novel Series* starts with For Nicky. Meet and fall in love with Nate and Nicky Morgan, twin brothers. Find For Nicky here: http://bit.ly/NickyAmazon

"Hey, Audrey, what's up? Come in." Audrey smiles, which seems a little fake, and comes on in. She's dressed to the nines as usual. Heels, tight skirt, tighter shirt, hair styled much bigger than you'd think is possible. I can smell her perfume and hairspray as she walks past me. Who dresses like this for a normal day? Audrey does, obviously. She looks me up and down. "Are you going somewhere, Beth?"

I tell her I have a date. She looks pissed for a moment, then gives me a smile that doesn't even begin to reach her eyes, and says, "Oh, that's nice. Who's the poor shmuck?"

Obviously, she's baiting me, but I don't think quickly enough and I just reply, "Nathaniel Morgan."

Audrey rolls her eyes. "Beth, sweetie, I'm going to try to say this in the nicest/sisterly love type of way. But, Nathan Morgan is way out of your league. You are dressed in a flannel shirt, you might as well wear a sign that says 'frumpy' on the front and 'won't ever get laid' on the back. Nate is an animal in bed, I should know. He needs sex. I doubt you're giving it to him yet. If you ever decide to try sex again, it will probably be as bad as it was with Austin. Not because Nate isn't good, because the good Lord knows that man is G.O.O.D in bed, but there's no way your 'basically a virgin' body can live up to what he's used to. Hell, the boy wore ME out and I have as much experience as he does, if not more. I'm not sure why he's hung around this long. Maybe he sees you as a challenge. Yeah, maybe he's decided to string you along long enough to get in your pants, but, Beth, he's not going to stick around. Nate needs hot sex, a variety of girls, no strings. I don't want you to get hurt when he fucks you and leaves you. Oh, God, Beth, seriously, stop with the teary puppy-dog eyes. I'm just telling you the truth." ~Libby {Beth} Decker in **For Nicky**

The sequel to For Nicky, Because of Beckett (this is Audrey's story and as much as you hate her in For Nicky, you will find yourself liking her in Because of Beckett and you will fall in love with Jeremiah Jordan!) Find <u>Because of Beckett</u> here: http://bit.ly/BeckettAmazon

The one girl he should stay as far away from as possible, the one girl who had made him feel more alive in one evening than he had in several years, the one girl who threatened his well-designed single-dad, good role model position in life was Audrey Decker. Instead of letting her off the hook and planning the party himself, he had practically begged her to stick with it and all but promised her there would be no problems. That was all well and good, he was truly glad she was going to take the party, except for one small problem, he hadn't been able to get her out of his mind; he couldn't stop thinking of those gorgeous blue eyes or her beautiful hair or luscious curves. His heart jumped into his throat when he saw her walking toward the shelter house; his breath hitched in his chest when her hand touched his knee; he wanted to hold her hand and start right back where they had left off the other night. But, they'd agreed that this was a business deal only, so he wouldn't complicate it. They'd get through the party and move on. They were living in the same town; they'd surely see each other. Jeremiah was determined to keep things cool between them so that the party would be a success and they could be friendly toward each other in social settings.

And then, he watched her eyes light up as she knelt down and opened her arms to Beckett. He was gone; hook, line, sinker. Audrey didn't strike him as the type to be particularly caring towards anyone, let alone a child with special needs.

But, there she was, on her knees, hugging his son... How was it, the woman he had just promised he wouldn't pursue, was on the ground hugging his child like his real mother never had? Jeremiah's gut clenched at the thought. He wanted this woman in his life. But, she'd made it clear that she wasn't interested and Jeremiah wondered if he had lost his chance to indicate any interest. So, he decided he'd have to settle for having her in his life as a friend. ~Jeremiah Jordan in **Because of Beckett**

The families celebrate the holidays in Christmas in Torey Hope, A Novella. Love and family and friendship abounds and readers get to learn of the older couples' love stories. Find Christmas in Torey Hope here: http://bit.ly/ChristmasAmazon

"Libby-girl, you never cease to amaze me. That was amazing." He kissed her and they proceeded to clean up and redress. "Now, we better get back to the house before everyone knows what I've been doing to you." Nate winked.

Libby's cheeks blushed but she said, "Nate, I'm pretty sure this is exactly what your mom had in mind when she sent us away for a bit."

"Well then, I'll have to sincerely thank my momma!" Nate kissed her lips as they headed back out the door, locking it soundly behind them.

"Uh, Mom, I'm all for reminiscing and I know you and Dad love each other, but could we please keep it G-rated. For the love of all that is good, please don't make me listen to sex stories involving you two." Jeremiah shuddered but smiled good-naturedly at his mother.

"What? We all had to see you and Audrey and Nate and Libby come in here glowing after your little 45 minute romp; I think a little steamy romance story about your dad and I would serve you right." Judy laughed at her son's expression. "Don't worry, I'll keep it clean." The whole group laughed at Jeremiah's visible relief.

Before the story could get started, Nate cleared his throat and said, "Mom, Dad, let's keep in mind that I've walked in on the two of you in some compromising positions that are now burned into my delicate mind; please don't add anymore trauma to my already scarred psyche." Everyone laughed at Nate's statement. "You all think I'm joking but I'm really not. You don't know the images that still float through my mind." Nate teased his parents and pulled Libby against him as they settled onto one of the couches.

If you loved Torey Hope, you're in luck! <u>Torey Hope</u>: *The Later Years* is now available. It contains stories revolving around the children of Nate/Libby, Jeremiah/Audrey, Nicky/Carly, and Kyle/Josie. Check out http://bit.ly/AmazonADEllis to find the stories. There will be four books in that series when it is complete.

ABOUT THE AUTHOR

A.D Ellis was born and raised in a small farming town in southern Indiana. An avid reader from the time she learned to read, A.D. could often be found curled up somewhere with her nose in a book. Most of her friends and family were not such book enthusiasts, so A.D. got used to dealing with snickers and joking comments about her constant reading habits.

A.D. always dreamed of being a teacher. Graduating from Indiana State University in 1999 and earning a Master's Degree from Indiana Wesleyan in 2003, she met her goal of entering the world of education. A.D. has been teaching in the inner city of Indianapolis, Indiana for 15 years. She spent the majority of her 15 years in fourth grade, but has now taken on the challenges of teaching 3rd and 4th grade alternative education students. A.D. loves teaching fractions, variables, probability, and graphing in Math. She loves almost all aspects of English Language Arts. Figurative language, theme, making predictions, drawing conclusions, inference, context clues, making writing come to life, A.D. loves it all! Her students don't always share in that enthusiasm.

A.D. met her husband in college in 1996 and they married in June of 2000. She lives in a south side suburb of Indianapolis, Indiana with her husband and two school-aged children. When she's not reading or writing with music blaring, she can be found shopping at thrift stores, reading to her children, and running.

A.D. began her writing journey in October 2013 and she is grateful for the friends and support she's found along the way.

Please connect with A.D. Ellis on Facebook. www.facebook.com/adellisauthor

ACKNOWLEDGMENTS

Where do I begin? First, I have to thank the readers. I love to read and I love to write, but I probably would have stopped after book 1 and 2 if it hadn't been for readers loving Torey Hope and its families. Because of my readers, I continue writing and telling these stories. I would probably write even if I had no readers, but it sure wouldn't be as fun and rewarding as it is with the fabulous readers I've gotten to meet along the way.

Second, I have to say thanks to my editor, Stephanne. She's been with me from the beginning and I appreciate her input and skills. Also to Kari for the gorgeous cover on <u>Loving Josie!</u> I also have to thank the numerous people who helped me out along the way and answered my questions over and over as I tried to figure this whole indie author thing out.

The friends I have made during this journey are far too

many to name; just know that I appreciate each and every one of you that I've had the pleasure of meeting. I feel blessed to have gotten to know some of you; without these books, I likely would have never met you.

The Ellis Elite Street Team—thank you for reading, supporting, and sharing my books.

My BETA readers—you all mean the world to me. Thank you for walking me through my freak outs, reading excerpts and letting me know I'm on the right path with my stories, and for loving Torey Hope just as much as I do! Oh, and thanks for being my second set of eyes to help catch all those tiny mistakes that get by sometimes! I truly value your thoughts, opinions, and input. Thank you from the bottom of my heart!

To the ARC readers—again, too many to name, but I appreciate you taking the time to sign up, read, and review Loving Josie. Some of you signed up because you had read my previous books and loved them. Some you had read my previous books and really not cared for them but signed up and took a chance anyway. Some of you had never heard of me and I appreciate you giving Loving Josie a chance.

My girls in the Indie Round Table, Indie Romance Writers, Indiana Authors and Blogger, and The Juice Box...having you all to turn to is beyond priceless and I'm so grateful to have you all. I feel blessed to have met some of you in real life and consider you colleagues/mentors/friends.

My IEZ girls—I truly don't think I could have done any of

this without you all. I not only consider you colleagues and friends, but you're like my family. One of these days, we're making an IEZ get together happen! You all mean the world to me and I love you from the bottom of my heart! Twirl and flourish ladies!

Last, but certainly not least, I want to thank my family and friends. I know it gets tiresome to see me constantly at the computer with my hot tea and headphones. I know you get tired of hearing me talk about "my books" when some of you are not really into reading at all. To those of you who have taken and chance and read my books, THANK YOU!! It means so much to have family and friends standing behind me, supporting me.

♥ A.D. Ellis

CONNECT WITH A.D. ELLIS

I LOVE, LOVE, LOVE hearing from happy readers! Please feel free to contact me on any and all social media.

Facebook--www.facebook.com/adellisauthor
Goodreads--www.goodreads.com/adellisauthor
Twitter--www.twitter.com/adellisauthor
Website--www.adellisauthor.webs.com
Amazon--http://bit.ly/ADEllisAmazon
Instagram--www.instagram.com/ADEllisAuthor
Pinterest— www.pinterest.com/ADEllisAuthor

SONG LIST FOR LOVING JOSIE:

Follow me on Spotify for the entire playlist.

NOTES

Kyle Martin dealt with depression as do many people. Julie, the girl getting the tattoo, suffered from depression. Josie, in some ways, had depression symptoms. Depression is not the same for all people and the treatment isn't a one-size-fits-all. If you or a loved one suffers from depression, I don't pretend to know all about it, but I do have people close to me who suffer to differing degrees and I know that talking about it and gathering information and treatment options is a good start.

Getting help for depression:

http://www.helpguide.org/mental/depression_signs_typ es_diagnosis_treatment.htm

As you may have guessed, the hospital scene and funeral scene for Izzy came from some personal experiences. I have not had personal experience with general organ donation, but

I know that I would be happy to know my organs were going to help others if I was no longer around to need them

Organ donation:

http://www.organdonor.gov/index.html

Another type of donation that I'd like to call attention to, although no one in this book dealt with it directly, is bone marrow donation. This is something I have personal experience with and I know just how important it is.

Bone marrow donation:

http://bethematch.org/

Finally, while we are on the subject of donation, I'd like to stress the importance of blood donation if you're healthy and able. My own son needed a blood transfusion as an infant and we are forever grateful for the donors who made that life-saving procedure possible.

Blood donation:

In Indiana, I use www.indianablood.org

Nationally, please look into the Red Cross: http://www.redcrossblood.org/donating-blood

LIBBY'S LITTLE BUTTER COOKIES

(this is the actual name of the recipe passed down in the author's family....it just so happened to work perfectly for Libby to suggest the cookies for Josie to make)

1 cup sugar

2 cups butter

Beat until creamy and fluffy.

Add 1 tablespoon vanilla. Add 2 teaspoons water. Mix in 4 cups flour.

Put mixture into refrigerator for at least 30 minutes.

Roll into small balls. Place balls 1 1/2 inches apart on cookie sheet lined with parchment paper. Using a fork dipped into flour press down in one direction and then lift fork/re-dip into flour and press down lightly to form cross cuts.

Bake at 325 for 12 minutes until LIGHT brown.

Can ice with icing made by mixing 1 tbs butter, 3/4 cup powdered sugar and just enough milk to make the frosting slightly runny. Drizzle onto cooled cookies.

Kyle's Famous Blueberry Pancakes

1 tablespoon lemon juice mixed into 2 cups milk - let sit until slightly curdled.

Melt 3 tablespoons unsalted butter - set aside
Mix 2 cups unbleached flour, 2 tablespoons sugar, 2 teaspoons baking powder, 1/2 teaspoon salt together.

Whisk 1 large egg into milk mixture and add melted butter.

Make a well into flour mixture and pour milk mixture into well and whisk very gently until just combined (will see lumps still) DON'T OVERMIX

Pour batter onto preheated lightly greased griddle. Turn only once.
If want to make blueberry pancakes sprinkle fresh or

frozen blueberries onto pancake batter when first poured onto griddle. Would need one cup of frozen or fresh blueberries for this recipe. If using frozen blueberries rinse and drain thoroughly before use.

www.ingramcontent.com/pod-product-compliance
Lightning Source LLC
Chambersburg PA
CBHW051328250626
47155CB00007B/2494